MOMMY

and the

MONEY

Also by Nancy Goldstone

Mommy and the Murder
Trading Up
Bad Business

MOMMY
and the
MONEY

A NOVEL

Nancy Goldstone

HarperCollins*Publishers*

HarperCollins books may be purchased for educational, business, or sales promotional use. For information please write: Special Markets Department, HarperCollins Publishers, Inc., 10 East 53rd Street, New York, NY 10022.

FIRST EDITION

Designed by Ruth Lee

Library of Congress Cataloging-in-Publication Data

Goldstone, Nancy Bazelon.
    Mommy and the Money : a novel / Nancy Goldstone. —1st ed.
      p. cm.
    Sequel to: Mommy and the murder.
    ISBN 0-06-017526-5
    I. Title.
PS3557.0427M64   1997
813'.54—dc20   96-29467

97 98 99 00 01 ❖/RRD 10 9 8 7 6 5 4 3 2 1

For Emily,
again and always

Prologue

"Hello, Elizabeth."

"Hello, Detective Fineburg." I paused. "Hello, Chief."

Chief Rudge inclined his head. "Ma'am," he acknowledged impassively.

"I suppose you know why we're here," said Detective Fineburg.

"Raffle tickets?" I suggested.

The chief flipped out his pad. "At approximately nine forty-seven P.M. last night a 911 phone call was received and forwarded to the Lenox Police Station," he began.

"We have a tape of the call," Detective Fineburg interjected. "We'd like you to listen to it."

The chief produced a small tape recorder from his pants pocket. He hit the play button. There was a lot of static. "This is an emergency," said a high-pitched voice, carefully enunciating each word. "Tell the Lenox police to go to the lot behind Route Seven and Housatonic. There's something there."

The chief clicked off the tape recorder.

"We did as the caller suggested," said Detective Fineburg. He paused. "You wouldn't, by any chance, have any idea what we found?" He looked at me expectantly.

I opened my mouth to speak but the chief beat me to it.

"A deceased male between the ages of thirty-five and forty-five," he reported, consulting his pad again.

"Thank you, Chief," said Detective Fineburg after a short silence.

The chief frowned and lowered his pad.

"In other words, Elizabeth," continued the detective, turning back to me, "we found a dead body."

"Oh," I said.

There was silence.

"The death did not appear to be of natural causes," the detective added.

"There were tire tracks down the front of his body," explained the chief.

"Oh," I said again.

More silence.

"You wouldn't happen to know anything about it, would you, Elizabeth?" asked Detective Fineburg finally.

"Should I know something about it?" I asked.

Detective Fineburg examined his right shoe. "Uh . . . we have a report that you were involved with the deceased," he said uncomfortably.

"Involvement of a highly *sexual* nature," noted the chief.

"And who told you that?" I demanded, outraged.

They both looked at me. "Everyone," they said.

Chapter

1

"Mommy?"

"Yes, sweetheart?"

"What's a handsome prince?" asked Emily.

It was a warm September night just after Labor Day. The windows of Emily's bedroom were open, and the ends of the soft pink ribbons of her curtains fluttered a little when the air blew in. It was just before bedtime, and the two of us were propped up against her pillow reading *More Tales of Amanda Pig* and snuggling. Emily smelled of mint toothpaste and raspberry Popsicle. It was my absolute favorite time of day.

The question caught me by surprise. There aren't any handsome princes in *Amanda Pig*. Just pigs.

"A handsome prince?" I repeated. "Uhh . . . well, a handsome prince is someone very special."

"What do you mean, 'special,' Mommy?"

"Let's see," I said, laying the book down and considering. "Well, special in the way he treats other people, especially you. Someone who is kind and strong and caring. But, also, special in the way you feel about him. Someone who makes you feel good when you're scared, for example."

"Like Mr. Bear?"

"Kind of," I said, ruffling Mr. Bear's fur. "But a handsome prince is usually a person."

"Oh," said Emily. She thought a moment. "Was Daddy a handsome prince?"

"Yes," I lied.

"But he died," she said.

"Yes, honey, he did. When you were very little."

"When I was two?" she asked.

"Even littler than that."

"But I'm a big girl now."

"Oh, yes," I assured her. "You're three. Three is much older than two."

"Three and a half," she corrected me. She thought a little more. "Do I have a handsome prince?" she asked.

"Not yet," I said, wiggling her nose with the tip of my finger. "Handsome princes are kind of hard to find. We're still looking for yours."

"And yours," she reminded me, giggling.

I tucked her in and turned on her teddy bear night-light. "Good night, sweetheart," I whispered, kissing her on the forehead. "Sleep well. Remember, tomorrow's your first day of school." Well, preschool, at any rate.

"Good night, Mommy," she echoed. "You sleep well, too."

When it came time to enroll Emily in preschool, I found that the Berkshires offered two main choices: the Hawthorne Day School and the Berkshire Magic Nursery. The Hawthorne Day School was the elite private school in the area. Run by Fawn Woodehouse, a tall, gaunt woman with short frosted hair and an underbite, the Hawthorne Day School catered to the county's small group of high-income, status-conscious residents. The Berkshire Magic Nursery, by comparison, was a local day-care unit expanded to include preschool. It was run on a shoestring by a well-meaning but perpetually harried woman named Kiki Karberry. It serviced a clientele comprised basically of two-parent working families.

Tuition at the Hawthorne Day School was three times that of the Berkshire Magic Nursery (for fewer hours) and, as a result, the differences between the two could not have been more pronounced. The Hawthorne Day School was housed in a magnificent stone edifice on twenty-four rolling acres that used to be the old Palermo estate. The Berkshire Magic Nursery was in an old ramshackle clapboard colonial smack in the middle of town. The Hawthorne Day School, a private elementary and middle school that accepted no one younger than three, smelled of fresh paint and baked goods. The Berkshire Magic Nursery, whose primary purpose was to take care of children aged eighteen months to four years, smelled of ammonia and overflowing diaper pails. The Hawthorne Day School, which offered only morning classes for three-year-olds, had two teachers for a class of ten children. As a result, the teachers there were calm and rested, wore colorful print dresses and ribbons in their neatly arranged hair. The Berkshire Magic Nursery, which tried to keep its rates down and operated along state guidelines, could afford only two teachers for nineteen children all day, every day. Their teachers wore cutoff blue jeans and, by afternoon, had acquired the sort of wild-eyed, deranged look common to rabid dogs.

I agonized for weeks over this choice. True, the Berkshire Magic Nursery was far from perfect. But enroll Emily in a chichi private school dedicated to the preservation of affluence and snobbery? Out of the question.

"Welcome to the Hawthorne Day School," the sign read.

"Okay, Em," I said the next morning, pulling the car into the parking lot. "We're here. Now, I want you to—"

"Where are we?" Emily interrupted.

"This is your new school, remember?" I reminded her as I nervously smoothed my skirt after helping her to clamber down from the car seat. I took her hand and began leading her across the parking lot to the main building. All around us prosperous-looking people were emerging from Lexuses and Cadillacs and Range Rovers, the men wearing suits and ties, the women in blazers and chinos and ridiculous little tartan mid-length shorts with knee socks, the children well-scrubbed and wearing miniature Patagonia jackets and carrying Power Ranger backpacks.

"Oh." Emily digested this. She eyed me. "Are you coming, too?" she asked.

"Just for today," I told her. "Today is an open house."

"Why?"

"Well, it's the first day of school and the teachers want to meet you and they want to meet me and they want us to meet all the other kids and all of their mommies and daddies—"

"Why?"

"Well, they want to get to know us and each other so that they're sure you'll have a good time and if we have any questions they can be sure to answer them—"

"Why?"

"Because that's their jobs, they're the teachers—"

"Why?"

I bent down and beeped her nose. She giggled. "That's why," I whispered, giving her a little hug before helping her up the stairs and into the building.

We passed through a stone archway and two massive carved-oak doors into what had once been the foyer of a huge private home. The floor was tiled, the walls white, the ceilings high. At one end of the room stood an imposing ornate antique mirror, and at the other was a table arrayed with flowers, fresh fruit and pastries, juice in glass pitchers, coffee in china cups, and several neat rows of little paper rectangles that said "Hi! My Name Is . . ."

Next to the table stood three matronly women wearing blue blazers and pearls over Laura Ashley dresses. One by one the parents filed past this trio. It was like the great-aunt section of a receiving line at a wedding.

The line surged forward; Emily and I found ourselves face-to-face with the first of the women. Her name tag said "Hi! My Name Is Fawn Woodehouse."

"Good morning!" she exclaimed in an overhearty tone common to political candidates and fitness instructors. "You must be Mrs.—"

"Umm, Halperin," I supplied. Now did not seem like the time to go into my marital status, or lack thereof.

"Mrs. Halperin. Of course." With admirable subtlety she cast a quick glance at a clipboard in her hand. "Elizabeth, isn't it?"

"That's right."

"And this must be Emily." Fawn secured our name tags and watched as I dutifully peeled off the backings and stuck them on our respective chests. Then she crouched down and smiled at Emily, who was busy examining her name tag. "We're so happy to have you here, Emily. All three of my daughters went to this school, and they all agree that the years they spent here were the happiest of their lives."

"Why?" asked Emily.

"HA!" Fawn guffawed. "ISN'T SHE ADORABLE! Let me introduce you to Mrs. Robinson," she said abruptly, throwing an arm around my shoulders and sort of pushing me along. "Mrs. Robinson is our principal here at HDS. Mrs. Robinson, this is Mrs. Halperin. She's a new mother in our Early Child-hood Division."

Mrs. Robinson, withered, fair, and slightly moist with the effort of appearing statesmanlike, grasped my hand as though she'd just been hurled overboard and I was the safety line.

"Mrs. Halperin," she began. "On behalf of all of us here at HDS, I want to thank you for making the choice to entrust your daughter's preschool training to the care of our staff. You should take pride in knowing that by doing so you will have provided your daughter with the best possible environment for her intellectual and social development." She paused and looked at me expectantly.

"Yes, I'm sure it will be a great help to her with her doctoral work," I agreed.

But Mrs. Robinson was already moving me along. "Mrs. Collinsworth will direct you to your classroom. Mrs. Collinsworth?"

The third member of the triumvirate stepped forward, grasped my hand, pumped it. Mrs. Collinsworth was a shorter, plumper version of Fawn. "The Preschool Threes Department is located two doors down to the left. Please feel free to help yourself to the refreshments. We're so pleased to have you as part of our family here at HDS."

And, with that, she smiled sincerely, put one arm around my shoulders, and deftly but firmly pushed me out of the line and down toward the corridor.

Hand in hand, Emily and I padded down the hall. We stopped in front of the second door on the left.

"This is it," I said. "Now, before we go in, I want to tell you something. You don't have to stay here if you don't want to. If you have any problems with it, anything at all, just say so and we'll leave. Okay?" I said.

"Okay," said Emily.

"Ready?" I asked.

"Weady," said Emily. She has a little trouble with her *r*'s.

I opened the door.

We both just stood in the doorway for a moment, blinking at the scene in front of us. Although a number of adults and children were already milling about, it was easy to see that the room was warm, cheerful, and spacious with delightfully cozy nooks sprinkled throughout. The walls were cream colored, with ogee molding and built-in bookshelves lined with rows of picture books. An old fireplace had been sealed, painted, and its interior adorned with stuffed animals and dolls and pillows perfect for quiet play or snuggling. There were smocks and easels and paints in one corner, blocks and Tinkertoys in another. Puppets with a real puppet theater. Musical instruments. A fish tank with exotic-looking fish. A turtle in a bowl. Dress-up clothes on hooks. A child-sized kitchen complete with stove, refrigerator, and sink, and fully equipped with utensils including ten authentic miniature wooden rolling pins. A train set. A globe. Fresh flowers on the mantel. A wooden floor so clean and polished that its boards glowed golden. Sunlight streaming through the high arched windows. It was, simply, the most inviting play space that I had ever seen.

"Oh," Emily breathed and made a beeline for the blocks.

I couldn't help smiling as I watched her concentrate on her building. The intent expression on the little heart-shaped face. The large, oddly serious, jewel-like blue eyes, the button nose, the rosebud mouth. Her curls—Emily's hair hung down her back when wet, but dry it sprung up, like honey-colored coils, to shoulder length. As usual, she'd selected her own clothes. This morning she was wearing a hot pink dress with olive green tights and red shoes. A string of blue plastic beads hung around her neck, and there were bright yellow barrettes in her hair. She looked like something from an old Carol Burnett skit.

Feeling my gaze upon her, she turned suddenly and held out her hand, her face lit up in a tremendous smile. "Look, Mommy—*purple* blocks! Have you ever seen *purple* blocks before?"

"Never," I agreed, smiling.

"And look, Mommy! They have numbers and letters on them." Emily, who has known her numbers and alphabet for some time, pointed to the numbers. "One, two, three," she read. Then she sighed with pleasure. "I can't even believe it. *Purple blocks*. Aren't they *adorable*," she concluded and immediately returned to her building.

Well, what do you know, I thought. Maybe this isn't going to be so bad after all.

"Mrs. Halperin?"

I turned. A stout dark-haired woman with red cheeks and an air of authority had her hand extended in my direction.

"Mrs. Halperin, I'm Penny Johnson, one of the teachers here in the Preschool Threes. I'm so pleased you could be with us today. Come right this way. You're just in time for art."

I glanced in the direction in which she was already herding me. A number of women and a few men were sitting self-consciously in some tiny chairs grouped around an equally tiny table.

"Do you prefer crayons or markers?" Penny continued as she showed me to my seat.

"Since I'm sure we are all very interested in learning something about each other, I thought now might be the right time to get acquainted," said Penny as soon as she had shepherded me over to the group and overseen the distribution of art materials. "Why don't we go around the table and introduce ourselves?" She turned to the woman on her right. "Now, let's see, you're Denise Costello . . . Amber's mother, is that right?"

Denise nodded and smiled nervously. She had a round, open face, with long curly black hair that she wore loose and flowing. She wore a green cardigan over a tweed skirt, knee socks, and penny loafers. Eyeing her closely, I saw that Denise was very pretty, if a little plump. She had a rock the size of Rhode Island on the fourth finger of her left hand.

"Umm, that's right." Denise had a soft, breathless way of

speaking, as though she'd just walked into a library after running a 10K.

"Can you tell us something about yourself, Denise?" Penny smiled encouragingly.

"Well, I'm not sure. . . . I guess the first thing I should say is that William—William's my husband, he wanted to be here this morning but he couldn't, he had to work—William's a personal injury lawyer—"

(I recognized the name as belonging to the person whose advertisement, featuring a serious but caring face, occupied the entire back cover of the local phone book: "William A. Costello/Attorney at Law *concentrating in* Personal Injury Law: Auto Accidents, Scars, Fractures & Burns, Slip & Fall, Defective Products, Medical Malpractice, Lead Paint Injuries, Head Injuries and Dog Bites.")

"—William thought HDS would be a good place for Amber, we've only been married four years by the way, we were married at Wheatleigh—" (the Berkshires' only four-star inn) "—we have a cottage in Maine, that's why we got the Range Rover, although now I'm thinking we need a Pathfinder—"

And so it went around the table. The Berkshire legal community was well represented in the Preschool Threes, although they were outdone by the medical establishment. (Two women were married to cardiologists, two to obstetricians, and one to a lower-back specialist versus three women either married to lawyers or lawyers themselves.) There were also a banker and the owners of an electrical contracting business.

Penny Johnson smiled. "Well, this is certainly a diverse group! I look forward to working with all of you during the school year. And now, we'd like to have some time alone with the children, to get them used to the idea of coming to school without their parents. So, if you don't mind, I'm going to ask you all to leave as soon as you've finished drawing something for your child. You may pick up your children after lunch. We will bring them out to the stone wall at twelve-thirty."

We all sat and dutifully drew pictures of rainbows and flowers and princesses and dragons. I drew a picture of our house with me sticking my head out one of the upstairs bedroom windows and Emily sticking her head out of the other. It didn't look much like either me or Emily, but it was the same picture she made me draw every time we drew at home, so I knew she'd recognize it. When we had finished we put down our markers and rose from our chairs. I was just turning toward Emily to say good-bye when Penny called me back. "Umm, Mrs. Halperin? May I speak to you for a moment?"

"You may if you call me Elizabeth."

"Elizabeth, then. Fine. Elizabeth, I'm afraid that one or two of the parents' background forms have been mislaid and that yours was among them. I need to fill in a little information on you." She took out a pen and clipboard. "Let me see, you said you live in Lenox?"

"That's right. At One-oh-five Upper Reservoir Road," I filled in.

"Great. And—let me see, yes, of course—Emily is your only child?"

"Yes."

"And I think you introduced yourself as a writer just now?"

"I've written a book, yes. Before that I—"

"Oh, good, I'm so glad I got that right. It's so easy to be confused about people's professions. There are so many of you and so few of us."

"Yes, of course."

"Now, what about Mr. Halperin? I see that he couldn't be here with us today."

"Uh—no."

"That's too bad, although of course we understand. Some of our parents have very high-powered careers. Still, I think I should mention that here in the Preschool Threes Department we strive for full parent participation. Even the busiest people give some of their time to the school."

I felt called upon to elaborate. "Actually, there is no Mr. Halperin," I volunteered.

"Oh." Penny stopped. Then she smiled and nodded. "I understand," she said.

"No, I don't think you do. There *was* a Mr. Hack—Emily's father—but he's not here either."

"Well, perhaps another time—"

"I doubt it. He's dead."

"Oh." Penny stopped again. "Oh, I'm so sorry. Was it sudden?"

"Kind of. He was shot," I told her.

"Oh!"

"At a Halloween party," I continued conversationally.

"Oh!" She had stopped writing.

"It was about two years ago. He was tied up in a sex triangle. I'm sure you read about it in the paper," I said.

"No, I—well, maybe . . ." Her hand had crept up to her throat.

"They never did catch who did it, you know."

"No? How terr—"

"I was a suspect for a while, but I can assure you that I've been completely exonerated," I added brightly.

"Uh, yes, of course—"

"I *was* living with someone else, but he's not around anymore, either."

Penny Johnson's lips worked. "Shot?" she finally managed.

"Worse," I pronounced.

"Dd-dead?"

I shook my head. "Moved to Boca Raton. Is there anything else?"

"No, no, that will—that's quite enough," said Penny Johnson.

* * *

What can I tell you about the months that preceded this open house? By all accounts I was a person to be envied. Howard's death had left me more than comfortable, and on top of that I'd earned a modest sum off a comic mystery I wrote, with the prospect of more for a sequel. I'd felt secure enough to abandon the cottage I had since before Emily was born in favor of a stately old colonial on one of the nicest country roads in all of Lenox. I now had French doors leading from the living room to the patio, my own apple trees, and a private deck for sunbathing.

When I moved, I sort of drifted away from some of my old friends. Pat was busy with her new job, Didi now had three children to occupy her, and Astrid had been relocated to Grand Rapids, Michigan. And then, I'd turned into something of a minor celebrity in town. People knew me. They asked me to things—charity benefits, ice-cream socials, garden committee meetings, Super Bowl parties. My name was mentioned as a possible candidate when a vacancy appeared on the board of the Lenox library, and the woman who ran the greeting card store asked my advice before expanding. Everywhere Emily and I turned we were petted and made to feel welcome by the local community. This was something of a feat considering that I was a Manhattan transferee who had lived less than four years in Lenox. Usually it takes that long just to make eye contact.

I should have been absolutely, unquestionably happy. I was getting to watch my daughter grow up in peaceful, beautiful surroundings; I had fulfilled a lifelong ambition and written a book, with enough success to encourage another; I had a loving, handsome, sensitive live-in boyfriend named Adam Rothstein who also happened to be Emily's pediatrician. Most people would have killed to be in my shoes. Actually, come to think of it, the police thought I had.

It takes a lot to mess up a situation as good as that one, but I am nothing if not talented.

*   *   *

It all started about six months after my book came out. I was working on the sequel. It wasn't going very well. Actually, that was something of an understatement. It wasn't going at all.

My first book, I realized belatedly, had been something of a fluke. Of course, it's nice to have language skills and an eye for odd characters, but the one really satisfying aspect of having your estranged husband die suddenly under mysteriously sexy circumstances, leaving you almost a million dollars so that the police suspect you of killing him, forcing you to go out and find who did it yourself in order to avoid life imprisonment in a maximum security penitentiary in Massachusetts, is that you don't have to go fishing around for a good plot. You just write what happened to you, and everybody believes you made it up on the grounds of something like that pretty much had to be made up.

But starting from scratch—that's a different story. What was I to write about? I had already tried, without success, a number of different drafts with creative plots. I had suffocated the woman who ran the ice-cream store in a vat of chocolate chip espresso bean frozen yogurt. I had knocked off a local artist by putting poison on the end of the paintbrushes that he habitually nibbled while working. I had pushed people off mountains, out of boats, into snowdrifts—to no avail. It all seemed silly and pointless and, worse, boring. Nothing anybody would want to think about, let alone pay money to read.

My inability to write at this time was particularly galling because it interfered with my own personal views of motherhood and career. When Emily was born, I had looked at her and realized that I could not simply go back to work after three months and leave her to the care of a nanny. I hadn't expected to feel that way; I'd expected to go right back to work. It was a completely personal decision.

But as strongly as I felt I shouldn't be working at three months, that's how strongly I felt I *should* be working at three years. It didn't matter that Emily and I could live quite comfortably off Howard's royalties; in fact, that only made matters worse. *I* wanted to make the money to support myself and Emily. I wanted to work, and have that effort rewarded. I wanted to be the kind of person whom Emily and I could be proud of.

So all this trying without succeeding was really starting to get to me. I was starting to wonder if I was going to blow my big chance to be a writer. I was starting to wonder if I had any talent at all. I was starting to wonder if the only way I was ever going to write another book was if somebody died right under my nose.

"Would you *please* be quiet!" I snapped.

Adam paused in the entranceway. It was about eight o'clock on a bitterly cold night this past February and he was just coming home from a day of poking tongue depressors down three-, four-, and five-year-old throats. I, by contrast, was sitting in the armchair by the woodstove in a pair of gray sweatpants and a stained white sweatshirt, a box of half-eaten Rice Chex at my side, and a yellow pad in my lap. It was the same position I'd occupied since I put Emily to bed over an hour ago.

Adam stood for a moment and waited. Evidently realizing that this was all the greeting he was going to get, he took off his coat and hung it on the coatrack. Then he came over to where I was ensconced and peered over my shoulder at the pad in my lap. "Getting somewhere?" he asked.

"What? Huh?" I frowned down at the paper, stuck my hand in the box of cereal, and chewed absently.

Adam gave up and made for the kitchen.

I stared down at my work for a few more minutes, then slammed down my pen. No matter how many times I asked him, he couldn't seem to understand that you can't bother someone when they're writing. I made a big show of dropping my notebook on the floor and heaving myself out of the chair. I stomped into the kitchen. Adam was just unscrewing the top to the peanut butter.

"Why are you eating that?" I asked.

"Why not? Is there anything else for dinner?" he replied.

"I didn't get to it. I was trying to work."

"Did you get anywhere?"

"I was starting to."

"You mean until I walked in," said Adam, spreading jam.

"Well, yes, now that you mention it."

"Sorry," he said. "After eleven hours I ran out of sick children for the day."

"What's that supposed to mean?"

Adam stared at me, chewing. He stopped and swallowed. "Has it occurred to you that there is something wrong with this relationship?"

"What do you mean?" I asked again. Then: "Oh. Right. You're saying it's all my fault."

"I didn't say that."

"You don't have to say it. It's pretty clear that's what you think."

Adam reached silently for the pickles.

"You think I'm being selfish and self-absorbed," I burst out, hands on my hips, as he calmly speared a gherkin. "That I'm not paying enough attention to you or the relationship. That I'm an untalented fake who sits around the house stuffing her face with Rice Chex. What do you want? Someone who cooks chateaubriand every night and meets you at the door in a negligee?"

Adam stood for a moment. He seemed to be considering it. "I'd settle for a 'Hello, how are you,'" he said finally. He paused. "Since an 'I love you' seems to be out of the question." And he turned and left the room.

A week later he packed up his things and left. That was the

last I heard of him, except for a postcard from Florida in April announcing the opening of his pediatric practice at the Mizener Center.

I don't think it would be an overstatement to say that recently I had been through more than the average person, but still, Adam's leaving was something of a shock. Thirty-four years old and this was the second time I'd been unceremoniously dumped in the past two years. True, Howard's departure had been a function of his own ambition and basically despicable personality. But the same could not be said of Adam. With Adam, *I* had been the aggressor. *I* had been the destructive partner. If anything, I realized with a sudden sickening percipience, *I* had behaved like . . . like . . . like *Howard*.

It took a little while, but after Adam left I made a vow. No more whiny self-absorption. No more self-destructive behavior. No more Rice Chex. If Providence ever took the time to smile down on me again when it came to matters of the heart, I would be *ready*.

Just send me someone, okay? Give me a second chance. I dreamed of Lancelot, of Clark Gable, of Cyrano de Bergerac.

What I got was Jonathon Nichols.

Chapter

2

"You're Elizabeth Halperin, aren't you?" he asked.

I looked up from my perusal of the program. I was at the reception for the opening of Shakespeare and Company's production of *A Midsummer Night's Dream*. Shakespeare and Company was a local troupe that performed regularly throughout the summer at Edith Wharton's house, the Mount. I always went to their openings. I love the Mount. When she was alive, Edith Wharton lay in bed on the third floor of this house and wrote. When she was finished she would throw the pages on the floor, and her stenographer would come around and gather them up and type them for her. Something about this idea appealed to me.

It was already crowded by the time I got there. The reception was being held in the drawing room. (Howard had proposed to me in this room, but I don't hold it against the place.) There were engravings of cupids on the ten-foot-high ceiling, Italian marble on the mantelpiece, and huge floor-to-ceiling, wall-to-wall windows, two of which had been flung open to reveal a wraparound terrace and polished stone steps curving down to the lawn and gardens. Looking out, I could see the outdoor stage where the play was to take place, the Japanese maples, the cedars and oaks darkening in the twilight, the heavy scrolled pots of geraniums, the white shirts of the ushers moving between chairs as they began seating people on the lawn for the performance.

"You're Elizabeth Halperin, aren't you?" he repeated. "Loved your book," he continued.

"Uh . . . thank you."

I took him in. He was about average height, with curly brown hair, a prominent nose, and a deep tan. It was a terrific tan. It was the best tan in the room. To accentuate it, he was wearing a white button-down shirt open at the neck, beige Armani slacks, perfectly shined Bally loafers, and a yellow cashmere sweater draped over his shoulders, with the sleeves folded precisely two inches below the top button of the shirt. He looked not so much dressed as put together. At the opening of his shirt collar, a small gold chain was visible.

Ugh.

"Something of a mystery buff myself," he confided, "although generally I stick to the classics. They're just better. I'm Jonathon Nichols, by the way," he continued, holding out his hand, another small gold chain dangling from his wrist. "Are you working on another book?"

"Uh, ye—"

"Oh, having some trouble getting started, huh? Yeah, that's tough," he commiserated. "It's always hard when I finally finish one project to get started on another."

"Really."

"Oh, yes. I give every project my undivided attention."

"You don't say."

"Since you're interested," he continued cheerfully, "I'll tell you what I'm doing now. I'm restoring Lenox."

"The whole town?"

"Maybe someday. Just part of it for now."

"Oh," I said bleakly. "That's you."

Now I remembered. It had been in the paper. Someone had come up from New York City and bought a huge piece of property on the corner of Housatonic Street and Route 7 with the intention of turning it into a mall.

"Ohhh," he said. "You're one of those."

"One of what?"

"A history snob."

"There is no such thing as a history snob," I said, and why am I having a conversation with this person? I thought.

"Oh, yes, there is," he said. "A history snob is a person who thinks that a two-hundred-year-old building, *any* two-hundred-year-old-building, even one which is in complete disrepair and isn't being used for anything anymore, is more attractive than, God forbid, a modern building which is actually capable of housing people or supporting a business."

Well, yes, I admitted grudgingly (to myself). Actually, that was exactly what I thought.

"Personally," he continued, "I find that sort of attitude a little dated, not to say defeatist. A Frank Lloyd Wright building is a national treasure today, but by your way of thinking he would have been better off restoring some old Victorians, which are only copies of other Victorians, anyway.

"For myself," he concluded, dashing off the rest of his white wine, "I'd like to think that those of us who happen to be around today are still capable of making a contribution, beyond simply acting as caretakers for the past. Besides, how would you feel if everyone suddenly decided not to publish any new books but instead reissued those written two hundred years ago, regardless of quality?"

I blinked at him.

"I rest my case. Shall we get our seats?"

He took my arm and steered me outside and down the stairs to where the chairs had been set up. It's open seating at

Shakespeare and Company, so a lot of people had gotten there before us. A young woman holding additional programs pointed out two seats still available toward the front. As we walked up the aisle, Jonathon smiled and said hello to a silver-haired patrician-looking woman in her seventies whom I recognized from the society pages of the *Berkshire Eagle* as being on the board of a number of cultural organizations, talked tennis with a man whom he introduced as Judge Clarkson, and shook hands with Ellsworth and Florence Hunkler, the unofficial doyen and doyenne of the Lenox Country Club set, who lived in a huge stone mansion at the top of Undermountain Mountain, where they entertained visiting celebrities during the summer.

"They hate me, you know," he confided gleefully as we sat down and I saw him wave to a man I recognized as one of the town's leading real estate lawyers.

"Who does?" I asked, startled.

"All of them." He gave a wave of his hand encompassing, apparently, most of the audience.

"Why?" I asked, although I was beginning to have my suspicions.

"Oh, there are all sorts of reasons. They hate me because I wasn't born here and, what's worse, because I'm from New York, because I'm a developer, because I'm tan. But most of all, they hate me because they have to be nice to me."

"Why do they have to be nice to you?"

He looked at me incredulously. "Because I have a lot of money." He paused. "Why else are people nice to anybody?" he asked.

At intermission he told me his philosophy of life.

"Here's my philosophy of life," said Jonathon Nichols. "If you stand out in traffic long enough, you'll get hit by a truck."

"What?" I said.

"Look. It's like this. About ten years ago, right after the riots in New York . . . "

"What riots?" I asked.

"What do you mean, what riots. There are always riots in New York. Anyway, you could pick up buildings in parts of the Bronx for next to nothing. Nobody wanted 'em. So what did I do? I bought 'em. And do you know why I bought 'em?"

"Because you had a lifelong ambition to be a slum lord?" I asked sweetly.

"No," he said. "Because I had *vision*." He paused for effect. "All my friends, everybody I knew in the business, thought I was crazy. 'You're crazy,' they all said to me. 'You're throwing your money down the sewer.' And do you know what I said to them?"

"I can't wait," I said.

"I said 'You stand out in traffic long enough, you get hit by a truck.' And you know what happened then? Every one of the buildings I bought came in. And in only four years. The Small Business Administration and HUD designated them as pilots in the Neighborhood Revitalization Program."

"How convenient," I said.

"Hey, scoff if you like, but that's vision. I *saved* those buildings. Without me, they would have been torn down, annihilated, and all the people living in them would have been thrown out on the street. Two thousand people lived in those buildings."

"And you made money off them."

"Don't give me that, Elizabeth. Those people are now living in clean, well-constructed apartments. The heat works, the toilets flush, and there's no lead in the paint. Of course I made money. You want a project to work, somebody's got to make money out of it. Don't tell me you're one of those people who think that projects should be undertaken for noble and altruistic motives. You know what you get with noble and altruistic? You get Chernobyl."

That stopped me. But then: "How did the government happen to pick your buildings?" I asked slowly.

He looked at me as if I'd just suggested acquiring a nose ring. "Because I paid them to, that's how," he said.

It is no excuse, of course, but I had been lonely for some time. Adam had left in February and here it was July. And it is much, much worse to be lonely in the Berkshires during the summer than in the winter. In the winter it's quiet. There's hardly anybody on the street, and the people you do meet are invariably cold and depressed and miserable. There's companionship, however warped, in being cold and depressed and miserable at the same time as everybody else.

But in the summer the Berkshires come alive. From Memorial Day to Labor Day, the whole county dresses up like a fashionable bride, albeit a seasoned one. There are fairs and carnivals, horse shows and art exhibits. There is music, dancing, theater. Grassy meadows to loll in, babbling brooks to wade through, cool forests to rest beside. The whole populated by a mass of people walking the streets, eating ice cream, holding hands, haggling over the price of pottery and antique spoons, and generally conducting themselves as happy, sunburned, carefree merrymakers. Being lonely under these circumstances is a little like Cinderella's finally making it to the ball only to find out they need someone to pass out the cheese twists.

And Jonathon Nichols was nothing if not persistent. He asked me to see the Martha Graham dance troupe's recital at Jacobs Pillow; Itzhak Perlman's performance at Tanglewood; Karen Allen's new play at Williamstown. He asked to take me sailing at Stockbridge Bowl, hiking up Bash-Bish Falls, and biking through Alford. He wanted to shepherd me through the Norman Rockwell Museum, Herman Melville's house, and even the historic Hancock Shaker Village, where he expressed considerable admiration for Shaker architecture. ("Look at that round barn! Did you ever see a building so perfectly in harmony with its surroundings and at the same time so absolutely suited to its purpose? Boy, can you imagine if those people had ever decided to build a mall?")

And then Emily liked him. Or at least she liked his truck. He had this big four-by-four Ford pickup truck that he tooled around in, by his own admission his most prized possession ("Most valuable truck in the county," he bragged). It was highly polished black with a thin racing stripe down the side, huge tires, and an array of lights over the cab that helped him to track down innocent creatures at night. Emily loved it. He let her climb all over it, sit in the driver's seat, and swing the steering wheel. "Look, Mommy, I'm driving to New York!" she announced.

In a way, I think I was doing penance for mistreating Adam. And, of course, it didn't help that I was still having trouble stringing together a series of cogent ideas for my mystery, the deadline for which was now approaching with a truly awful inevitability. Day after day I sat down to work, day after day I struggled, day after day I—there is no other word for it— failed. Under those circumstances, ardent male attention can be so seductive that a person is almost able to overlook the character of the male supplying it.

Still, there was never any question of Jonathon Nichols being anything more to me than . . . well, than someone to sit next to at the theater. I used to argue with myself about it sometimes. "Why don't you try to like him a little better?" I'd reason with myself, with my new post-Adam outlook. "He's a perfectly attractive man. Some people would even call him good-looking." "You kiss him, then," I'd retort, and that would effectively end the argument.

Still, this arrangement worked just fine until the night of August twenty-eighth.

* * *

The night of August twenty-eighth was unutterably beautiful. Magical, really, as only the Berkshires can be when the extravagance of summer rallies itself for a final burst of glory. A heat wave had just broken and the night air was suddenly cool, sweet, and refreshing, a silken scarf against your skin. There was a moon, too, that night, and stars, and just the trace of a rose garden in the air.

It was the kind of night that beckons you out of your house. The kind of night that whispers to you through the window, that murmurs to you as you brush your hair in front of your mirror. The kind of night where nature conspires to rid you of rational thought and entices you to fall in love.

I went out for dinner with Jonathon Nichols that night. We had a bottle of wine. Afterward, I took a walk with him in the moonlight. He took me to his construction site.

Some of the excavation had already begun. We found seats on some cinder blocks.

"Isn't this great?" Jonathon exulted.

I looked around. There was a backhoe, a trailer, a line of Portosans, and a lot of dirt.

"Wait a minute. I almost forgot," he said, and jumped up. He ran over to his truck and removed a Styrofoam cooler. He hurried back, resumed his seat, and flung open the lid. "I have just the thing for a romantic evening," he assured me, reaching in and pulling out a bottle of Dom Pérignon and two champagne flutes.

I love champagne. It is crass and weak of me, I know, but I love champagne.

The backhoe started to look better to me.

He poured. "What shall we toast?" he said. "Ah. I know. To the new Lenox."

What the hell. "To the new Lenox," I repeated, and drank.

"That's where the theater will be." He pointed. "And there's the ice-cream store—"

"Ice-cream store? But Lenox already has an ice-cream

store. What about the people who own that one—"

He made a face. "That one? Mom and pop. Small pota-toes." He waved an arm. "We'll have a *real* one. Right next to the sushi bar—" He interrupted himself. "Do you know what this mall is going to do for this town? The jobs, the revenue." He stopped. "Do you know, we're importing real teak for the archways on the storefronts?"

"Teak? But isn't that endangered? Can you do that?"

He made another face. "Everybody does it."

I drank some more champagne.

"And can you believe that there are some people in this town who tried to keep me from doing this?"

"No kidding," I said.

"Oh, yeah. They're blind, provincial . . . that's how the town got to be the way it is. No vision."

Actually, I'd always liked Lenox the way it was. I drank some more champagne.

"One day they're all going to thank me," he said solemnly.

It wasn't until two o'clock in the morning while I was hastily flinging on my clothes that I realized I had been completely undone by half a bottle of champagne, a sky full of stars, and a vacant lot.

The phone rang at eight-thirty the next morning.

"Guess who!"

Oh, God. "Hi."

"Did I wake you up?"

"No."

"Oh, because I slept great. Afterwards, of course."

Afterwards. Right. Snicker, snicker, snicker. "I'm glad to hear that," I said.

"Thought you might want some breakfast!"

Really, he was as chipper as if he had just evicted somebody. It was revolting.

"No, thank you," I replied. "I'm really not very hungry this morning."

"You're not? No kidding. I'm starving. I guess I worked up more of an appetite than you." He chortled. "But, then, men usually do most of the work, don't they?" He chortled again.

"*What?*"

"Oh, you know, all that . . . oh, never mind. How about we wait a couple of hours, then, and make it brunch?"

"No, I don't think so . . . "

"Dinner then."

"Uh—I've decided to fast today," I told him.

"No kidding. Is that something you always do after—"

"No. Only on special occasions."

"Well, when are you going to eat again, then?" he asked.

"I'll let you know," I said, and hung up.

The sound of the receiver slamming into its cradle caused Emily, who was having her breakfast, to look up from her blueberries.

"Why do you have a sad face, Mommy?" she piped up, cocking her head to one side.

"It's not really a sad face, honey."

"It's not a *happy* face," she observed.

I sighed and sat down next to her. "The truth is, Em," I began, brushing a curl off her forehead, "that—" What was the truth? "That—" I ran quickly through a variety of responses, each of them completely unacceptable. "That—that I made a big mistake last night."

"What do you mean, a big mistake?" Emily asked.

"Well, it's kind of hard to explain. It was a grown-up mistake," I said.

"What's a grown-up mistake?" asked Emily, scooping up some blueberries with her Mickey Mouse spoon, two of which actually made it into her mouth.

"Well, there are kid mistakes and grown-up mistakes," I explained, making a quick save with the side of my foot. "You make kid mistakes like dropping blueberries on the floor or running so fast you trip over your own feet or putting your dress on backward. I make grown-up mistakes."

"Like what?"

"Like making someone think I like them more than I actually do," I finished, rather desperately. Who needs a shrink when you've got a three-year-old? I thought.

Emily swallowed and digested this information. "*Who* did you make think you liked them?" she asked.

I sighed. "Jonathon. Mr. Nichols, I mean."

"Why don't you like Mr. Nichols, Mommy?"

"I didn't say I didn't like him at all. Of course I like him. I just don't like him in a certain way."

"*What* way?"

"The way . . . the way you'd like a handsome prince," I said. Always use mistakes as a learning exercise, I reminded myself. "But, see, I did something last night that might make him think I thought he was my handsome prince, when, of course, he wasn't. So that was the big mistake. I know it's hard to understand, but sometimes giving the wrong impression is actually the worst thing you can do to someone."

Emily sat quietly. I could see the wheels working in her brain. Then she spoke.

"But you never spit except when you're brushing your teeth," she said.

For the next week, I was haunted by Jonathon Nichols. Not only did he call every day, it was like he'd planted a homing device in my shoe. I went to the market; he'd catch me in front of the tomatoes. I dropped off my laundry at the dry cleaner's; he'd pop out of the copying place next door. I took Emily to the bakery for a cookie; there he'd be munching a Danish.

It got so that I looked for places where I was pretty sure he wouldn't be. That's difficult in the Berkshires, where everybody does the same things. But I had hit on what I thought was a sure bet.

"Where are we going, Mommy?" Emily asked as I strapped her into her car seat and threw the picnic basket and a blanket in the backseat of the Jeep.

"We're going to look at forty years' worth of feminist sculpture, sweetie," I said, and drove to Chesterwood.

Chesterwood, the home of Daniel Chester French, the artist who sculpted the model for the Lincoln Memorial, is a principal Berkshire tourist attraction. Set up on a hill is a large white house where the sculptor lived, the original studio where he worked and served tea to notable figures (unlike most artists, Daniel Chester French was celebrated in his own time and made quite a splash in society), and a loftlike building that serves as a gallery.

But what's really nice about Chesterwood are the extensive grounds. There's so much room that the administrators allow local artists to display their work by setting up statues all around. Emily and I scouted around until we found a nice secluded spot, right in front of a huge steel egg-shaped mass to which little wrought-iron spermlike creatures were attached. ("*Woman Under Siege,*" the little placard in front of it announced.) I was feeling pretty good about my little subterfuge as I laid the cloth and unpacked the picnic basket when suddenly I heard an all-too-familiar voice.

"Hi!"

"Look, Mommy! It's Mr. Nichols," said Emily through bits of peanut butter and jelly.

He stepped out from behind a tree and plunked himself down comfortably on the blanket. "Imagine meeting you two here!" he exclaimed as he removed his shoes. "You never told me you like sculpture, Elizabeth. If you'd told me you were coming I could have given you a lift in the truck." He winked at Emily. "Maybe I can give you a ride back, though."

"Ohhh," breathed Emily, lighting up.

I looked at him. It was now or never. "Look, Jonathon . . ." I began.

But he was already talking. "I shouldn't be telling you this," he said, moving closer and lowering his voice. "But I've got something really big on my plate."

"That's nice, Jonathon. But we need to talk about—"

"You're an intelligent woman so you know there's no such thing as a sure thing, but, believe me, this is as close as they come," he continued, ignoring my efforts to change the subject.

"I'm happy for you, Jonathon. Now about our—"

"Nobody else could put this together the way I am. Juggling all the pieces, you know. The big bucks. The investors. The risks."

I gave up. "I take it you're not talking about the mall," I said.

"The mall? That's peanuts." He sniffed. "This is something much bigger. And you know what I'm going to do? I'm going to sneak you into this. I shouldn't do it, but I will." He put his arm around me. "Now if that's not enough to show you—"

"Jonathon Nichols."

We turned. There stood a graying woman in her forties wearing an A-line green skirt, a short-sleeved pink shirt, and a flowered scarf, all of which I recognized as coming from the Talbots right in town. The scarf was fastened at the neck with a little silver pin in the shape of a pig, also from Talbots. I recognized her from the town meeting. It was Marion Hollister Thornewood, our local selectwoman.

Jonathon dropped his arm from about my shoulder as if I had just developed a loathsome skin disease. He was on his feet so fast I didn't even see his legs move.

"Marion!" he exclaimed warmly, grasping her hand in both of his. "How lovely to see you here."

Marion Hollister Thornewood considered him. She had a round fleshy face and wore no makeup except for some orange lipstick that only served to accentuate the frown lines on either side of her chin. A pair of tortoiseshell glasses hung from a cord around her neck, and she tapped her teeth with them thoughtfully before she spoke.

"And how surprising to see you here, Jonathon," she replied.

"I wouldn't miss it," he assured her solemnly. "In fact, I'm considering purchasing this one for the mall." He turned and contemplated the huge steel egg.

"Oh, yes," I agreed. "Be sure and put it right in front of the sushi bar."

Jonathon shot me a look.

Marion turned to me and smiled. "Hi, I'm Marion Hollister Thornewood," she said, holding out a hand. "I'm sorry, I know I've seen you around town—"

"Elizabeth Halperin," I replied, shaking hands.

"A pleasure to meet you, Elizabeth." She had a firm grip. Then she turned back to Jonathon. "I can't tell you how happy I am to have run into you like this, Jonathon," she said. "We— I mean, those of us on the select committee—have a couple of questions about the new mall."

"Shoot," said Jonathon comfortably.

"Well, we're wondering about the progress. Frankly, we need to know if it is still running on schedule. It seems to be moving very slowly—"

"Oh, Marion, if that's been bothering you, I wish you'd come to me sooner," said Jonathon. "I want you to know that everything is actually coming along *ahead* of schedule. The site itself is only a small part of the overall deal, you know. There's material and labor and, oh, quite a number of factors which are running full steam ahead."

"So, then, you are still planning to meet a November opening date?" Marion asked.

"Without question," said Jonathon solemnly.

"Good. The committee has been quite concerned. They thought perhaps you had bitten off more than you could chew, if you don't mind a cliché."

Jonathon took her hand again. "Marion, I can swear to you that I am completely, totally involved with the mall. I am giving it my undivided, twenty-four-hours-a-day, seven-days-a-week attention," he intoned. "There is absolutely nothing else on my plate."

Then, turning slightly away so that she couldn't see, he winked at me.

Why I couldn't just tell him to buzz off, I'll never know. Probably it was because I felt so . . . complicit. I didn't want him to accuse me of leading him on. And, after all, it had been my fault, not his. He hadn't been deceitful about his feelings. I had.

So I employed the age-old technique for getting out of a relationship. I stalled.

That is, until I went to get my teeth cleaned.

"I'll be with you in a moment," Roberta, the dental hygienist, sang out from the hallway after the receptionist had shown me into an examining room. "Just sit down and make yourself comfortable."

I sat down in the dentist's chair and looked around for something to do. There was an old copy of *Cosmopolitan* by the window. I reached over and started leafing through it. I was just starting "Why Women Who Love Men Hate Their Clothes," when Roberta came in behind me.

"All set?" She took a seat beside me and began laying out her instruments on a tray. Roberta was short, blond, and petite. She wore the regulation goggles, mask, and gloves, so everything she said was slightly muffled. "Could you open, please, Elizabeth?" she asked.

I opened.

"How's Emily?" Roberta asked, her hands deep in my mouth.

"Ah ah," I replied.

"Good. She must be getting pretty big by now. What is she, three?"

"Ah ah ah ah," I said.

"Three and a half. No kidding." Roberta handed me a cup. "You can rinse," she suggested.

I rinsed.

"Weather's been nice, hasn't it?"

"Ah."

"It's been a nice summer."

"Ah ah."

"Of course, I hear it's been a *real* nice summer for some of us."

I turned to look at her. Even with the mask and the goggles and all, there was no doubt about it. Roberta was smirking.

Now, it just so happened that for the past week or so, I had had a feeling that I was being talked about. There had never been anything definite, nothing that I could really put my finger on, just there had seemed to be, oh, I don't know, little indications. Knots of people that broke up when I entered the grocery store. Whispers. Little looks. Why, I'd felt it in the reception area here at the dentist's, I remembered now. Something in the way Kate behind the desk had greeted me when I walked in. Her smile . . .

"What do you mean?" I demanded, forgetting to open.

"Oh, nothing. Just something a little bird told me," she cooed maddeningly, trying to get her fingers into my mouth again.

But I was having none of it. "Roberta," I warned.

"Well, you know what a small town this is."

"Roberta."

"Things get around."

"Roberta."

"Jonathon Nichols was in the other day," she said, finally.

"Really."

"You know how friendly he is with Dr. Lipp," she continued.

"Is he."

"He said. . . . Are you sure you want to hear this?"

"Just go on, Roberta."

"All right. . . . He said you two are an item. He said you're really hot stuff. He said you did it with him outside at his construction site. He said–"

"That'll do, Roberta."

"You're not upset, are you?"

"You can do my teeth now, Roberta."

"Because I'm sure he meant it to be complimentary."

"Just do my teeth, Roberta."

Roberta did my teeth for a while in silence. But after she had finished flossing, she leaned a little closer. "Want to tell me about him?" she whispered.

"Absolutely."

"What?" She almost fell into my lap in her eagerness to hear.

"Jonathon Nichols . . ." I began solemnly, removing the little paper bib around my neck with deliberation.

"Yes?"

"Jonathon Nichols . . ." I was out of the chair, heading to the doorway.

"What? What?"

"Jonathon Nichols is dead meat," I intoned with finality, and stalked out of the office.

That does it, I fumed, as I marched down Church Street toward my car. The gloves are off. No more Mr. Nice Guy.

Just imagine my having had scruples about his feelings! Worrying about hurting him! While all this time he was off detailing the highlights of our encounter to the general population as if he was performing a public service!

Speaking of which, where was Romeo, anyway? I looked around. By rights he should be lurking in some doorway waiting for me. Was that him with the chocolate-covered cheesecake around the corner over by Wholesome Harold's? No . . . how about down the block at Body & Soul? Was that him in the electric massage chair? No. Too bad. I might have been able to fix the wiring and give him a *real* charge.

No matter. There'd be a message from him on my answering machine when I got home for sure. How should I do it? I wondered grimly as I got into the car. By phone? No. Too passive. Invite him over? Not a chance. A meeting on neutral ground, I decided. Yes. That was best.

But when I got home there was no message on my machine. And, though I waited around all afternoon and on into the evening, he never called that day. Nor the next day. Nor the next.

He had just . . . disappeared.

Chapter

3

"Please note that the HDS Fall Fair will be held this Saturday, September 18th," read the sheet of paper I found in Emily's lunch box along with the remnants of her peanut butter and jelly sandwich and half of a mashed banana. It was a typewritten letter from the school.

The Fall Fair is the Parent Association's most important fund-raiser. It is a Berkshire County tradition which brings many prospective families to the campus for the first time. It is a joyous and festive day that depends on the helping hands of every single parent.

We are all truly blessed to be part of a school community that clearly celebrates children. Thank you, one and all, for reaching out to help us make the Hawthorne Day School the wonderful educational institution it is.

With all best wishes,
Fawn Woodehouse
Administrator

Then, underneath in pen was scrawled: "You have been assigned to work at the baked goods counter from 8:30 to noon. Please make a note of it on your calendar."

Since Berkshire County is a place where country fairs are held with the frequency of photo ops in an election year, you might not think that notification of yet another impending festival would be cause for much excitement. But the Hawthorne Day School fair was different. It was *the* fair for children. There were pony rides and games and all kinds of crafts. There were homemade candy apples and fudge and caramel corn, clowns and gymnasts and women dressed up in long skirts and aprons with little pockets from which they produced prizes. The adults had stuff like a silent auction, a band for dancing, and a used-book table. Inured as I was to carnivals, I had always loved the Hawthorne Day School Fall Fair.

And this year promised to be the best. Emily was the perfect age. She could ooh and aah over the petting zoo. She could throw a bean bag into a hole and win a prize. She could light up at the prospect of a balloon. Taking Emily to the fair was such a pleasant prospect that it even made me feel better about the message from my literary agent on my answering machine this morning. "Elizabeth, honey, how's the new manuscript coming?" she'd cooed in her most maternal tones. You know when they get maternal with you you're in trouble.

But how could I work behind the bake sale counter and take Emily around at the same time? I mentioned my dilemma to Penny Johnson the next morning while dropping Emily off at school. Fawn Woodehouse, who often made a point of drifting through the preschool threes' room during arrival and departure hours, overheard me.

"I'm sorry, I can't do it this year," I was just saying to Penny when Fawn interrupted.

"You can't?" said Fawn, somehow managing to smile and

frown at the same time. "But we were so counting on you."

"Well, I'm going to the fair, of course," I said. "It's just . . . I'm taking Emily."

"Of course, I understand," said Fawn, smile broadening, "but I'd like you, just for the moment, to put yourself in my— in all of our—shoes. This is what independent education is. Giving is simply a fact of life if we have any hope of maintaining our standards, which as you know are much higher than in the public sector. It is desperately important that every parent give as much as they can." Her smile deepened further. "And, really, Elizabeth, working at the fall fair is a joyous experience. It's an opportunity to relish. You get to help, not just your own child, but *all* the children. You get to experience *all* of their joy."

"Well, of course, I'd love to help, Fawn, but . . . but . . . I'll never be able to get a baby-sitter on such short notice," I replied lamely.

"Oh, is *that* the problem?" Fawn smiled. "Oh, thank you for bringing that to my attention. I'm sure we can find someone to take Emily around while you work. Penny?"

Penny consulted her clipboard. "Denise Costello is free that morning," she pointed out. "She's been assigned to the afternoon shift."

"Oh, I wouldn't want to inconvenience her," I said quickly. "I mean, she might have something to do in the morning."

"Oh, I'm sure Denise would love to help," Fawn assured me. "She has a wonderful appreciation of the sense of giving."

It turned out that Denise had nothing to do that morning, was already taking her daughter Amber to the fair, and would be happy to chaperone Emily as well. I was stuck.

"There," said Fawn when it was all arranged. "That's one of the really wonderful things about this school. The sense of community. Oh, and by the way," she continued, "it's always nice for parents working behind the counter to contribute something toward the bake sale. . . . Cupcakes are always welcome."

* * *

And that's how I came to be standing glumly in front of the baked goods counter at eight-thirty Saturday morning, Emily dancing at my side, a large white box containing twenty-four devil's food cupcakes (which I'd had to bake during the time I specifically set aside to work on my novel) in my arms, waiting for Denise to come and take *my* child to the fair.

Of course it was a beautiful day. Blue sky, warm but not hot, a few leaves turning. They'd done a perfectly lovely job. The grounds were festive with balloons and streamers and flags. The petting zoo had a real llama.

"Elizabeth?" It was Denise and Amber. They were wearing matching Polo shirts and shorts. They even had matching socks.

"Oh, hi, Elizabeth. Hi, Emily," said Denise. "Amber, say hi to Emily and Mrs. Halperin. Elizabeth, isn't this just the most wonderful day for the fall fair? You know, I told William he should try and make it but he's so dedicated to his clients. I worry about his health, I really do. He works so hard, I just don't know what—"

"*Mom,*" Amber whined, pulling on her arm.

"Just a moment, sweetheart. You're a writer, aren't you, Elizabeth? I think that's so exciting. William does some writing, of course—he's a personal injury lawyer—and I've always admired anyone—"

"*Mom.* We want to *go.*"

"Of course you do, sweetheart. I guess we'd better get going," she said to me. She smiled down at the girls. "Where would you like to go first?" she asked.

"THE PONY RIDE!" Emily and Amber sang out in unison.

"Okay, let's go."

"Thank you for taking Emily," I said. "And, by the way, I'll be happy to look after Amber for you this afternoon."

"This afternoon?" repeated Denise as she took each girl by the hand.

"Yes. Aren't you working the afternoon shift?" I asked.

"Oh, no," said Denise. "I told them I couldn't. We're all leaving for the Cape right after lunch."

"*Mom.*"

"Good-bye, honey," I called to Emily's retreating back. "Have fun . . . "

"Umm . . . Elizabeth?"

I turned. There was Fawn Woodehouse. I recognized the Laura Ashley.

"Elizabeth, I believe you have a customer," Fawn Woodehouse said.

I turned further. A boy of perhaps eight was standing in front of the counter waving a dollar bill at me like it was a red cape and I was the bull. "Gimme some cookies," he demanded.

Two hours later, I had seen (and served) nearly everyone I knew in town. This was partly because of the fact that the baked goods counter was the first booth inside the entrance gate and partly because the first thing anyone does at a country fair is eat.

"Excuse me," said my next customer politely.

I looked up. Standing in front of me was a tall, thin, balding man of over sixty, tanned and fit, wearing a white tennis outfit with a little Wimbledon emblem on the left sleeve. He had a tennis bag slung over his shoulder. His face was as wrinkled as a raisin (too much sun when he was younger, I supposed), and he wore a hearing aid in one ear. He was accompanied by another male sexagenarian, this one short and round and rosy, also dressed in tennis attire. Together they looked something like an old tomato walking next to a wilted carrot.

Grandfathers, I thought. "Yes?" I said aloud. "May I help you?"

"I hope so," replied the tall thin one. He leaned closer. "Do you play tennis?" he asked conspiratorially.

Tennis? "I'm afraid not."

"That's too bad." His face fell. "We're looking for a third, you see."

A third? To play tennis? "How do you play tennis with three people?" I asked.

"You don't. You need four. We were hoping you had a friend," he admitted.

I looked at him.

"I'm joking, actually."

I nodded.

"We really wanted you and your friend for sex," he continued.

I stared.

He cocked his head in the direction of the short round one. "My friend Frank is too shy to ask," he confided.

"Obviously not your problem," I noted.

"Oh, no. I'm very shy. I have a great deal of trouble talking to women," he said.

Frank spoke up. He pointed to his friend's hearing aid. "Actually, Ed has a great deal of trouble *hearing* women," he said, smiling affably.

I looked from one to the other. "Do you want something to eat?"

"See, Frank?" said Ed. "I told you she was a good sport."

I laughed. It irritated me to do so, but I couldn't help myself.

"Seriously now," Ed continued. "We're strangers in town. What can we do for fun around here?"

"Have you tried the pony ride?" I suggested.

"Will you go with me? I need someone to hold my hand," he said.

"Actually," said Frank, "we're looking for a nice restaurant for dinner."

"Oh, yes," said Ed. "Now tell me. Do you like Mexican food? We're looking for a Mexican restaurant. We're meeting a friend for dinner."

"Perhaps you know him," said Frank. "His name is Jonathon Nichols."

I stared at him hard, but he returned my gaze innocently. "Yes, I know Jonathon Nichols," I said evenly.

Frank brightened. "Have you seen him lately?" he asked. He looked around him. "He isn't here now, is he?"

"No, I haven't seen him."

"Why are we talking about him?" Ed demanded. "I'd rather talk about us." He reached (unsuccessfully) for my hand. "Are you sure I couldn't interest you in a burrito, my dear?"

"Quite sure."

"I promise to behave myself."

"Too bad," I said. "And just when I was weakening."

About fifteen minutes after they left I was approached by another couple, this time a man and a woman. He had a beard and wire-rimmed glasses. The woman, obviously his wife, was about four inches shorter, with a round pretty face. They were of middle age, dressed in black, with bodies reminiscent of Emily's stuffed bears. They looked like the kind of people for whom eating was a very important part of their lives.

"Pardon me," said the man in an indeterminate English accent that seemed to have originated somewhere in Hungary, after anxiously spanning the countertop, "what would you recommend?"

"The lemon poppy-seed muffins have gotten very good reviews," I replied.

He nodded sagely. "I will by all means try one, then."

I handed him the muffin. The woman, who had been standing behind his left shoulder, stepped around him to get to the counter. "I think I'll have a brownie," she said.

I handed her the brownie just as the man lifted his muffin into the air. "'*O di*,'" he recited, "'*reddite mi hoc pro pietate mea.*'" He paused. "'Gods, grant me this thing for my piety,'" he translated, and bit. "Catullus," he added.

"Uh-huh," I said.

"A Roman poet," he continued by way of explanation, through crumbs. "Lived to be thirty. The Scott Fitzgerald of his day. Of course, his day was 60 B.C. Are you a student of Rome, by any chance?"

"No, I'm afraid not."

"A pity. So few are. This is excellent, by the way. A lovely muffin."

"I'm glad you like it," I said, looking around trying to figure out if these people really had children. "That'll be a dollar," I added.

"We're together," he said. "How much for the brownie?"

"No, no, it's a dollar for both," I explained. "Fifty cents each."

"How very reasonable," he said. "I'll have another."

"Me, too," said his wife, still chewing.

"I understand this is a school fair," said the man, after securing the second muffin. "Are you from the area?"

No, I thought. They imported me from California to sell muffins. "Yes," I said.

"Ah. But you don't speak like a native."

"I moved here from New York about four years ago," I said.

"That seems to be a popular activity, moving from New York to the Berkshires. A good friend and associate of mine has done that as well."

"Who?" I asked.

"In your travels have you ever run into Jonathon Nichols?" he asked.

This isn't happening, I thought. "No," I said coldly.

"Perhaps you've seen him without knowing it. He's about five foot—"

"NO," I interrupted firmly.

"Ah," said the man. "I see." He paused. "A pity. We were hoping to run into him."

"I'm sorry. I can't help you."

"Of course you can't. As you say, you don't know him." He turned to his companion. "Shall we be going?" They started to move on, but then turned back. "'*Agnosco veteris vestigia flammae*. I feel again a spark of that ancient flame.' Virgil. A contemporary of Catullus, much more well known. Perhaps just one more of those excellent muffins to sustain us . . . "

"Me, too," said his wife.

More people came and went. I caught sight of Emily getting her face painted at a booth across from the ring toss. I hope they give her a rainbow, I worried. She always gets a rainbow painted on her left cheek when she gets her face painted. Maybe I should just go over and make sure . . .

"Excuse me," rasped a nasal voice.

I sighed and turned back to my cookies. "Yes . . ." I began, and then stopped.

A short, painfully thin woman stood in front of me. Her long hair was caught back in a ponytail held by a jeweled clip. It was a shade of red that does not occur naturally in this solar system. Her eyes, plastered with blue eye shadow and ringed by black liner and mascara, were small and spaced closely together. Her mouth was wide and painted tomato red, as were her long, clawlike fingernails. She was wearing a turquoise sweat suit with a pink logo that read "La Costa."

"May I get you something?" I recovered.

With obvious effort, the woman pulled her lips back into a smile. "Do you have anything diet?" she growled.

"Uh . . . I don't think so," I said.

"Okay," she said, making no attempt to suppress her irritation. She squinted at the table and then pointed abruptly to the Rice Krispies Treats. "I'll take one of those."

I handed it to her. "That'll be fifty cents."

She accepted the sticky bar but made no move to leave.

Instead, she looked me up and down and then leaned forward slightly.

"Such a charming little country fair," she observed in an ingratiating tone, or as ingratiating a tone as someone who otherwise sounded like a German shepherd could have. "I just love little country fairs like this one, don't you? They're so— so—"

"Country?" I supplied helpfully.

"Exactly. So *country*." She pulled her lips back a second time. "By the way, *love* your T-shirt."

"Thank you."

She pecked a single kernel of Rice Krispie from the bar with one enameled fingertip and popped it into her mouth. "Actually, I was wondering if you could help me. I'm new in town and I'm looking for someone named—"

Not again, I thought.

"—Elizabeth Halperin," the woman finished.

I opened my mouth to say "I'm Elizabeth Halperin," then closed it again. Instead: "Are you a friend of hers?" I asked.

There was a pause, then:

"She's one of my oldest and dearest friends," the woman assured me. "We go way back. I mean, *way* back."

I nodded slowly. "She left," I said firmly.

Relief finally appeared in the form of Penny Johnson, a tray of sugar cookies with little faces made of M&M's in her arms. I escaped from the bake stand and stood in the center of the school yard, looking around for my daughter. It didn't take long to spot her. She was climbing on the monkey bars. Denise and Amber stood nearby. "C'mon, Emily," I heard Amber wheedle. "I want to get popcorn now."

I ran over. "Hi, everybody. Hey, Em," I said, coming up from underneath the monkey bars. "It's me. Mommy. Remember?"

"Look at me, Mommy!" Emily hung upside down by her knees.

"Excellent job," I told her. "Did you have fun?"

Amber came over and regarded me solemnly. "Emily won't get popcorn," she reported.

"She might be a little—" I started to answer, then stopped.

Standing a short distance away was the most attractive man I'd ever seen. Really, he was mesmerizing. He was very tall and powerfully built, athletic, but not in a bodybuilder sort of way. His features were strong, sharply etched and intelligent. There was something about his face and the way he carried himself that was both assured and daring. His hair was going silver but his brows were still very dark—a striking combination. He was wearing a soft, gray turtleneck and charcoal gray slacks. Set against the backdrop of all the other parents slouching around in their jeans and windbreakers and sneakers he looked like he had just stepped out of an ad for Chivas Regal or Grey Poupon or something.

He was looking around with a strange expression of amusement and irreverence. Having a wonderful time taking it all in, not really searching for anything in particular, but somehow on the alert. It was the sort of look that Robin Hood probably wore whenever he went undercover at the sheriff of Nottingham's garden parties.

He caught me looking at him and his forehead crinkled up for a second.

"Look at me now, Mommy!"

Embarrassed to be caught staring, I turned quickly to my daughter. Emily was hanging by one arm and one leg. "Very good, sweetheart," I said, and immediately looked back to see if he was still looking at me.

He was. In fact, he was doing more than looking. He was starting to walk over.

"Emily, let's go get popcorn NOW," Amber demanded, reaching up and pulling on Emily's skirt.

"No!" Emily has a stubborn streak. Howard's side of the family, no doubt.

Amber pulled harder.

Denise stepped forward. "Amber, honey, don't do that. It's dangerous."

Emily took a swipe at Amber.

"No!" howled Amber, trying to pinch.

"Don't!" wailed Emily, swaying unsteadily.

I quickly reached up and untangled Emily from the monkey bars, one eye on the rapidly approaching stranger. "That's enough. Say thank you to Mrs. Costello," I said. Actually, pleaded is the more accurate term.

"No!" shouted Emily, turning her head away.

"Pooh!" spat Amber.

"Amber!" scolded Denise.

"Pooh back!" sputtered Emily.

"Emily!" And I wonder why I don't meet interesting men, I thought in desperation.

"Thank you, that would be charming."

We all turned at the sound of his voice. Emily, who was in my arms, stopped struggling. Amber, who was pulling at her mother, became quiet. Denise and I just stared. What kind of accent is that? I wondered. Not American. Not English. Scottish? Welsh?

Denise spoke first. "Umm, excuse me?" she said. I saw her run her hand through her hair reflexively.

"To see that I was a stranger in town and ask me to dinner," he continued, looking right at me.

It took a few moments, but by degrees I realized that my mouth was open. I shut it so hard my teeth chinked.

Denise looked from one of us to the other. "Amber and I will just be running along," she announced, although she made no move to leave.

"Right. Shall we say the Cottage Café at ten o'clock? I'm afraid I have a business appointment in the evening which prevents me from making an earlier engagement," he said, his eyes twinkling at me.

"Oh," said Denise.

"I look forward to seeing you. And may I add that it has been a distinct pleasure to meet all of you," he added, and with a little nod of his head, walked off in the direction of the parking lot.

We all stood there and watched as he got into a vintage two-seater convertible Jaguar roadster in British racing green, expertly backed up, and flew out onto the road. Then Denise looked at me.

"Who was *that*?" she asked.

"I have no idea," I replied, still shading my eyes and staring in the direction of the Jag.

"You mean, a perfect stranger came up out of nowhere and asked you out to dinner just like that?" Denise squealed.

"It would appear so, yes."

Denise took a step forward. "Are you going?"

I lowered my hand from my eyes, shifted Emily in my arms, and turned back to her.

"Of course I'm not going," I said virtuously.

By eight-thirty that evening, every decent item of clothing I owned lay spread out on the bed. I stood in my underwear and looked at Emily. "So, what do you think?" I asked anxiously.

Without hesitation she reached out one grubby hand. "The beautiful long black dress," she sighed.

I rescued it just in time. "You always pick this one," I accused her. "You just like it because it's long."

"No, I like it because it's long and *black*," she corrected me. "I *love* black."

Great. I'm raising Dracula, I thought. I held it up to the mirror. "I don't know, Em," I worried. "It's kind of . . . obvious."

"What do you mean, 'obvious'?"

"Well, you know, it's tight and low-cut and has that slit up the front. . . . Never mind." I reached over and plucked a sedate navy blue dress with cap sleeves from the pile on the bed. "Now, this one would be much more sensible." I held it up next to the black one. "What do you think?" I wanted to know.

"Yuck," said Emily.

"Don't say 'yuck,'" I reproved her automatically. "It's impolite." We both heard a knock on the front door. "COME IN, SOJI!" I hollered out the window. "IT'S NOT LOCKED." Soji was Emily's baby-sitter. Short for Sojourner.

"Soji!" Emily sprang down the stairs.

I stood holding the two dresses for another moment in front of the mirror. Then I tossed the navy blue on the bed.

"Yuck," I said.

Half an hour later I sashayed rather unsteadily down the stairs. I had decided to go all the way and wear my new black high heels, purchased the previous April during a particularly expensive fit of despondency over the departed Adam and my nonexistent love life. This was the first time I'd felt like wearing them. During all those dates with Jonathon Nichols I hadn't once even thought of them.

I was a little uncomfortable about the shoes—about the whole outfit, actually. Nobody dressed like this in the Berkshires. For one thing, it's impractical. In the winter it's too cold, and in the summer the heels make little holes in people's lawns. But it's more than that. There's a large, aging hippie contingent in the Berkshires who make a virtue of Birkenstock sandals and blue jeans with holes in the knees and who frown on vain affectation in the form of fur coats, stiletto heels, and fluoride in the water.

But tonight I didn't care. Tonight I wanted to look . . . well, not glamorous, exactly, but sophisticated—in a romantic sort of way. It was as though some part of myself that had been hid-

den away was reasserting itself, demanding to be dusted off
and used. The part of me that yearned for excitement, for
adventure, for a little harmless recklessness . . . What a dope
I'm being. He's probably an insurance salesman, I thought as I
clomped down the stairs.

Soji and Emily were on the sofa reading when I made my
appearance. Emily looked up at the clatter of the heels on the
wood floor.

"Ooohh, look at Mommy!"

Soji, who was nineteen and very cool, also glanced up. She
was wearing long cutoff shorts, a beaded ankle bracelet above
bare feet, and a T-shirt with an M. C. Escher print of lizards on
the front. She took one look at me and I immediately felt about
as romantically sophisticated as one of Emily's Barbie dolls.

"Planning a big night?" she inquired.

I will not be intimidated by a nineteen-year-old, I resolved.

"Uhh—it's a formal affair," I lied.

I was saved from further humiliation by the sound of the
phone ringing.

"I'll get it," I volunteered quickly, and tottered off into the
kitchen. "Hello?" I said into the receiver.

"Elizabeth?"

I paused. "Hello, Jonathon," I said coldly and with as much
dignity as I could muster in the presence of Soji's disapproving
gaze.

"Elizabeth, I have to see you. Right now."

"I can't. I'm going out."

"Please."

"I'm sorry, but—"

"It's very important. You know I wouldn't ask you if it wasn't."

No, as a matter of fact, I don't know that, I thought. "What
is it, Jonathon?" I asked.

"I can't tell you over the phone."

"Why not?"

"There isn't time. I'm taking a big risk as it is."

"What risk?"

"Listen. I promise I'll tell you all about it as soon as you get here."

"Get where?"

"The site. I need for you to meet me at the site. Right now."

At the site? "Forget it," I said flatly.

"Please, Elizabeth," Jonathon pleaded. "It's a matter of life and death."

"Right."

"No, really. I need your help. Promise you'll come."

"NO."

"Elizabeth, I'm in trouble! If you were in trouble, don't you think I'd help you?"

"Listen, Jonathon—"

But the line was dead.

It was already dark when I got there. I gingerly picked my way through Jonathon Nichols's construction site doing my best not to ruin my heels. I can't believe I'm doing this, I groused to myself as I just barely avoided the gravel pit.

Actually, though, I knew why I was there. I was glad to have the chance to see him one last time. This time he was going to get an earful. I'm sorry you're in trouble, I mentally rehearsed, but that's no excuse for blabbing about me all over town. This is it. We're finished. (Not that we ever started.) Pretend I don't live here anymore. Pretend we don't know each other. Pretend . . .

I stumbled over something in the dark and my heel caught. "Goddamn it," I swore. I twisted around to extricate myself when I saw what it was that I'd tripped over.

It was a body. A dead body. A dead body lying on the ground with big, deep tread marks on it.

It was Jonathon Nichols. He had been hit by a truck.

Chapter

4

Oh, God. "Jonathon!" I sort of squeaked and leaped back.

He didn't answer, of course. He was lying on his back, staring straight up at the sky. There was a very surprised look on his face.

All the anger drained out of me in a split second and was replaced by overwhelming remorse. Poor Jonathon! How could it have happened? I wondered. An accident? What kind of traffic accident could occur at a deserted construction site? I looked around. There was nothing that could have done something like this except the backhoe, and that clearly hadn't been moved, since there were no tracks around it. The moon peeked out from behind a cloud for a moment, and I squinted down at the ground in front of me . . . the tracks led away from Jonathon's body, out of the lot . . . a hit-and-run, I realized. In a deserted lot. A deliberate hit-and-run.

I could feel myself shaking. The moon went back behind the cloud and it got dark again. The construction site was very still. It was on a side road off Route 7, and since this was after season, there wasn't a car in sight. There was no sound but my own breathing. I scooted back a few feet, but I almost tripped over a cinder block. I was hot and cold at the same time, my heart pounding.

I realized I was all alone in a vacant lot with a murder victim, a relatively *recent* murder victim. That meant the murderer might still be around. And me loafing around the scene of the crime dressed like Demi Moore about to seduce an unsuspecting accountant.

I took off. Heels or no heels, I fled. I stumbled over ruts and ditches and discarded bits of metal, but I didn't stop running until I was back in my car with the doors and windows locked.

What to do? Go to the police, of course. I started the car, turned on the headlights and squealed my way out of the lot and onto Housatonic Street.

The light at Route 7 was against me. I sat there and waited, panting, straining to see if anyone was following me. Hurry, hurry.

The light turned green. I put my foot all the way down on the accelerator and careened across the intersection. Three more blocks and here was the left onto Church Street. Town was deserted, but the police station was only about thirty seconds away now.

A right onto Walker. Half a block down. There it was, on the left. I started to turn the wheel—

And then drove right past it.

In the approximately four minutes it had taken me to drive from the construction site to the police station, after I had ascertained that, in fact, no one was following me, a thought had occurred to me. And that thought was how—well, how *odd* it was going to look when I told Chief Rudge—he's the chief of police here in Lenox—how odd it was going to look when I reported that I'd arranged to meet Jonathon Nichols in a vacant lot and found him dead when I got there.

If I'd been an ordinary citizen of Lenox—that is, if I had not already been suspected of murdering my late husband—there would have been no problem. I would simply have gone into the station, told the police what I knew, driven back with them, shown them the body, and been on my way.

But I was no ordinary citizen. Since no one had ever been convicted of Howard's murder, the case was technically still open. And Chief Rudge made no secret of the fact that he still thought I'd done it and was just waiting for me to make a mistake so he could nail me. Police chiefs in small towns, I'd discovered, don't *like* having two-year-old unsolved murder cases lying around the district. They think it makes them look bad, which, of course, it does.

As a result, for a long time now I had been the recipient of the chief's extra-special personal attention. This is not like having the extra-special personal attention of someone desirable, like your hairdresser or your literary agent. The chief's extra-special personal attention generally took the form of such petty harassments as giving me the fisheye while I was having pancakes with Emily at the Village Snack Shop, driving his squad car back and forth in front of my house at odd hours, and writing me up for having a two-week-old expired registration on my car, which probably gave me the distinction of being the only person in New England to be so ticketed.

Now here comes another corpse with whom I was personally involved. I mean, let's face it, it just doesn't look right. I banged my head on the steering wheel of my Jeep and cursed myself all over again for that confounded night with Jonathon Nichols. If it wasn't for that, I might not have a problem. But as things stood, the police might very well have heard the rumor that I—well, who knew where they went to get their teeth cleaned. I just couldn't take the risk that they'd associate me with the crime.

And yet I had to report the discovery of the body. What to do?

And then it came to me. An anonymous phone call. Perfect. The police would find out that Jonathon had been murdered almost as quickly as if I'd told them myself. After all, I reasoned, Jonathon was already dead, so there wasn't anything I could do for him beyond alerting the authorities, and who said I had to do that in person? It's not like I knew anything about it. All I needed was an out-of-the-way phone and a disguised voice. And, since I was already on my way to the Cottage Café, there seemed no reason not to just go ahead and use a phone near that location. The Cottage Café was all the way in Southfield, nearly half an hour away. They'd never trace me there. And I'd have an alibi. I could say I was meeting someone there, as I was.

I swear to you that not once during this period did I even consider the fact that if I went to the police they would most certainly have detained me long enough that I would have missed my date.

I stopped at the first pay phone I found in Southfield. It was in front of the general store, which is about a block away from the restaurant. There wasn't anyone around at that time of night and all the lights were off inside. I rummaged around in my purse for a quarter, put it in, and dialed 911. It rang. Remember, I warned myself, don't use your own voice.

"Nine one one," the operator reported.

"I have an emergency message for the Lenox police," I said, in my assumed voice. "Tell them to go to the vacant lot at Route Seven and Housatonic. There's been some trouble. There's been—"

"Who is this?" interrupted the operator.

"Tell them to go right away. Tell them it's an emergency. Tell them there's a—there's a"—I couldn't bring myself to say it—"there's something there. At the vacant lot."

"Where are you calling from?"

"Just tell them. It's an emergency," I repeated, and hung up.

It was only after I'd gotten back into my car and driven nearly to the door of the restaurant that I realized the voice I'd assumed was that of Miss Piggy.

The Cottage Café is a small, intimate restaurant set out in Southfield, which, even by Berkshire standards, is the middle of nowhere. I had lived in the area three years before I'd even heard of it. It has lace tablecloths, lots of plants and flowers, cream walls with exposed beams, and soft lighting. Jazz plays huskily in the background, and there are shelves lined with old books on the walls. It's the perfect place for a romantic tryst.

There were only two tables occupied when I burst in through the door. At one of them sat a party of four. At the other was the man from the fair.

"Can I help you?" asked the hostess.

"Uhh, I'm meeting that man over there . . ." I fumbled. She was looking at me a little strangely. Must be the heels, I thought.

"Of course," said the hostess, dropping her eyes uncomfortably. "Right this way."

She led me across the room. He was at a wicker table at the far corner. A bottle of wine sat in an ice bucket beside him.

"Hello, Elizabeth."

"Hi," I said, trying to remember if I'd mentioned my name before. I was pretty sure I hadn't.

"I'm glad you could make it. It looks like you had some difficulty getting here." He paused. "You did drive, didn't you?"

"Yes." Why did he have the same expression as the hostess?

"Perhaps you would care to freshen up before you sit down."

Reflexively, I looked down at myself. The front of my dress was streaked with dirt. The sexy slit in the front opened to reveal a big hole in my stockings from where I'd stumbled over the gravel pit on my way out of the lot. I became aware that my hair was hanging limply in my face, and when I went to push it back I saw bits of gravel clinging to the mud on my hands. As for my shoes . . . "I'll just go freshen up a bit before I sit down," I volunteered.

I went into the bathroom, ditched the pantyhose into the wastebasket, scraped the shoes with paper towels, and washed up as best I could. Then I stood in front of the mirror and addressed my reflection. "Take a deep breath," I said aloud. "Try not to think about it. And, for goodness sake, whatever you do, act *naturally*."

I went back to the table.

"Please, sit down," he said, and held the chair for me.

"Thank you."

He had removed the wine from the ice bucket and was pouring me a glass. He held up the bottle. It had a ZD on it. "This is an excellent . . . "

He paused as I tipped back my glass and drained it. I set it down and he refilled it. I thought about Jonathon Nichols's body and took another long sip.

"Right. Don't feel the need to restrain yourself. I have another bottle being chilled," he said, and poured again.

Act naturally. "I don't always drink like this," I pointed out quickly.

"Really. How do you drink?"

"I mean, so fast. It's just that . . . it's so . . . the wine's excellent. What kind is it?" I recovered.

"California. Chardonnay. I always make it a point to drink the wine of whatever country I'm in. It was a little inconvenient in Afghanistan."

"Oh, right," I said blankly. I looked across the table at him. He was even better looking than I remembered. He'd changed his clothes since the fair and was now wearing an expensive-looking sport jacket, a white shirt, and a wonderful silk tie of a shade of blue that fell somewhere between sapphire and turquoise. His eyes were gray under the dark brows. At the moment they were gazing frankly and steadily into mine. They might have been holding up a sign that read, "Trust Me."

Instinctively, I felt the words *I just saw a dead body* starting to come my lips.

Instead: "How do you know my name?" I asked.

"You mentioned it."

"I did not."

"Oh. I thought you did."

"I know you didn't mention your name," I said, giving up.

"Oh. Sorry. Smith."

Smith, I thought. Right. "Joe Smith?" I offered, sipping.

"No, Simon. Simon Montgomery, actually," he said.

"Oh," I said.

The waitress came and brought bread. There was a momentary silence after she left. Then I filled it.

"I just saw a dead body," I blurted out.

He took a sip of his wine. "Yes, I know," he said calmly.

I stared at him.

"You just saw Jonathon Nichols sprawled in a construction site," he continued. "It must have been ghastly for you."

I pushed my chair back, got up, and started to move for the door.

"No, no, Elizabeth. Sit down. Have some more wine. I didn't kill him."

I remained standing but turned back to the table.

"Believe me, the last thing I wanted in the world was a dead Jonathon Nichols."

I cautiously resumed my chair.

"Why is that?" I asked. "And how do you know he's dead, anyway?"

"Because I was at the site before you. You were not the only person who had an appointment with Jonathon Nichols tonight."

"What were you there for?"

"Same thing you were. The money."

"What money? I wasn't there for any money. I was there for . . . well, for something else," I said. "Uh, another reason, I mean. No, I . . . what money?" I asked.

"The money Jonathon Nichols stole," said Simon, calmly breaking off a piece of bread. "Would you care for some? Bread, I mean. Not money."

I stuck out my hand and he put a piece of bread in it. "Jonathon stole money from you?" I asked, automatically taking a bite.

"Among a number of others, yes."

The visitors to the cookie stand popped into my head. "How much money?" I asked, chewing methodically.

"All together? Oh, I don't know exactly. Somewhere in the neighborhood of thirty million dollars."

My jaw started to drop, then snapped shut when I realized I still had a piece of bread in it. "Jonathon Nichols stole thirty million dollars?"

"No, not precisely. Jonathon Nichols doesn't exist."

"You mean he's dead."

"No. I mean Jonathon Nichols never existed."

"I'm a little confused," I said.

"Jonathon Nichols is, or, more precisely, *was* Irving Meltzman."

Irving Meltzman? I slept with somebody named *Irving Meltzman?* This isn't happening, I thought. "I don't believe you," I said.

Simon lifted the lapel of his jacket and removed an envelope from the inside pocket. "This is a photograph of Irving Meltzman," he said, handing it to me.

I looked at the picture. It showed an overweight, balding man of indeterminate middle age wearing a hideous green-checked suit.

"This is not Jonathon Nichols," I said flatly and with great relief, trying to return the photo.

But he didn't take it. "Look again," he said, reaching for his wineglass. "Look closer."

I looked closer.

"Think thinner," Simon suggested, taking a sip. "Think tanner. Think hair transplant."

I blinked suddenly. Come to think of it, there was something about the face. . . . No, it couldn't be. . . .

"Irving Meltzman," said Simon as I continued to stare down frozenly at the photograph, "was a New Jersey real estate developer who made something of a name for himself in the eighties. Perhaps you remember him from your own halcyon days on Wall Street?"

"No, I—" I stopped. "Wait a minute. How do you know I worked on—"

"No, of course not. I remember now you traded commodities. You would have been watching corn futures and gold bullion and so forth, wouldn't you, not apartment complexes. He would have known that about you, of course," Simon reflected.

"He? What about you? How is it you know so much about me?"

"What? Oh. I read the little biography of you on the inside flap of your book jacket. Quite a nice read, actually. The book, not the biography."

"Oh. Oh," I said. "Thank you."

"Not at all. Of course, then came the nineties and Irving found himself overextended . . . which was not especially unusual," Simon noted, switching back once again to the topic of the murder victim. "What was unusual was the way Irving handled it. By the way"—he paused, looking at me solicitously—"would you prefer I call him Jonathon?"

No, I thought. I'll take my humiliation straight. "Irving's fine," I said.

"As I was saying, then, instead of retrenching like everyone else, Irving expanded. Talked his way into a thirty-million-dollar New Jersey hotel project."

"What do you mean, 'talked his way into'?" I asked. "I mean, if everybody knew that real estate prices were way down, why would anyone invest in a new hotel, particularly such an expensive one?"

"Well, money is always looking for a good return, and Irving Meltzman promised a substantial one. Then again, he had a good track record—conservative, reliable—up until that point, at any rate. But mostly what Irving Meltzman had going for him was his ability to talk investors into projects. He was quite a good talker, I believe. I understand that he even managed to talk you into a thing or two."

I let that one go by.

"But this time," Simon said, "Irving was neither reliable nor conservative. This time, Irving Meltzman took his thirty million dollars and dropped out of sight completely. That was three years ago. We've been looking for him ever since." He paused. "It was only by chance that we discovered him at all."

"What kind of chance? And what do you mean we?" I asked.

He reached into his other pocket and unfolded a newspaper article. It was from the *New York Times*. "VALUES CLASH OVER NEW ENGLAND DEVELOPMENT," the title read. Then, underneath, in smaller print, "Berkshire Developer Unleashes Local Passions with Mall Proposal." The grainy photo to the right of the story was captioned "Lenox developer Jonathon Nichols at the site of his proposed mall."

I squinted at the photograph. "You recognized him from *this?*" I asked.

"If he had taken thirty million dollars of your money, you'd have recognized him, too."

"But if he was in hiding, why on earth would he allow himself to be photographed by the *Times?*"

Simon shrugged. "Perhaps he felt so comfortable with his

new identity that he didn't think it would matter," he said. "Perhaps he thought we'd given up looking for him altogether, although that seems unlikely. I can't imagine anyone giving up thirty million dollars so easily. Perhaps . . . "

"Perhaps he couldn't help himself," I said in an undertone, staring down at the paper.

"Pardon?"

"Jon—Irving was like that, you know. He loved the action. I can't imagine him standing on the sidelines living a quiet life. He hustled people just to stay in practice."

Simon smiled. He had a great smile. I felt myself tingle a little. "I knew I had the right woman."

"The right woman for what?" I asked, tingling a little more.

"For the moment, let's just say the right woman to help me get the thirty million dollars back." He leaned back in his chair. "He didn't mention anything about it to you, did he?"

"Of course not."

"Think back. It might not have been straightforward. He might have bragged about it in a circuitous way." He paused. "You know Irving."

"Oh, no, you don't," I said, waving the remainder of my bread at him. "I'm not having anything to do with this."

"I'm afraid you have no choice, Elizabeth."

"Oh, yes, I—" I stopped. There was something in his tone. "What do you mean, I have no choice?" I demanded.

The gray eyes looked steadily into mine. I felt myself kind of melting toward him. "I'm afraid that I'm not the only one who thinks you know something about the money."

"But I don't know anything about the money!" So much for melting.

"No one is going to believe that. You were with him all summer. You were seen everywhere together. He made no secret of his affection for you. If the key to the location of the money wasn't on him at the time of his death—and I have reason to believe it wasn't—then he hid it somewhere. It is quite possible that he took someone into his confidence. In these cases it is usually a woman. You are the obvious choice."

I stared at him. "But that means . . . "

"Exactly. They'll come after you." He paused. "And one of them is a murderer."

Chapter

5

It is just amazing what a night's rest and a sunny morning will do for a person's perspective.

In my case, it turned around by about 180 degrees. Only eight hours earlier, sitting at the Cottage Café with Simon, visions of armed murderers running amok in the Berkshires, I had seriously considered packing Emily off in the dead of night and whisking her away to safety. I could take her to my parents in L.A., I thought. But no, that'd be the first place they'd look, I realized. (Hey, I've seen *The Terminator*.) What about leaving the country? Mexico, South America, that sort of thing? Forget it. Emily's diet consisted strictly of peanut butter and jelly and buttered noodles. She'd starve to death in a foreign country. What was left? I'd wondered as I pushed my roast chicken and garlic mashed potatoes absently around my plate with the fork. Nebraska and the Witness Protection Program?

But in the calm light of Sunday morning with the sun streaming through the dotted curtains, the clear blue sky of early autumn visible through the lace, the sound of robins chirping and Emily spooning Cheerios and chatting happily with Grover, I relaxed and had a chance to reassess the situation. And what I thought was: What am I worried about? This is Lenox, for goodness sake. Lenox. Where people wear sturdy, sensible shoes and polyester baseball caps and the major event of the season is the croquet match at the Lenox Club. Nothing really bad ever happens in Lenox. For that matter, not much of anything at all ever happens in Lenox.

True, Jonathon—er, Irving—was dead, but had he *really* been murdered? Might I not have overreacted a teensy weensy bit to the sight of the body the night before at the construction site? Maybe it really had been an accident. Maybe he hadn't really been run over. Maybe it just *looked* like he'd been run over but he'd actually had a heart attack or something, and then someone drove over him in the dark by accident and that's what made those tire marks. . . .

Okay, so he really was murdered. That didn't mean the rest of the story held water. I mean, thirty million dollars. If a person had thirty million dollars stashed away somewhere, would they really stay in Lenox and try to put up a Wal-Mart? I ask you. Does it make sense? With that kind of money, if a person had to get lost and stay lost, wouldn't they get lost somewhere interesting, like the South of France, for example? That's what I'd do.

Well, there's one way to find out, I thought.

"TAAaaaa . . . DAAAaaa . . . "

WAMC is the Berkshires' only classical music station. On Sunday mornings it is hosted by Septimus Bartholomew. No one would ever accuse Septimus Bartholomew of pandering to the masses. He is a middle-aged man who always sounds sententious and world-weary, like someone who could have accomplished great feats of international diplomacy if he had not been called upon so often to officiate at solemn occasions such as tub parades and funeral services for dead house pets. However, the one thing that Septimus Bartholomew always did on Sunday mornings with rigid constancy was to read the local news at eight o'clock. At that hour, everybody else was carrying either a church sermon or Casey's Top Forty.

DDDUUUuuuummm.

The music ended. There was a pause, then:

"That was . . . *Gurre Lieder*," mourned Septimus Bartholomew. "A song cycle by Schoenberg to poems by J. P. Jacobsen." Pause. "The poems . . . are based on the Danish legend of King Waldemar IV, who . . . lived in the castle of Gurra. . . . When the king falls in love with the princess Tove, the queen plots and accomplishes Tove's death . . . which is announced in a song of the Forest Dove . . . part one." Pause. "Part two contains Waldemar's lament . . . and rebellion against God . . . for which, in part three, he is sentenced to hunt nightly with ghosts." Long pause. "From the Danish, of course," concluded Septimus Bartholomew somberly.

Pity I missed it, I thought.

"And now, for the news."

I braced myself.

"Town officials . . . have recently closed the debate . . . on the widening of Route Seven . . . with the caveat . . . that it may be reopened at any time . . . by a two-thirds majority . . . "

Not that.

"All those . . . wishing to participate . . . in the Lenox Garden Club's . . . annual pumpkin show . . . should fill out . . . an application form . . . at the . . . "

Not that.

"Police are investigating . . . the suspicious death . . . of Lenox developer . . . Jonathon Nichols . . . "

That.

"Mr. Nichols . . . was found late last night . . . at his construction site at the corner of Housatonic Street and Route

Seven . . . apparently the victim . . . of a freak traffic accident . . . "

Hmm, I thought.

"Mr. Nichols . . . had recently stirred up some controversy . . . with his plan to erect a large shopping mall . . . on the outskirts of Lenox's historic downtown shopping district . . . Lenox Police Chief Ned Rudge . . . has promised a full investigation into the matter . . . and now . . . a lively *Clausula,* a form of early thirteenth century music based on a short section of a Gregorian chant. . . . TAAAaaaa . . . DDDAAAaaaa . . . "

I leaned over and switched off the radio.

Of course, I thought. The mall. It was the obvious motive. One of the local tradespeople, justifiably upset at the possibility of losing his or her livelihood to Jonathon's endangered-wood monstrosity, experiences a momentary absence of sanity, focuses all his or her hatred on the developer, and runs the guy over with a pickup. Or it could have been a disgruntled construction worker who *wasn't* hired for the project, who drank a few too many beers with his pals in the afternoon, got himself all worked up over his grievance, and decided to take revenge. It could even have been one of those aristocratic elderly women with the blue hair and the sweaters flung over their shoulders à la Grace Kelly who have lived here forever and who you always see at the town meetings mourning the passing of time and fighting any sort of change tooth and nail. That was the beauty of the crime, I realized. Almost anybody has the strength and acuity to put their foot down on a gas pedal.

Still, Simon had been so convincing . . . Simon. Oh, yes, Simon. Now *there* was something to think about.

Kissing is pretty important to me. I'm not going to go into a long treatise on it or anything, but there it is. It's probably just one of those infantile hang-ups I have left over from junior high, like worrying about whether I'm dressed correctly or have food stuck in my teeth when I go out. It's ridiculous, misguided, shallow . . . and still the first and last requirement by which I measure a potential relationship. Before I kiss someone, I think about what it would be *like* to kiss them. Then, when I do actually kiss someone, I take that kiss and compare it to some of its predecessors (was it as good as that night in the eleventh grade with Dennis Mooney?). Finally, I see what kind of aftereffect the kiss had. Do I want to try it again? Or do I find myself thinking about other things, like what to get my folks for Christmas this year?

Not last night, though. Last night, after the Cottage Café, Simon followed me home to make sure I was all right. We were on my front doorstep outwardly murmuring polite nothings to each other while internally I was furiously working through the problem of whether to ask him in or not. Out of the question, I had just decided. I don't care how attractive he is, I don't care how romantic the circumstances, I don't care how much you want to, never ever let what amounts to a complete stranger in the door on the first date. . . . He leaned in a little closer.

"Would you like to come in?" I asked.

He leaned in so close that I could feel the heat off his skin . . . or was it mine? "I'd like to," he said, smiling down at me. He kind of tipped my chin up and looked deeply into my eyes. It was a completely hackneyed gesture. I knew it was a hackneyed gesture. Unfortunately, it was an extremely effective hackneyed gesture.

He paused. "But I don't think so. Not tonight."

"Of course not," I murmured inanely, still mesmerized by his eyes on mine. "I mean, that's what I meant. I meant, would you like to come in some other night, I mean . . . "

Then he took me in his arms and—

"Mommy?"

I blinked a little and the room came into focus. Where was I? Oh, yes, Sunday morning. The sun streaming in . . . "Yes, sweetheart?"

"What are you doing, Mommy?" Emily demanded, peering at me around her grape juice. "Your mouth is moving but you aren't saying anything."

"What am I doing?" I coughed. Then I swooped down on her in her chair and tickled her. She giggled and squirmed. "I was daydreaming. That's what I was doing. And you caught me."

"Stop, Mommy!" Giggle, giggle, giggle. "Listen." She held up her Big Bird cup. "One—two—three," she read. "Four—five—six—seven—eight—nine—ten!"

"Great!" I exclaimed as I lifted her up from her chair and snuggled her in my arms. "You are getting so good at numbers! Have you been practicing at school?"

"Oh, no," said Emily. "We don't do numbers at school."

"You don't?" Several thousand dollars a year and she doesn't get numbers? I thought. Am I supposed to pay extra for that? "Tell you what, puddin'," I said with sudden inspiration, "we'll do anything you like this morning."

"Anything?" asked Emily, arching her eyebrows, suspicious of such an open-ended offer.

"Yep. You name it. Color, paint, read, go for a hike . . . "

"I want to dance to *Swan Lake*," said Emily abruptly.

Swan Lake was Emily's favorite ballet. She'd showed such an interest in it that I'd bought her a video of Nina Anani-ashvili dancing Odette with a Russian ballet troupe. Now, I know that most children her age are more interested in *101 Dalmatians* or *Bambi* or something, but not Emily. Emily liked to see real people dancing and wearing ornate costumes. She'll probably end up either a prima ballerina or a rap star.

"Really? It's such a lovely day. Don't you want to go outside and—"

"I want to dance," Emily insisted. "*Swan Lake*."

"Well, all right, if that's what you really—"

"I do! I do!" Emily wriggled out of my arms in excitement

and scampered up the stairs. "ONLY DON'T PUT IT ON UNTIL I'M WEADY!" she hollered over her shoulder.

"DON'T WORRY, I WON'T," I hollered back.

Okay, I can live with Tchaikovsky for an hour or so this morning. (It certainly beat Gregorian chants.) I went over to the television and switched on the VCR. Then I'll get her out to the playground. I located *Swan Lake* from the bottom drawer of the television cabinet and popped the tape halfway into the insert hole. Then I filled a mug with hazelnut coffee and walked over to the window with the intention of loitering over the view of my apple trees until such time as I was called upon to start the show.

If the apple trees were picturesque, I never saw them. I never got past the driveway. That's because a Lenox police car was parked just behind the mailbox, and there stood Chief Rudge and Detective Fineburg, pads in hand, circling slowly and intently around my Jeep.

I froze. My body temperature went from nice and cozy to arctic while the first sip of hazelnut was still in my throat.

What were they doing here? How had they traced me so quickly? What did they—the call. The 911 call. That was it. They'd recognized my voice, tracked me down. I had an overwhelming desire to beat my head against the window, like Charlie Brown. Stupid, stupid, stupid. Here I'd been obsessing over phantom killers when the real threat was now scrutinizing my Jeep. Why hadn't I just gone and done the sensible thing and reported the crime in person? I reproached myself. Now they'd nail me for sure on—on what? Running from a crime scene, not identifying myself, probably. What was that? Accessory after the fact? Maybe I could get out of it. Maybe I could say I just panicked and . . .

As I watched, the chief and the detective stopped circling suddenly and bent over together to examine my tires. Then the chief got down on his knees in between the front and rear axles. Detective Fineburg squatted down beside him and handed him a flashlight. Suddenly, the chief disappeared under the car altogether. All you could see of him were his shiny regulation black lace-ups and his white socks.

I squinted down at my car. Even from that distance I could plainly see the tracks of dirt running along the chassis.

Oh my God, I thought. They're not going to try to get me for failing to *report* a murder.

They're going to try to get me for the *murder*.

"Looking to take it for a test drive, Detective?" I called from the doorway with a nonchalance I did not feel. Might as well bluff it out, I thought.

Detective Fineburg looked up. The chief got out from under the car.

Chief Rudge is a short, balding, middle-aged man with ramrod posture and ears that stick out even when he's wearing his police cap, which is just about always. I'd never seen him out of uniform, not even for the annual charity softball game against the fire department. Detective Fineburg, on the other hand, is tall and gangly, with wild curly black hair shot through with squiggles of white. His choice of attire was more liberal. Today he was wearing a blue-and-white-checked shirt, a houndstooth jacket with his trademark elbow patches, forest-green L. L. Bean corduroys, a tie with pumpkins on it, and work boots. He looked as though half of him was going to build a deck and the other half was going to lecture at NYU.

"Good morning, Elizabeth," hailed the detective, smiling. It was an easy smile. Sure, I thought. *He's* happy. Probably's got me all lined up.

Detective Fineburg waved in the general direction of my apple trees, all the while not budging from his spot at the rear of my car. "Beautiful morning, isn't it?"

"Lovely," I agreed. I opened the door wider. "Would you care to come in?" I invited them cordially, trying to behave as if the neighbors had somehow gotten turned around and mistakenly stumbled onto my driveway. "I've got a pot of coffee on," I added. Oh, that's good, Elizabeth, I congratulated myself. That's a nice little touch.

Now I happen to know, from my previous run-in with the police department, that the one thing you should never, ever do is volunteer anything, certainly not admittance to your home. But anything to get them away from the car.

"Thank you, Elizabeth," returned the detective, "I think we will," and to my great relief, he and the chief turned away from my Jeep and began to climb the front steps leading to the house.

I squeezed back and let them go past me.

"Chief," I nodded, smiling.

"Ma'am," he acknowledged brusquely. He and the detective stopped in the foyer and looked around.

I had a chance to get a better look at them then. The chief's eyelids were at half-mast. Detective Fineburg had black circles under his eyes. Their clothes were rumpled. Bits of dirt and gravel clung to their shoes. They had just come from the site, I realized. They must have been up all night.

"Why don't we go into the living room?" I suggested.

"Sure," said the detective.

The chief frowned but followed along behind us anyway.

Detective Fineburg sniffed approvingly as we walked into the room. "Coffee smells wonderful," he said.

"It's hazelnut," I said. "I hope that's okay."

"That'll be great," he said.

"Chief? How do you take your coffee?"

The chief, who had assumed a military stance next to the flowered ottoman with his arms behind his back and his feet apart, addressed his response to the air above my head. "No coffee, ma'am," he said impassively.

"Detective Fineburg?"

"Milk and sugar. Oh, and got any of those cookies from last time?"

"I'll check," I promised.

When I got back with a tray, the detective had seated himself on the sofa, but the chief was still standing in his previous position.

"Same old Elizabeth, I see," said Detective Fineburg, with a nod toward my bookshelves. "Always the reader." He shook his head. "Whew! I think you've got even more books than the last time I saw you. Of course, that was in the smaller house," he added.

I most particularly did not want to discuss my new house and all my new books since we all knew I could afford them only because Howard had been murdered, a crime which at least two people in the room thought I'd gotten away with. So I simply handed Detective Fineburg his coffee and cookies and watched as he took an appreciative bite.

"You've gotten thinner, Detective," I said, examining him. "I hope they're not working you too hard."

He looked a little sheepish. "I guess I haven't been eating as well since the divorce."

"You're divorced?" I asked, surprised.

"Two months now."

"I'm sorry."

"Yeah, it's tough. Especially about the girls." He swallowed. "I only get to see them on the weekends now."

"Oh, that must be so hard," I said, and meant it. I couldn't imagine seeing Emily only on the weekends. "How old are they now?"

"Brooke is seven and Mariel's five. They're being really great about it. At least, Brooke is. Mariel's acting up a lot."

"That might be the best thing for her," I said. "It has to be terribly upsetting for Brooke, too, and if she's hiding her feelings—"

"Yes, that's exactly what I'm worrying about—"

"If we might just ask you a few questions, ma'am," interjected the chief.

"Uhh, right," said Detective Fineburg. He swallowed the last of his cookie. "I suppose you know why we're here," he said.

I sat down in an armchair between them and folded my hands primly in my lap. Here it comes, I thought.

The chief flipped out his pad. "At approximately nine forty-seven P.M. last night a 911 phone call was received and forwarded to the Lenox Police Station," he began.

I tried to study their faces covertly as they produced and then played the 911 tape. Were they just setting me up? Did they already know I'd made the call and were waiting for me to hang myself? I didn't think so. Of course, it is always difficult to identify your own voice, but in this case, the sounds coming off the tape didn't even sound human. Actually, as they talked, I started to relax a little. They didn't seem to have much idea about anything. There was certainly no mention of Irving Meltzman or thirty million dollars. Then they got to the part about me and Irv—er, Jonathon.

"You see our problem," Detective Fineburg concluded. "Jonathon Nichols is dead. And you were involved with him."

"Involvement of a *highly* sexual nature," repeated the chief.

"We dated once or twice," I said flatly.

"He was a controversial figure," said the detective. "He must have made a few enemies with his mall proposal. Did he ever mention—"

"Will you please give an account of your whereabouts last night, ma'am?" broke in the chief.

Detective Fineburg looked at him, surprised.

The chief held his ground, pencil raised against pad. "Ma'am?" he prompted.

I held myself perfectly casually. "Why?"

"We have a report, ma'am, that you threatened bodily harm to the victim in the presence of others."

I looked to Detective Fineburg for enlightenment, but Detective Fineburg was looking at the chief.

"What are you talking about?" I demanded.

The chief flipped a few pages back on his pad. "You were expressly heard saying 'Jonathon Nichols is dead meat,'" he said, reading from his notes.

I started to protest, but the words did have a familiar ring. "Expressly heard by whom?" I pressed.

"Miss Roberta Rudge."

"Who?" asked Detective Fineburg.

"Miss Rudge is employed as an oral hygiene technician at the offices of—"

"You mean Roberta at the dentist?" I asked, light finally dawning. "Roberta's last name is Rudge? She's related to you?"

"That is not material," said the chief.

"You can't be serious," I protested.

Detective Fineburg shifted on the sofa. "Perhaps it would be better if—where were you last night, Elizabeth?"

"I had a date."

"With who?" asked the chief, flipping his pad ahead again.

I realized immediately that if I told them who I had gone out with, the next question would be where had we gone, and then they would know instantly that I had made the 911 call.

"Ask your cousin," I told him.

"Elizabeth–" began Detective Fineburg.

"I am not going to answer that question," I interrupted him. "It's not material. And besides, it's none of your business." I saw Chief Rudge scribbling anyway. "What are you writing?" I demanded.

"I'm just noting your lack of cooperation in a homicide investigation," he replied.

"I am not not cooperating. I just don't see that it is any of your business—"

"During your date, Elizabeth, you weren't by any chance at the mall site, were you?" asked Detective Fineburg.

I almost said, "I don't go on dates to vacant lots," when I remembered about that one night with Jonathon. "No," I said, relieved that what I was saying was at least technically true. I hadn't gone to the site *during* my date. I had gone right *before* my date.

Chief Rudge put down his pencil and pad and removed a small white envelope from the pocket of his pants. He opened the envelope and showed me its contents. "This dirt was taken from your tires and lower chassis," he said. "It exactly matches the dirt at the mall site."

I looked into the envelope. "It's just dirt," I said. "It could have come from anywhere. Dirt is dirt."

"Not to the trained investigator," said the chief, closing the envelope carefully and returning it to his pocket. "What kind of footwear did you wear on the evening in question, ma'am?" he continued relentlessly.

"Footwear?" I repeated stupidly.

"Do you own a pair of high heels, ma'am?"

I blinked at him. Now, how could he know—

"Elizabeth, I have to tell you that you're getting yourself into some pretty serious trouble here," said Detective Fineburg.

"I suggest you cooperate, ma'am," seconded the chief.

"If you think you're protecting someone—"

"We know you had a grudge against the deceased—"

"It's better to come clean—"

"There are reports—"

"I'M WEADY!"

We all turned.

There stood Emily, at the top of the stairs. She'd emptied her closet of finery. She was wearing a pink sequined leotard with a white tulle skirt, red tights, black ballet slippers, the wings from her angel costume, a silver birthday crown, and several colored necklaces, and was carrying her magic wand.

The chief and the detective gaped.

Aware that she had an audience, my daughter assumed what she considered to be a theatrical expression. That is to say, she simpered slowly down the stairs, executed a couple of arabesques that looked something like she was trying to kick a fly out of the way, and swept into such a deep curtsy that she ended up falling on her nose.

I crossed over to her and picked her up. Then I turned back to my inquisitors.

"Am I a suspect in this case?" I demanded.

There was no reply. The chief and Detective Fineburg looked at each other.

"Has your investigation proceeded to the point where you are prepared to charge me with the crime?"

There was another pause. The chief opened his mouth to respond, but Detective Fineburg shot him a look and they both kept silent.

"In that case, gentlemen," I said, "I suggest you find someone else to interview. Good morning."

Chapter

6

"*Good morning*, Emily. *Good morning*, Elizabeth."

It was eight-ten Monday morning. Penny Johnson stood at the entrance to the Preschool Threes' classroom, as she did each day that school was in session, greeting her charges.

"Good morning," I returned grimly, prying Emily out of her jacket. Under the best of circumstances, I am not particularly chipper at that hour of the morning. Add to this that I had just spent the greater part of the previous evening tossing and turning over the question of whether it was possible for Chief Rudge to pin Jonathon Nichols's murder on me, and you will get a sense of my mood.

But Emily was all smiles. "*Good morning*, Mrs. Johnson," she piped up, peering interestedly around the corner of the coatroom to see what was going on at the little table in the main room where most of her schoolmates were already gathered.

Penny Johnson bent down toward Emily. "We're baking gingerbread men this morning," she informed her. "Would you like to have a turn stirring the dough?"

"Sure!" Emily sang out.

Really, they were as chummy as a pair of nylon hose with static cling. I felt a distinct pang of jealousy.

"All right. Go in and have a seat next to Valerie and I'll be right with you," said Penny Johnson.

Emily turned to go.

"Just a moment," I interrupted her departure. "Aren't you forgetting something?"

Emily looked at me quizzically.

"How about a 'good-bye, Mommy'?" I suggested.

Emily smiled. I felt better. "Good-bye, Mommy."

"And a kiss."

She reached up and I bent down. I snuck in a hug as well. "Have a good day," I told her.

"Okay, Mommy." She was nearly hopping up and down in her impatience.

I let her go and watched as she raced inside. The smell of gingerbread wafted back after her. Then I turned to Penny.

"Do you have a minute?" I asked. "I'd like to talk to you about something."

Penny folded her arms in front of her and cocked her head to one side. "Of course," she said. "What seems to be the problem?"

"Well, it's not really a problem," I said. "It's just that Emily told me she's not learning about numbers at school, and I was wondering if that's true."

"Oh, I see." Penny Johnson smiled and nodded. "Yes, that's true. We don't believe that we should pressure children into academic achievement in the Preschool Threes."

"Well, of course, I don't believe in pressure either," I said. "But Emily *likes* numbers. She *wants* to learn about them. I don't see why she shouldn't be encouraged to learn—"

"Thank you for bringing this to our attention, Elizabeth." I turned. There was Fawn Woodehouse. The woman has an internal radar unit, I thought. "We appreciate your input. This school survives on parental input."

"Well, I just thought—"

"But I'm sure you also understand that we are professional educators who have devoted an enormous amount of time and effort to discussing the needs of preschool children. And we have concluded that what preschool children need most is the stressing of social skills and a *nurturing* environment." She smiled.

"Well, of course, I also believe in *nurturing*," I said. "But Emily is proud that she knows her numbers. I just don't see why she can't be nurtured and learn a few numbers at the same—"

"Why don't we discuss this some time later? My office is always open. This school survives on parental input," said Fawn, moving to the side.

At that moment the door opened and Amber Costello charged in, with Denise several steps behind.

"*Good morning*, Amber," said Penny. "How are you this morning?"

"I brought my show-and-tell," Amber announced, shrugging out of her coat and leaving it on the floor while she retrieved her knapsack from her mother. She burrowed inside it for a moment and came up with a Snow White dress. Not the JCPenney nightgown knockoff, either. The real McCoy, which I happen to know from personal inspection at the Disney store the previous Halloween costs fifty-two dollars.

"How lovely," said Penny. "Is it new?"

"Daddy got it for me. He's very happy because somebody tripped and fell in the street," said Amber.

"No, honey," Denise corrected her, picking Amber's coat up off the floor. "He's happy because he won *a case* for someone who tripped and fell in the street."

Amber did not appear to appreciate the nicety of this distinction.

"Elizabeth! I'm glad I ran into you. I was going to call you," said Denise as she thrust a lunch box, paper bag snack, and extra sweatshirt into Amber's cubby. She dropped her voice and leaned toward me, her eyes on Penny, who was busy with Amber, and Fawn, who had moved slightly off to the side. "I wanted to tell you that you were right not to go out with that man," she whispered.

"That man?" I repeated blankly.

"You know, the one from the fair. The one you said you didn't know but who asked you out to dinner anyway."

"Oh, *that* man," I said. I paused. It took a moment for the effect of her words to hit home. Then: "Whatever are you talking about, Denise?" I demanded.

"I saw him yesterday. Amber and I met a few of her friends and their parents at the lake yesterday, and he was there too. Not with us, of course, but at the lake. In a canoe," Denise paused. "He was with a woman," she added.

"Oh!" I said, struggling as much with the knowledge that there had been a play date to which Emily had not been invited as with the thought that Simon had spent Sunday with someone else.

"She wasn't very attractive," Denise continued loyally.

"Oh?"

"But they did seem very . . . close," said Denise.

"Oh," I said.

"Not that they did anything." Denise hurried along. "Not in public, anyway. But, you know, you can just tell when two people are—"

"I got it, Denise."

"Well, I just thought you should know. Personally, I thought you were crazy when you said you weren't going to go out with him. I mean, it was so romantic and all, but, I just wanted to tell you how smart you were about the whole thing."

"Thank you, Denise." I started to walk out.

Denise followed. "I mean, I really admire your strength of character. Not too many women I know would have had the foresight to—"

"Elizabeth! Denise!"

We both turned back to her. Fawn Woodehouse was waving a large manila envelope in our direction.

"It's time for our annual fund drive again," she declared. "Now, which of you wants to sell the gift wrap?"

That creep, I fumed as I slammed into the Jeep and roared out of the Hawthorne School parking lot to the severe detriment of some newly planted mums near the side of the road. In spite of my preoccupation with the police, I'd still spent half the day yesterday listening for the phone, or maybe even a knock on the door. And after all that talk about wanting to protect me and being around for me and then having the nerve to kiss me like that at the front door! I didn't notice *me* on any canoe yesterday. The closest thing to water I came to yesterday was Emily splashing me in the bath.

Served me right for being taken in, I thought as I headed to town. Probably the creep made a habit of going around to women and telling them fantastic stories in order to pick them up, the way other men had lines. Thank goodness, I thought virtuously, it hadn't gone any further than a kiss.

Thank you, Denise, I thought. You did me a big favor. Caught me before I got in too deep. This way I can walk away without a second thought. Good. Now that's decided. I feel much better. *Much* better.

I made a quick turn onto Housatonic Street, raced down the block, squealed into a parking space, and went to drown my sorrows in a steaming plate of blueberry pancakes.

The Village Snack Shop is a long, thin rectangle, bounded on one side by an old-fashioned counter and on the other by a set of four booths. In between are a couple of tables, including a long one that seats eight.

Although a number of people were waiting for takeout coffee and doughnuts at the cash register and the counter was filled with single diners, there was hardly anybody at a table, so I ran over to Al's Variety Shop two doors down to secure a *Berkshire Eagle* first. No sense not reading up on the murder while I was getting fat, I decided. I came back with my paper, took a seat at the back booth, and placed my order. Then I opened the paper.

LENOX DEVELOPER FOUND DEAD AT CONSTRUCTION SITE, read the lead story in the Berkshires section.

The door opened and I was vaguely aware that a troop of people came in and took over the large table to my right, but I was intent upon my reading and bent down over the paper in order to concentrate better.

> Lenox developer Jonathon Nichols was found dead of mysterious causes late Saturday night. His body was discovered at the site of his proposed mall on the corner of Housatonic Street and Route 7, apparently the victim of a hit-and-run accident.
>
> The body was recovered after police responded to an anonymous 911 emergency call placed shortly after nine o'clock Saturday evening. The caller, who refused to identify him- or herself, did not specifically mention Jonathon Nichols or a murder, but simply directed police to investigate the construction site.
>
> No vehicle was found on the premises, but Lenox Police Chief Ned Rudge confirmed that the size and tread of tire tracks left at the site would indicate that the accident was caused by either a four-wheel drive vehicle, a van, or a pickup truck. Also found at the site in the vicinity of the body were tracks consistent with a pair of high-heeled shoes, leading authorities to think that a woman was involved.

Oh, shit.

Mr. Nichols and his mall had been the subject of some controversy over the past few months. Although Lenox Selectwoman Marion Hollister Thornewood reports that, on the whole, the new mall would have had a positive effect on the economy, certain sectors, most notably shopping and consumer goods, would have been hit hard by competition from the new mall. "Of course, that does not excuse anyone's going out and taking the law into his or her own hands," Ms. Thornewood said. When asked if the Board of Selectmen would continue with the project despite the loss of Mr. Nichols, Ms. Thornewood answered with a resounding "Of course. The Board has decided that this mall is good for Lenox," she added, "and that takes priority."

Police are following a number of leads. Anyone with any knowledge of the incident should call . . .

I leaned back in my seat, still staring down at the article in the paper in front of me. Tracks consistent with a pair of high heels! Just my luck to choose that night to try out those wretched shoes. Well, it's okay, I'll just throw them out or burn them or . . . but wait a minute. Had someone seen me wearing them Saturday night and already reported it to the police? That would explain Chief Rudge and Detective Fineburg coming to my house to question me. No wonder the chief had asked about my "footwear"! I might just as well have left a little note at the site saying "Elizabeth was here."

But as worried as I was about the shoes, there was something else about the newspaper report that bothered me. Something not quite right, something I couldn't put my finger on, some piece out of place in the mystery. I had just started to read it again when I heard a voice somewhere to my right.

"So, what'll you have, Chief?"

I froze. Then I pulled the newspaper up over my face and glanced cautiously around it. There were four men seated at the large table in the center aisle. Three of them I recognized as Lenox town selectmen. The big heavyset man in the jeans and the neatly pressed blue work shirt opened at the throat and the Nikes was definitely Joe Cobb, the head of the selectmen, Lenox's most senior elected official. He was easy to spot with his wavy dark hair, delicate pink-and-white skin, round youthful face, and large protruding belly. He'd always reminded me of one of those bloated tourist-fed trout that get hauled out of Stockbridge Bowl by local fishermen now and then. The other two were older . . . I squinted. That was Paul Mahoney holding his trademark unlit cigar between his teeth and Forrest McNulty with the gray hair, bulldog posture, and sunburned neck. But the fourth man at the table, the man who *wasn't* a selectman, the one with his back to me wearing the light blue shirt with the dark blue epaulettes, that one was—

"Bran muffin," Chief Rudge grunted.

The waitress nodded sympathetically and turned. "TWO POACHED TWO SUNNY ONE WITH BACON FRENCH TOAST TWO SCRAMBLED AND A BRAN MUFFIN FOR THE CHIEF!" she hollered to the short-order cook.

The short-order cook nodded sympathetically and started cracking eggs.

"It couldn't have happened that way," announced Forrest McNulty, obviously continuing a prior conversation. He'd always reminded me of Wilford Brimley, only without the charm.

"Why not?" asked Paul Mahoney, taking the cigar out of his mouth and then putting it back in again. There's no smoking at the Village Snack Shop. "People get killed all the time."

I leaned a little closer, being careful to keep the newspaper up.

"But no murderer would go through all that right after

they killed somebody. It just doesn't make sense," argued Joe Cobb, who was universally known as Cubby, God knows why.

"Why not?" Paul shrugged. "We knew she was smart."

She? I thought. Then it hit me. Oh my God, they're talking about me. They think I—

"Yeah," agreed Forrest again, opening one of those little individual containers of half-and-half and pouring the contents into his coffee mug. "I think she would have taken the time. It covered up what really happened." He reached for another half-and-half.

So the police had known all the time about the 911 call and the high heels and now the selectmen knew. That meant the whole town knew. The chief and Detective Fineburg must have just been setting me up yesterday. Playing with me.

"What do you think, Chief?" asked Paul.

The chief paused and I held my breath.

"Seemed a little suspicious to me," he admitted. "I think Sipowicz had it right."

Sipowicz? I thought. Who the hell is Sipowicz?

"Yeah," sighed Joe Cobb. "They never should have let David Caruso get away."

"Oh, I don't know," remarked Paul, laying the cigar next to his fork in order to reach for his orange juice. "I think Jimmy Smits is better."

The chief grunted. "What difference does it make? *NYPD Blue* is still the best show on television."

"Your pancakes," announced the waitress in a loud voice, standing over me with a steaming plate and a pitcher of syrup.

As inconspicuously as possible I enveloped the pancakes behind the newspaper. The long table had dispensed with the subject of prime-time crime shows and had turned to other matters.

". . . and I sure wish we could do something about all those telephone poles over there on Route Twenty, I just hate to see all those telephone poles," Forrest McNulty was saying when suddenly the door to the Village Snack Shop opened and in walked a new customer.

It was a white-haired man, short and gnarled but thick, with hunched shoulders and massive bowlegs, dressed in a dirty lumber shirt and jeans, who leaned slightly forward and tottered so unsteadily that he gave the appearance of a tree uprooted by lightning who was walking in to complain of the matter. He went right over to the table with the chief and the selectmen. I saw them all exchange a quick low glance before greeting him.

"Good morning, Timmy," said Cubby politely.

"Morning," echoed the other two selectmen.

"Morning, Tim," grunted the chief.

Tim whoever-he-was (I'd never seen him before) raised a finger at the table. "Don't you fellers 'good mornin'' me," he began in a quarrelsome voice. "I got somethin' to say to you." He frowned, insofar as it was possible for a face that lined to change expression.

·"Sure, Timmy," said Cubby easily. "Sit down. What seems to be the problem?"

"You fellers know very well what the problem is," retorted Timmy, ignoring the offer to sit. "What about my land?"

"What about it?" asked Forrest McNulty.

"When am I gettin' paid for it? That's what."

Paul Mahoney squinted up at Tree Man. "What! Didn't Nichols pay you?" he exclaimed, taking the cigar out of his mouth again in surprise.

"Not a red cent," returned the old man. "And now that feller's dead and I want my money."

Cubby sighed. "I'm sorry about the sale, Timmy," he said. "I really am. We all are," looking around the table. Everyone nodded sympathetically. "I know you've been looking to sell that piece for some time—"

"I ain't lookin' to sell. I sold it," said Timmy.

"What'd Nichols agree to pay again, Timmy?" asked Paul Mahoney.

"Million two," answered Timmy.

"All I'm trying to say, Timmy," Joe Cobb continued gently, "is that I'm not sure there's anything we can do for—"

But Timmy had cut him off. "It's up to you people to take care of this," he argued. "What about that money he paid you?"

"Now, Timmy, you know that hundred thousand belongs to the town," Cubby reminded him. "That was for permits."

"What does he need permits for?" Timmy demanded. "He's dead. That's a good price for that land. I ain't moving on it. That land's been in my family for years. I already come down three hundred thousand. It's a million two," he repeated. "That's just what that feller Nichols was going to pay me."

"But he didn't pay you, Timmy," Cubby reminded him.

"You fellers better do somethin'."

"Tell you what, Timmy," said Joe Cobb. "I'm not making any promises, but we'll put our heads together and see what we can do. We'll discuss it."

"Well, I don't know. . . ." Timmy paused. "They could put a nice prison or jail in there," he said significantly.

This was a standard threat in Lenox. Whenever somebody had a piece of land to sell that the board was threatening to hold up for some reason, they would hint around about offering the property to the Commonwealth of Massachusetts for the purpose of putting up a penal institution. It made everybody in town, but especially the old ladies with the blue hair, go crazy.

"I don't see a jail going in there, Timmy," said Cubby firmly.

"You run along now and get your breakfast, Tim," said the chief, speaking for the first time.

Timmy looked at him, then turned toward the door. "It's up to you fellers to do somethin'," I heard him mutter on his way out.

There was a momentary silence after he'd left. Then Cubby turned to the chief.

"Did that fellow Nichols leave anything?"

"Can't tell yet."

"We got any leads at all?"

"Some," grunted the chief. He swallowed what remained of his bran muffin, wiped his mouth, and stood up. "Got to get going." The chief nodded to the rest of the table.

Cubby stood up as well. "Mind if I hitch a ride?" I heard him ask. "Truck's in the shop today." He lowered his voice. "We can talk on the way," I heard him say.

The two ambled to the front where the waitress stood behind the cash register. "Bye, Cubby. So long, Chief. You have a good day," she said after they paid.

Cubby smiled warmly. The chief raised his cap and led the way out the door.

I lowered the paper and took a reflexive bite of my pancakes. *Truck's in the shop.* Something about that line triggered—Of course! The piece that was missing from the puzzle. Saturday night when I went to meet Jonathon—

"Excuse me," a voice interrupted my thoughts. "Is this seat free?"

I looked up. There were the two grandfathers, the tall skinny one and the short plump one—what were their names again? Ed and Frank?—from the Hawthorne School fair. They were dressed in identical tennis outfits again, although this time they each carried a racquet.

"I was just leaving," I volunteered, folding my paper and starting to get up.

"Was it something Frank said?" Ed asked, sliding onto the bench across from me.

"No, but—"

The waitress appeared. "Have a good game?" she asked, nodding toward the racquets as Frank slid in beside Ed.

"Wonderful. I was brilliant," Ed told her.

"I won," said Frank modestly.

"Oh, you mean tennis," said Ed.

"What can I get you?" asked the waitress.

"That depends. What are you offering?" asked Ed.

"Breakfast. Lunch doesn't start until eleven-thirty," she informed him.

"In that case, I'll have whole wheat toast and coffee," said Ed. "I'm watching my figure," he confided.

"Me, too," said Frank. "I mean, I'm watching his figure, too."

"I'm so happy for you," said the waitress, and went to get the coffee.

"Well, I'll just be getting along. . . ." I began, gathering up my things again.

"Don't you want to know why we're here?" asked Frank, looking hurt.

"You told me. You're looking for sex," I reminded him.

"Do you have any?" asked Ed hopefully.

The waitress returned with the toast and coffee. "Anything else?" she asked.

"You're too late," Ed told her. "This young lady," he indicated me with a nod of the head, "has just agreed to provide sex."

"Lucky her," commented the waitress, and left.

As soon as she was out of earshot, Ed leaned forward. "We're very glad we found you."

"Really," I said.

"Oh, yes, we've been looking all over for you," Frank seconded. "We have something very important to tell you." He paused. "You're in danger."

"Excuse me?" I said, looking from one to the other.

"I'm afraid it's true, my dear," said Ed. He delved into the pocket of his tennis shorts and came up with his wallet. He flipped it open to an identity card. "FBI," he said, handing me the wallet.

Frank also produced a card. "Special agents Pasquini and Plishtin," he said helpfully, handing it to me.

I laughed.

"Don't be fooled by our debonair appearances," warned Ed. "Go ahead, check out the IDs."

I examined the cards. "Ed Pasquini, Special Agent, Federal Bureau of Investigation," said one. It had Ed's picture on it and some numbers. "Frank Plishtin, Special Agent," said the one with Frank's picture on it.

"I thought FBI agents aren't allowed to tell people who they are," I said suspiciously.

"That's the CIA, my dear," said Ed, recovering his card. "A different department altogether."

"Mostly golfers," agreed Frank, holding out his hand for his card.

I handed it to him reluctantly. The documentation certainly looked authentic (although how would I know?), but these two as FBI agents? Give me a break.

Ed regarded me. "I take it that you are not fully convinced that you are speaking with official members of the U.S. government," he said.

"Anybody can have a card made up," I observed.

Ed nodded. "That's true," he agreed. He paused. "Well, is there anything we can do to make you more comfortable?"

"You might try calling the office," Frank interjected.

"The office?"

"The Bureau," Ed explained. "I'm afraid there isn't a local number, but you may call Washington if you like and ask about us."

"You mean, they give out the names of their agents just like that?" I asked.

"Well, not to just anyone. But we'll call ahead and authorize them to tell you. Call information yourself to get the number, so that you are sure, and then ask for Mr. Atwater."

"Oh," I said, a bit uncertainly.

I hadn't expected this. I had been ready to sort of play along with them, but here they had offered such a concrete, sensible method of corroboration. Could it be that they really *were* FBI agents?

But Ed was continuing to speak. "In the meantime," he was saying, "I don't suppose it would hurt you to listen to what we have to say."

"I suppose not," I admitted.

"All right, then—" Ed broke off and regarded Frank, who was slathering a piece of toast with butter. "What are you doing? Trying to give yourself another bypass operation?" he asked.

"It's dry," said Frank with his mouth full.

"Do you think you could take a minute and get the file out?" asked Ed.

Frank carefully wiped his hands on a paper napkin, unzipped the carrying case for his racquet, removed an unmarked manila envelope, and handed it to Ed. Ed produced a pair of horn-rimmed reading glasses from the pocket of his tennis shirt, put them on, opened the file, took out a sheaf of papers, and began to read.

"Jonathon Nichols, a.k.a. Irving Meltzman, was under indictment for twenty-three counts of mail and securities fraud, embezzlement, and misappropriation of funds relating to a real estate project in New Jersey when he turned fugitive three years ago," he read. "As it was believed at that time that he crossed state lines, his apprehension came under federal jurisdiction."

"That means the FBI took over the case," Frank interjected.

"Specifically, Meltzman was accused of taking thirty million dollars from investors, mostly widows and elderly pensioners," Ed continued.

"I hate when they do that," said Frank. "Target the elderly, I mean." He looked at Ed. "Don't you agree?"

"A real jerk," Ed agreed. He looked back down at his papers. "The Bureau was in the process of pursuing a number of important leads when the suspect's body was found Saturday night in a vacant lot. Fingerprints taken that night confirm the identity of Irving Meltzman, a.k.a. Jonathon Nichols."

"Do the police know that?" I broke in.

"The Bureau always works closely with local law enforcement personnel in order to maintain the highest degree of cooperation and maximum efficiency," said Ed.

"We told 'em last night," Frank confided.

"And about the money?" I persisted. "They know about the money?"

"The Bureau retains the right to withhold information not pertinent to ongoing investigations," Ed explained.

"We work close but not that close," Frank translated.

"So why are you telling me?" I demanded.

"The Bureau values civilian cooperation. Also you were known to have gained the"—Ed coughed—"confidence of the fugitive."

I will never sleep with anyone again, I vowed silently.

Ed put the papers down. "It's imperative for your safety that we find that money before the perpetrator does."

"Perpetrator?" I asked. "But don't the police think I killed Jon—er, Irving?"

Ed and Frank looked surprised.

"You?" said Frank. "Who said anything about your killing Meltzman?"

"Well, I just thought . . . the way they came over and interrogated me on Sunday . . ." I floundered. It suddenly seemed silly to say that the chief was out to get me.

"*Did* you kill Meltzman?" asked Frank.

"Of course not!"

"Don't get touchy," said Frank. "It was just a question."

"We know who killed Meltzman," said Ed flatly. "Irving Meltzman had a partner," he said.

"Foreign fellow," Frank added.

"Meltzman was supposed to split fifty-fifty with this partner. However, he did not see fit to do so," said Ed.

"Consequently the partner has been looking for him for some time," confirmed Frank. "He found him Saturday night."

Ed detached a five-by-seven photograph from his file and handed it to me.

"This is a picture of the man who killed Irving Meltzman," he said.

I looked down at the photograph in my hand.

It was Simon.

Chapter

7

"Is something wrong?" asked Frank.

"You know this man?" asked Ed.

"This was Irving Meltzman's partner? This man?" I asked. Then: "If you know that he's the killer, why don't you just arrest him?" I demanded.

Ed shrugged. "Not enough proof yet."

"Got to make the case," explained Frank.

"So you see, my dear," said Ed, retrieving the photograph and slipping the papers back into the manila envelope, "it would be very helpful if you could help us find the money, before . . ." He let the sentence trail off.

"Oh," I said.

"So where is it?" asked Ed.

"I have no idea," I said.

"Did you ever see him with a small key?" asked Ed.

"Did he talk about a hiding place?" asked Frank.

"Did he offer to buy you things?"

"Did he discuss his investments with you?"

"Did he seem interested in the price of gold?"

"Was he buying paintings?"

"Did he give you jewelry?"

"Did he mention his will?"

"Was he collecting antiques?"

"Did he seem interested in stamps—?"

"STOP!" I said. "He wasn't interested in any of those things," I told them. "He was only interested in the mall and . . . "

"Yes, my dear?" Ed pressed. "You were about to say?"

"Well, I don't know if it will help or not, but he did mention a new project he was working on," I said.

"A new project?" Ed frowned.

"What did he say about it?" Frank prompted.

I tried to remember. "Well, it was going to be big, very big," I recalled. "And . . . and . . . "

"Bigger than the mall?" suggested Ed.

"*Much* bigger. Big bucks, he called it. He wanted me to invest in it. He said"—I squinted—"he said it was the closest thing to a sure bet that there could be and that he was juggling the risks." I stopped.

"That's it?" asked Ed.

"That's it," I replied.

"He didn't tell you what it was?"

I shook my head.

"He didn't tell you how much?"

I shook my head again.

Frank looked at Ed. "It's not very much," he said.

Ed shrugged. "It's better than nothing."

They started to slide out of their seats.

"Wait a minute," I said. "You said I was in danger. What about protection?"

"Don't worry," said Ed. "We'll have someone looking out for you." He stopped sliding for a moment. "And I wouldn't talk about this with anyone," he added.

"For your own sake," echoed Frank.

"Not even the police," Ed warned.

"It might confuse them," said Frank.

"Just let us handle them."

"But if there's a problem," I persisted.

"Don't worry. We'll be in touch," they promised.

I watched them take their respective checks to the cash register. As the waitress rang them up, I saw Ed lean closer to her.

"You don't by any chance play tennis, do you, my dear?" I heard him say.

I waited until they had left and then got up and paid my check. But I did not go home. It had occurred to me, while I was listening, that I was allowing myself to be fed entirely too much information secondhand. While it had been a relief to hear that at least two people did not suspect me of Jonathon's murder, in fact, had somebody else in mind altogether, it was less comforting to have Simon's warning corroborated. There is no getting around the fact that it can make a person quite uneasy, not to say paranoid, to be told she is in danger from two highly different sources.

But what was truth and what was fiction? Who was Irving Meltzman? What exactly had he done? Who had a motive for killing him? Strike that. There were apparently any number of people who had a motive for killing him. So who had the best motive, the real motive?

Answers to questions like that do not appear in the *Berkshire Eagle*. Answers to questions like that demand research.

So I did not go home. Instead, I went to the library.

The Lenox library is located on Main Street, across the street from a savings bank and next door to a bridal shop, about two minutes' walk from the Village Snack Shop. It is big and old and registered as a national historic landmark. It is also in a constant state of renovation, or at least, the appearance of renovation, since restoring a historic landmark is much more complicated than restoring, say, your garage. Everything has to be just so, and people on various committees have to pass on everything from architectural designs to the brand of lightbulbs. Consequently, the old paint is scraped away, but the new paint isn't applied because no one can agree on just the right shade of colonial red. Shelves are torn off walls, but the decision as to what will go in their place won't be made until next year, so they just leave the holes. Scaffolding is put up every couple of years to fix the roof, but every year they ask for donations to fix the roof. It's kind of like watching that TV program *This Old House*, only in reverse.

The library doesn't open until ten o'clock, so I had to loiter in the entranceway reading the tourist brochures for Tanglewood and Main Street Sports and Leisure for a few minutes until they unlocked the door. At least it was still season. After Columbus Day they don't bother opening at all on Mondays.

As soon as I heard the lock on the door click, I zipped inside.

"Do you have back issues of the *Wall Street Journal*?" I asked the woman behind the main desk.

"I'm not sure. You'll have to ask the librarian," she replied. She turned to a makeshift partition on the right. "Paige," she called, "there's someone here who needs help."

Immediately, a small brown head popped out from behind the partition. "How may I help you?" Paige asked. She was all of twenty-five.

"Do you have back issues of the *Wall Street Journal*?" I repeated.

"On microfiche," she replied, and with that, the rest of Paige popped out. Someone had obviously told her that the way to garner respect for one's authority on the job was to dress severely, because she was wearing a heavy gray wool skirt that broke below the knee, flats, and a white blouse buttoned all the way up to its Peter Pan collar. All that was missing was the support hose.

She led the way to the library's one viewer. "How far back do you want to go?" she asked.

I considered. Everybody had talked about what Irving had done in the nineties, but if he'd truly made a name for himself in real estate, he might have gotten himself profiled some time in the eighties, before the crash. "Umm, 1985?" I tried.

Her face fell. "We only go back to 1991," she confessed. You would have thought she was admitting to larceny.

"That's okay," I reassured her, even though it meant I was probably in for a trip to New York or Boston in order to get the information I wanted.

She showed me the film. Each separate little oblong contained one issue of the newspaper. There were two file cabinets full of little oblongs.

"Do you know how to work the machine?" she asked, turning it on for me. Then, before I could answer, "See, you just put the film in here like this"—she put the film in there like that—"and then you move it up and down and back and forth to view it."

"Thank you. I've got it," I said, shrugging out of my coat and going to work immediately scanning the first issue, those two file cabinets firmly imprinted on my mind. And the *Journal* doesn't even publish on the weekends, I thought.

She hung around my shoulder. "You can print it if you want," she added, pointing to a button marked Print.

"Thank you."

"Maybe if you told me what you're looking for."

"I don't think so," I said, my eyes fixed on the viewer. "The *Wall Street Journal*, January 2, 1991 . . . "

Still she hovered. "You're the one who wrote that mystery, right?" she asked finally.

I looked up.

"I read it," she announced. "It was great."

"Uh, thank you," I said, flattered.

She leaned a little forward. "Are you doing research on the next one?" she asked.

"Uhh—"

"I was an English major in college," she volunteered.

"Really."

"I love mysteries. That's why I got the job here. It's not much money, but you get to meet such interesting people."

"Uh-huh."

"Being a librarian is a little like being a detective, don't you think? I mean, not really, of course, but often you do have to find things. You know, like if a book is misfiled or if it isn't returned or someone is looking for—"

I gave up. "Actually, I'm looking for articles about a specific person," I said. "I don't suppose you could help me."

"Of course!" She beamed. "Have you tried our new Proquest database?" she asked.

"Lenox has a computer database?" I asked, surprised.

She nodded and pointed to a PC a few feet away, in a corner where bits of plaster were peeling off the walls. "National magazines and journals going back to 1986," she declared proudly.

We got up to check it out.

"See, you just sit here," Paige explained, pointing to a swivel chair in front of the desk, and then, in her excitement, sitting in it herself, "and turn it on like this," she turned it on, "and then you wait for the Proquest logo. . . ." Up came the Proquest logo. "What name did you say you were looking for?"

"Uh, Irving Meltzman," I said.

"Irving Meltzman," she repeated with a total lack of recognition. "How do you spell that?" She typed the letters in, hit the enter key, and sighed with pleasure. "It's so much easier when you have a name," she confided. "Otherwise you have to give it a general area of interest and by degrees make it more specific, and that's so much harder."

"Yes, I can see where it would be," I agreed, leaning over her shoulder and squinting at the screen.

"Now, let's see, it should be coming up any moment now . . . ah-ha!"

Ah-ha indeed. Proquest claimed it had three stories on file that contained the name Irving Meltzman:

"SAVVY INVESTOR TURNS GRANITE INTO GOLD," *Barron's*, June 1987.

"KING OF CO-OP GETS NEW LEASE ON LIFE," *Business Week*, November 1991.

"WHAT TO WEAR TO YOUR BANKRUPTCY PRO-CEEDING," *GQ*, March 1993.

"Can we read them?" I asked.

"Let's see," said Paige, moving the cursor to the *Business Week* title. "CD-ROM GP095," she read. "Yep. We have that one." She pointed the cursor at *GQ*. "CD-ROM BS153. We have that one, too." She paged up to the *Barron's* title and hit enter.

"This record's image not available," the computer reported.

"What does that mean?" I asked.

Paige frowned. "It means we don't have it," she said. Then she brightened. "But I can get it for you on an interlibrary loan," she offered.

"How long will that take?" I asked.

Her face fell again. "About three weeks," she admitted.

"Let's look at the other two," I said.

She reached into a cabinet to the right of the machine, procured a disc, and slipped it into the CD-ROM drive. The cover of *Business Week* for the week of November 13, 1991, came up. We paged to the table of contents. There it was. Page 12.

KING OF CO-OP GETS NEW LEASE ON LIFE

Irving Meltzman, the New Jersey financier who for a short time became known as the "King of Co-op" because of a penchant for buying cheap, low-cost institutional housing such as welfare hotels and mental hospitals, evicting the old tenants, and then converting the structures into one- and two-bedroom luxury apartment houses—

That does sound like Jonathon, I admitted to myself.

—has just been given a new lease on life. Specifically, it is the lease on 58 Rolling Hills in Cedar City, New Jersey.

Mr. Meltzman claims to have brought together an international consortium to fund the development of a huge resort in this quiet New Jersey township. The plans call for a 350-room luxury hotel. Most of the rooms will be suites, and all will contain such amenities as working fireplaces, Jacuzzis, mirrored ceilings, and multiple fax machines, including one in the bathroom. "In today's fast-paced, high-powered business environment, you can't afford to be more than an arm's reach from your business at any time," Mr. Meltzman noted. In addition to the hotel, there will be two man-made lakes on the property, one for boating and fishing, the other sand-bottomed with a beach for sunbathing. Trails for cross-country skiing, hiking, and biking will be marked and, over time, two PGA-approved and -ranked golf courses will be added.

Asked about the makeup of the investing group, Mr. Meltzman reported that it consisted of private bankers, wealthy foreign investors, and, in some cases, scions of some of Europe's leading families. "A real highbrow, elite kind of a group," Meltzman assured a group of citizens packed into a local gymnasium to discuss zoning regulations and tax revenues from the project. "Not a deadbeat in the bunch," he added.

Although the high-stakes developer refused to comment on the dollar amount being invested—

That's a first, I thought.

—Sources close to him indicate that the total cost for construction and development should be in the neighborhood of—

No, don't tell me. Let me guess.

—Thirty million dollars.

"Is this helpful?" Paige, who had been reading over my shoulder—no, that's not quite right since she was the one still sitting in the chair. Paige, over whose shoulder I had been reading, asked.

"Definitely."

"Good," she settled back, pleased.

Meltzman's new venture has come as something of a surprise to Wall Street analysts who predicted earlier this year that, as a result of falling real estate prices and mismanagement, developers like Meltzman might have to retrench. In Meltzman's case, bankruptcy protection had seemed the logical choice, given his highly leveraged position on earlier deals. But Meltzman indicated that he was in no way pulling back. "Retrenching?" he asked. "Me? Retrenching is something auto mechanics do to tires."

Despite the naysayers, Meltzman remains confident that this latest gamble will pay off. "It's like this," he told the gathering in the gymnasium, "to succeed in this business, you've got to have *vision*. A philosophy of life. And my philosophy of life is: If you stand out in traffic long enough, you're going to get hit by a—

"That'll do," I said quickly to Paige.

She nodded and removed the disc. "You want to see the *GQ* piece?" she asked.

"Sure."

GQ was disappointing. There was only a passing reference to Irving Meltzman. It seemed that, right before he became a fugitive and dropped out of sight, he'd appeared in court wearing a plaid suit.

I sighed.

"Do you still want the *Barron's* article?" Paige asked.

I can probably get all of this off the Internet, I realized belatedly. Of course, I'd have to figure out how to get on the Internet first. "Sure," I said.

I was rewarded with a big smile. "Why don't I just print out these other two for you?" she said, reaching toward the CD cabinet to the right of the machine.

"Thanks."

"And if you want, I can keep a look out for you. Would you like me to start a file on this guy or something?"

"That's okay," I said quickly. There was such a thing as too much help. The one thing I didn't want was for it to get back to Chief Rudge that I was investigating Irving Meltzman's background.

"Are you sure? It's no trouble. I go through the newspapers and journals anyway—"

"*Please* don't bother."

"But it's no bother at all—"

"Really." I smiled. "These two pieces will do it for me," I said, grabbing the papers out of the machine. "You've been such a help," I added.

"You think so?" she murmured.

I went back to the microfiche reader, put away the *Wall Street Journal* disc, and started to slip into my coat.

"Pardon me," said a foreign male voice behind me.

I turned. There were the pudgy man and woman from the fair. What is this, I thought, a cupcake reunion? Aloud I said: "Yes?"

"I see you are doing some research," observed the man.

"Actually, I was just leaving."

"I wonder if we might speak with you for a moment before you go."

"It's important," added the woman.

"Uh, all right—" I started to sit down in the chair, but the man shook his head.

"Could we go somewhere more private?" he asked.

"More private?" I looked around. Except for Paige, who had gone back to her desk, there was no one but the three of us in sight.

"This way," said the woman, leading the way to the stacks.

We followed her up the stairs and into the nonfiction aisles at the back of the building. When the two of them were satisfied that we were alone, the man turned to me.

"May I be frank?" he asked.

"As long as you're not Ed."

"Pardon?"

"Sorry. A private joke."

"Ah! American humor." He nodded understandingly.

"Let me guess," I said wearily. "You're here to tell me that Jonathon Nichols isn't really Jonathon Nichols at all, he's somebody named Irving Meltzman. And that he embezzled thirty million dollars. And that you are here to get it back and that I am in danger. And, oh, yes, if I help you, you'll protect me. Right?"

The man smiled. Actually, he had rather a sweet smile under the beard. "'*Grau, teurer Freund, ist alle Theorie/Und grun des Lebens goldner Buam*,'" he quoted.

"Catallus again?" I guessed.

"Goethe, actually. From *Faust*. 'All theory, dear friend, is gray, but the golden tree of actual life springs ever green,'" he translated.

"I don't quite understand," I said. "Are you saying my theory is gray or my life is green?"

He laughed and put out a hand. "Allow me to introduce

myself. My name is Tumenas. Alejandro Tumenas." We shook hands. He put his arm around the woman and brought her forward. "And this is my wife, Kristina."

"I'm sure this all sounds rather fantastic to you," said Kristina. She had an accent, too, come to think of it. Brooklyn.

"Not at all," I assured her. "I always come to the 900 section for private conversations."

She nodded slowly. "Please believe me," she said. "We wouldn't involve you if there were any other choice."

"Of course not," I agreed, and waited.

She stared at me for a moment and then turned to her husband. "Let's go, Alejandro," she said. "We will just take our chances."

"I think perhaps you are right," said Alejandro slowly. He nodded at me. "We are sorry for disturbing you," he said.

They are using guilt, Elizabeth, I told myself sternly as I watched them turn away. It is a well-known and obvious ploy. For heaven's sake, don't fall for it.

"No, wait," I said before they'd even reached the end of the stack. "I'm sorry."

They came back.

"Go ahead," I urged. "Tell me."

They told me.

They told me that Alejandro had been born in Germany and that his parents were forced to flee Hitler for political reasons when he was only three. That after the Allied victory, his family had lost everything, yet his parents scraped and sacrificed so that he could go to boarding school in England. How he grew up lonely and different, away from his family. How he applied himself to his studies and became one of the youngest accepted to Oxford, where he distinguished himself in classics.

They told me how Kristina, also a refugee child, emigrated to Brooklyn after the war. How she lived in abject poverty for many years before winning a scholarship abroad. How they met, how happy they were.

Anyone can make up a story like this, I reminded myself while they were speaking. They do it all the time on PBS.

Then came the cold war. Alejandro felt he had to do something to fight injustice. He helped organize an underground movement to smuggle people out of Eastern Europe. He himself went to set it up, but there was a spy. Someone turned him in. He spent fifteen years in a German jail. Kristina was wild with worry. They were barely allowed to communicate. Letters were infrequent, and those that got through were censored.

Of course, it's a good story, I admitted.

Then came the collapse of Communism. Alejandro was freed. Although his old post at Oxford had of course been filled, the university found another position for him. He brought a number of political prisoners and their families out of Germany with him, and he and Kristina tried to help the others get established.

I mean, it is the kind of story you *want* to believe.

The refugees knew nothing of the capitalist world. Alejandro and Kristina took it upon themselves to educate and advise them. He used his own funds, the advance from a book he'd written on the Golden Age of Greece, to help set them up. Grateful for the help, the others turned over what moneys they had to Alejandro to invest.

Rumors of a big financial deal overseas were floating around the university at that time. . . . Some American developer, a man with a long list of successes to his name, was promising large dividends from a real estate deal . . . it would make such a difference to the families . . . many of Europe's key families were investing . . . it was supposed to be a sure thing. . . .

Alejandro waved an arm in conclusion. "But it isn't for ourselves we are here. What is money to us?" He put his arm around Kristina. "We have been through so much together, the loss of our savings is nothing. It is the others, don't you see? I cannot allow them to suffer for my mistake."

There was a pause and they looked at me.

"I . . . uh . . ." I floundered. It suddenly was not as easy as I thought to ask for proof. "I'd like to, you know—"

"I wish we had a way to substantiate our story." Alejandro deliberated. Then he brightened. "Ah but . . . just perhaps . . ." He squinted at the bookshelves in front of him and then paced down the aisles deliberately until he reached one several feet away. "Yes!" he exclaimed suddenly, reaching out with one hand and extracting a volume from the lower left-hand side. "Perhaps this will help," he said, offering me the book.

I took it in my hands and looked down at it.

Aristophanes, Euripides and the Five Stages of Greek Religion, said the title. Published by Oxford University Press. Written by . . .

Professor Alejandro Tumenas.

"Won't you help us?" Kristina pleaded.

It wasn't until later, much later, after I'd promised to do whatever I could for the Tumenases, after I'd picked Emily up at school and romped with her at a playground and fed her some dinner and put her to bed, after I'd reread the articles on Irving Meltzman three times and was brushing my teeth that I finally remembered the clue I'd uncovered at the Village Snack Shop earlier that morning, the piece of the puzzle that was missing, the point that had bothered me.

Last Saturday evening, when I'd arrived at the site, mine had been the only car in sight.

So how had Jonathon gotten to the site if he had not driven his own truck?

And if he did drive his own truck . . . where was it?

Chapter

8

I was still puzzling over the question of the missing truck Wednesday morning at breakfast when I suddenly remembered Denise's remark about the other children having a play date to which Emily had not been included.

I raised my coffee cup and scrutinized my daughter. She didn't *look* unhappy. She didn't *look* like she was being ostracized. Of course, she was only three and a half. It was a question of how much she was capable of understanding. Let's face it, this was the child who only last month had awakened me in the middle of the night to ask for a whale. She might not know she was being excluded from the other children's extracurricular activities.

But now that I thought about it, I remembered how cliquey school could be. How much children wanted to be part of the group, how it could affect their self-esteem, even at the tender age of three, to be left out. How it was the unhappy, left-out, low-self-esteem children who used drugs and robbed banks and so forth.

I put down my coffee cup. "Um, Em?" I ventured.

Emily, who was busy picking the raisins out of her cereal bowl, didn't look up.

"Emily."

Emily looked up. "Yes, Mommy?" she piped. Those incredibly blue eyes blinked at me.

"Listen, Em, I wanted to ask you . . . so, how's school going?" I affected a bright, cheerful, carefree tone.

Emily's head disappeared into her cereal bowl again.

"What I mean is," I tried again, "well, who did you play with yesterday, for instance?"

Emily's head came up and she considered. "I played with Mrs. Johnson," she announced.

Mrs. Johnson? But she's the teacher. "She's the teacher, Em," I said.

"I know that," Emily said.

"I meant, of the kids," I continued patiently. "Which of the kids did you play with yesterday?"

Long pause.

"Well, I didn't play with Rebecca," she declared finally.

"No? Why not?"

"Well, she was playing with David."

So it was true. The other children *were* excluding Emily.

"Did you *want* to play with Rebecca and David?" I asked tenderly. "Did it make you feel bad when they didn't play with you?"

"Uh—not really."

She's hiding her feelings. Worse and worse. "Are you sure?" I asked anxiously.

"Well, David bites," she explained.

"Sounds like a cogent rationale to me," said a cheerful voice behind us.

I whirled around in my chair. Simon was standing in the doorway to the kitchen. "How did you get in?" I demanded.

He was dressed in an elegant dark suit, complete with white

shirt and vivid tie, this one in alternating shades of violet and emerald. He was so recently shaved that his cheeks were still pink from the exercise, and his hair lay sleekly against the sides of his head. He was scrubbed and clean and polished and he exuded such animal high spirits, robust health, and extraordinary good looks that he positively glowed.

As I stared at him, he grinned at me. That nice, frank, trust-me-I'm-here-for-you grin.

I forgot completely that here was the man who had been Irving Meltzman's partner in crime and most likely the person who'd rammed him with a four-wheel-drive vehicle only a few days before; a hardened criminal, a fugitive from the law, who was wanted by the FBI and the CIA and Interpol and God knows who else; the man who I had been warned was dangerous, who would stop at nothing to regain the lost millions, who had probably targeted me as the next entry on his hit list.

I did not, however, forget that here was the man Denise had seen at the lake on Sunday squiring some other woman around in a canoe.

"What's the matter, lose your canoe?" I asked, picking up the breakfast dishes and carrying them to the sink.

Emily remained at her place. "Who is that man, Mommy?" she asked.

"Nobody, honey," I told her.

"He must be *somebody*," she insisted.

"My name is Smith," said Simon, coming toward Emily. "Simon Montgomery Smith." He crouched down next to her. "And I've got something in my pocket."

"What?" asked Emily.

"I don't know. Why don't you put your hand in and find out?" He held out his jacket pocket.

Now I remembered the part about him being a dangerous, hardened criminal.

"Uh, Emily . . ." I began, nervously.

But Emily had already stuck her hand in the proffered

pocket and emerged with a little package. She ripped off the wrapping paper. Out came a little white stuffed toy.

"Ohh, it's a buuunnny," she said ecstatically. "I *love* him," she said, hugging the bit of imitation fur to her cheek.

"It's a puppet, too," said Simon, sticking his hand into the toy. "Hello, Emily," the puppet said in a squeaky voice.

"Hello, bunny," Emily returned gravely.

"Would you like to be my friend?" asked the bunny.

"Oh, yes."

"Time for school," I announced.

"Killjoy," said the bunny.

"May I take the bunny to school with me, Mommy? Please?"

"Yes, but only if you hurry," I told her. I turned to Simon. "Thank you for the gift," I said, in a tone that implied anything but, "but I'm afraid we have to be going."

"Why don't I just tag along?"

"I don't think that would be a very good idea," I said.

"Why not? It's on the way, isn't it?"

"What's on the way?"

"Emily's school."

"On the way to what?" I asked.

"To Irving Meltzman's house," he said.

"Who's going to Irving Meltzman's house?" I demanded.

"We are," he said.

Irving Meltzman's house turned out to be a large, extremely tasteful redbrick country manor on one of those discreet little unmarked dirt roads where all the really rich people live but which from the main street look like an abandoned cross-country ski trail. It had a stone fence, rosebushes, a white-pillared facade, and several feet of screaming neon yellow Crime Scene: Do Not Enter police tape wrapped across the front steps. We drove about a quarter mile past, and Simon pulled his Jaguar off on a little path that led into the woods.

"What do you do, Simon?" I asked suddenly.

"Pardon?"

"For a living, I mean. What do you do?"

"Well, you might think of me as an outside consultant. Someone you hire when you want something done privately."

"You're a private detective?" I guessed.

"Certainly not," said Simon.

"You weren't, by any chance, Irving Meltzman's partner?" I asked lightly.

"Who told you that?"

"I'm just asking," I told him.

"Elizabeth, you're not being honest with me. How can I help you if you're not honest with me? Now, what have you heard?"

"Who were you at the lake with?" I demanded.

"What?"

"You took a woman canoeing on Stockbridge Bowl Sunday morning."

"Is that what this is all about?"

"Of course, it's none of my business, but since we're on the subject of *honesty*—" I continued obstinately.

Simon laughed. Then he leaned over and kissed me. Then he did it again. Finally, he stopped.

"Shall we go?" he said.

"How do you plan to get in?" I whispered as we walked back toward Irving's house. There wasn't any particular need to whisper—especially since Simon had insisted that we trek through the woods rather than stay on the road—but since the kisses I'd started getting into the spirit of the thing.

"Let's try the back door, shall we?" He paused as we came out into Irving's yard and scanned the rear of the house. "Where *is* the back door?" Simon asked.

"How should I know? I've never been here before."

"Never been here before? What kind of girlfriend were you?"

"An extremely reluctant one," I told him.

We found the back door. It was on the side. There wasn't any police tape on it.

Simon tried the handle. I noticed that he had slipped on a pair of leather gloves. "Locked," he said.

I started hunting around under the welcome mat, behind the flower pot, across the windowsill. Simon watched me blankly.

"No one keeps their key under a flower pot," he said patiently, just as I got on my tiptoes to reach up to the top of a post.

I came down with a key. I fit it into the lock. It turned. The door opened.

"This is Lenox," I said.

We crept inside. Simon closed the door behind us and bolted it.

We found ourselves standing in Irving's kitchen. It was a large flagged-stone affair with wooden beams, a six-foot cherry wood Shaker table, brand-new appliances, and gleaming copper pots hanging from the ceiling. The sun streamed in through oversized windows, making it unnecessary to turn on the electric light. It was perfectly quiet.

"What are we looking for?" I whispered.

"Anything. Nothing. Whatever might give us a clue to the money," Simon whispered back. "Here, take these," he said, handing me a pair of gloves.

I slid my hands into the gloves and we started going through the kitchen. I opened drawers containing silverware, Saran Wrap, paper napkins. I poked into the broom closet. Simon ran through the pots and pans and peered into the sugar bowl. Nothing unusual.

"Perhaps it would be better to split up," he suggested.

"Why don't you take the rooms upstairs and I'll take those on this level?"

"What about the basement?"

"We'll run through it on the way out."

I nodded and slipped out of the kitchen while Simon started on the dining room. As I walked through to the foyer, it did not escape my notice that the rooms Simon had elected to search included the library, the den, and Irving's office.

I found the main staircase and headed up to the second floor. I paused at the top. To the left were four bedrooms and two baths. To the right were some French doors that clearly led to the master bedroom suite. I turned right.

Irving's bedroom was impressive. I'd always known he had money, of course, and he wore expensive clothes, but I had no idea that he lived like *this*. His closet was bigger than my bedroom, and he had dozens of pants and jackets and ties hanging from little quilted hangers. The bathroom was huge and consisted of a marble floor, claw-foot tub, Jacuzzi, separate shower, and double sink. The French doors opened up onto a sitting area, complete with a stone fireplace and French provincial furniture. Then you went through some more doors before finally coming to the bedroom. The bedroom furnishings were an abrupt departure from the rest of the house; the bed was huge and covered in red Chinese silk, and there were oriental screens along the wall and a mirrored ceiling. It looked like an uneasy alliance between Madonna and Fu Manchu.

I started in the sitting room. There was an ornate writing table with three drawers. I pulled them open one at a time. The one on the left contained boxes of stationery. I peeked into some of the boxes. There was a different heading stamped across the top of each: Jonathon Nichols Investments, Jonathon Nichols Real Estate Development, Jonathon Nichols Money Management.

In the center drawer were an assortment of pens and pencils, some paper clips, a ruler, laundry tickets, a package of Wrigley's Spearmint gum, and a box of condoms in mixed colors. The drawer to the right held a small box of Fanny Farmer chocolates, an opened package of pistachios sealed with a rubber band, several small bottles of liquor, such as are distributed on airplanes, and more condoms in mixed colors.

May this be a lesson to you, Elizabeth, I thought.

A survey of the bathroom revealed a lot of Aramis, some dirty socks, and a ring around the Jacuzzi.

That left the bedroom.

I started with the drawers. Irving had a lot of drawers. There were drawers for socks and drawers for underwear and drawers for shirts that had just come back from the laundry. There were sweater drawers and handkerchief drawers.

Unfortunately, there were no incriminating paper drawers.

It was much the same with the closet. Lots of pockets . . . with nothing in them.

I came out of the closet and went back into the bedroom for a last look. Nothing. Then I crept back out of the room toward the landing.

At the top of the stairs I stopped and listened. I could hear the sounds of paper rustling. Very quietly, I made my way downstairs. At the entrance to the library I stopped again. The sounds of rustling paper were louder.

All at once, I stuck my head in the door. "Nothing upstairs," I chirped. Then: "What have you got there, Simon?" I asked innocently.

"Elizabeth. I was just about to call you," said Simon.

He was bent over some papers on a desk in the corner. He straightened up and very nonchalantly took his hand out of the inside pocket of his suit jacket. To the side was a safe that had been set in the wall behind some books. The safe's door was wide open.

"How'd you get it open?" I asked, gesturing toward the safe.

"Trade secret."

"What are you looking at?"

"Come and see," he said.

I crossed the room and looked over his shoulder. There were some papers with figures and names on them. "Are these about the mall?" I asked.

"Looks that way. Recognize any of these names?"

"Well, no, I mean—why, yes." I pointed at the names Ellsworth and Florence Hunkler. "These are local people," I said. "This one, too." I showed him Judge Clarkson. "And this one. And this one." Next to each name was an amount. "What does it mean?" I asked.

"I'm not sure, but I think this is a list of investors for the mall," said Simon.

"Investors? But I thought Irving was supposed to be putting up the money."

"Well, he might have been, but I doubt it," said Simon. "Looks to me like he was rounding up wealthy locals to do the dirty work for him." Simon frowned down at the paper. "Not only that, he was keeping about twenty percent as a management fee," he noted. "If he really collected all of this money, he was doing pretty well for himself. According to these papers, a substantial sum was invested."

"How much?" I asked. "All together, I mean."

"After his cut? About a hundred thousand dollars."

A hundred thousand dollars, I thought. Exactly the amount he put down as a deposit to get his permits. "And what are these?" I asked, pointing to a different pile that appeared to consist of newspaper clippings.

"Articles about the economic climate in the Berkshires, wealthy investors, that sort of thing," Simon answered, riffling through the papers. "It's probably how he located his pigeons. Here's one I'm sure you'll find interesting," he commented dryly.

I looked at the paper he handed me. It was a copy of a piece that had run about me in a local weekly soon after Howard died. "LOCAL WOMAN INHERITS FORTUNE," the headline read.

I felt my cheeks burn. "You're saying he only went out with me for my money?"

"I'm not saying anything of the sort. He didn't ask you for money, did he?"

"No," I lied. My whole face was hot by this time.

"There you go." Simon started putting the papers back into the safe. He worked quickly and efficiently.

"Is that all there is?" I asked, watching him.

"It would seem so."

"Nothing about a new, larger project?"

Simon shook his head. "Nothing," he reported. He took the last file and slipped it into place.

"No clue to the missing thirty million?" I persisted. "No mention of a safe deposit box or a bank account or even a stamp collection?"

Simon closed the safe, swung the dial on the combination lock, replaced the books. Then he grabbed my elbow. "It's getting late," he said. "Let's get out of here."

Too late. At that moment we heard a car pull into the driveway.

"Stay here," Simon ordered. In two quick, catlike steps he was at the window. He put his hand around one of the heavy curtains and ever so slowly and carefully parted it slightly. "We have visitors," he reported.

I came over to where he was standing and peeked around his shoulder. Two men had gotten out of a police car and were heading to the front door. It was Chief Rudge and Detective Fineburg. "What'll we do?" I whispered.

"This way."

We scurried out of the library and into the main hall. I could see the handle of the front door starting to turn. Detective Fineburg's voice floated faintly through the wood. "Think maybe we can get that safe open this time, Chief?" I heard him ask.

"If that locksmith ever shows up," I heard the chief reply, and, with that, the door started to swing open.

I froze in my tracks. Simon, who was already into the kitchen and therefore out of sight of the front door, stopped and beckoned to me. But I knew I wasn't going to make it. They were going to catch the tail end of me going through that kitchen door, and that was going to be the end of my life as a single mother and the beginning of my career as a convicted felon. . . . The door was almost open. . . .

"Wait," I heard Detective Fineburg say at the same time I heard the sound of another car pulling into the driveway, "here he comes now."

I heard the chief grunt, "About time," and the front door stopped opening.

I escaped into the kitchen and out the back with Simon.

I didn't say much on the car ride home. My near brush with the police had left me chastened. What was I doing risking my freedom, my life with Emily, for Irving Meltzman's millions? What did his crime have to do with me? The answer to that was easy: nothing. Enough's enough, Elizabeth, I told myself as Simon pulled the Jag into my driveway. You've had your fun. Now get out of it.

Simon turned off the motor and looked over at me. "Are you all right?" he asked.

"Yes," I said. Then: "No. I don't know." I rubbed my forehead. "Listen," I said, "don't take this wrong, you're a lovely man and under ordinary circumstances I would love to get to know you better, but I think this is where I duck out. It's getting a little too—"

"Interesting?" Simon supplied helpfully. "Sorry. I know that last bit was a little sticky for you."

"Well, they already think I killed my husband, so I'm sure you'll excuse me if I quit trying to be Mata Hari—"

"Mata Hari was a spy."

"Well, Sherlock Holmes then—"

"Sherlock Holmes was a man."

"Well, whoever I've been pretending to be, and just go back to being plain old boring Elizabeth Halperin, mother of Emily, frustrated mystery writer, and general screw-up."

"Are you sure?"

"I'm sure."

"All right, then."

I got out of the car. Simon got out of the car.

"What are you doing?" I asked.

"I'm walking you to your front door."

"That's unnecessary."

"Not to me."

"Fine. You can walk me to my front door," I said.

We walked to the front door. I put my key in the lock and stuck out my hand. Simon took it. We shook.

"It was nice meeting you," I said.

"The pleasure has been all mine."

I nodded and turned away. I pushed the door open, stepped into the entranceway and stared.

In the time that I had been gone with Simon, my house had been completely ransacked.

Chapter

9

The inside of the house had been turned upside down. The sofa pillows were on the floor and the rugs were on the sofa. The lamps had been stripped of their shades, the phones were off their hooks, the bric-a-brac were in pieces on the floor. The bookshelves had been tipped over and my books—my wonderful books—were lying helter-skelter on the floor. Big Bird was lying nose down with wings outstretched at the top of the stairs. He'd obviously been trying to get away and had been tripped from behind.

Simon peered in over my shoulder. "I hadn't realized you were so domestic, Elizabeth," he said, stepping in behind me.

"Who—who—" I sputtered.

"Tsk, tsk," said Simon, moving around me and examining the debris. He righted one of the bookshelves and then bent down and picked up my copy of *A Christmas Carol*. "Not his best, you know," he said.

"What are you talking about?"

"Dickens."

"Why are we talking about Dickens?" I demanded. "My house is a mess. My stuff is all over the floor. For all I know, a professional assassin is waiting for me upstairs. Why would you choose this moment to talk about Dickens?"

"I thought it might be diverting."

"I don't want to be diverted! I want my house back!"

"As to the part about the professional assassin," Simon continued calmly, as though he hadn't heard my outburst, "I don't think you have to worry. Whoever did this is gone. And this is hardly a professional job," he added.

"You're saying some teenager suddenly took it into his head to come and trash my house?"

"No. I'm just saying that if a professional decided to look over your house while you were out you'd never know. The people who did this weren't looking for anything."

"Then why—"

"I'm not saying that they didn't have hopes of finding something, but, well, frankly, Elizabeth, when someone does something like this—so obviously, I mean—it just means that they're sending you a message," said Simon.

"A message?" I repeated blankly. "What? They never heard of an answering machine? A fax?" Then I blinked at him. "You mean they're trying—"

"To scare you. Yes."

"They think I have the money," I said dully.

"Yes."

"They want me to know that they think I have the money."

"Yes."

"And they think that if they do something like this, I'll give it to them," I said.

"Well, maybe not just this," said Simon. "Of course, they hope that this will be enough. No one likes to escalate, unless they're psychotic, which, at the moment we have no evidence of—"

But I had caught the key word. "Escalate?" I sort of squeaked.

Simon put down the Dickens and crossed the room to stand in front of me. "I tried to tell you," he said gently.

"Escalate? You mean, like kill me?"

"Well, that wouldn't be particularly useful at this point, since they think you have the money—"

"They killed Irving."

"Yes, that is a puzzle," Simon agreed. "There was no benefit to doing so. He clearly hadn't told them where the money was since they're still looking for it."

"Maybe he told them something," I said. "Maybe they thought they knew where the money was and that's why they killed him."

"Yes. Perhaps." Simon paused. "Come on," he said finally. "I'll help you clean up."

It was a mammoth job. The living room was the least of it. We put away pots and pans and dried beans in the kitchen, tablecloths and candlesticks in the dining room. The furniture was straightened and the CDs rearranged. We scooped all the clothes off the staircase. Upstairs, we put Emily's mattress back on her bed and folded her blankie. Big Bird went back to his accustomed place in the rocking chair. Finally, we made it to my bedroom.

"There you are," said Simon, coming up behind me. I'd sent him downstairs for a broom.

I turned so quickly I almost bumped into his shoulder.

"Listen," I said, "you've done enough. I can't thank you enough . . . "

But Simon was looking around the room. "Interesting taste," he noted. He looked at me. He was very close.

"It's the bedroom," I pointed out idiotically.

"Yes. I see that." He moved infinitesimally closer. "That's the bed," he said softly.

"Well, yes, as a matter of fact—"

"It's not even made."

"No, it—"

"And we've worked so hard this morning."

"Yes, we—"

"But, of course, you have to get Emily soon," he said, bending down toward me and lifting my face up toward his.

"Not that soon," I said.

Fifty minutes later, I made a supreme effort and threw off the covers. Immediately, Simon sat up and pulled me back down.

"Time to get Emily?" he murmured.

"Umm . . ." I murmured back.

"So soon?"

"Uh-huh . . . "

"Five more minutes."

"I can't . . . "

"Three more minutes."

"Out of the question . . . "

Fifteen minutes later I raised my head, got a good look at the clock, and shot out of bed. I tore around the room looking for my clothes. The room was still pretty messy from the ransacking.

Simon watched me as I picked through piles. "I think your shirt is over there," he said, pointing over by the bureau.

"Oh, right."

"And your pants are over here," he continued, scooping a pair of jeans off the floor by the bed.

"Thanks." I was suddenly shy. I grabbed a pile of clothes off the floor and held them in front of me, like a shield. Then I kind of backed my way into the bathroom. "It won't take me a minute . . . " I said.

"Shall I come with you?"

"To the bathroom?"

"Well, of course, nothing would please me more, but I meant to pick up Emily."

"Oh, no." All I needed to further my reputation was to show up at the Hawthorne Day School with Simon. "Why don't you wait here?" I suggested. Then I thought about Emily's coming home and finding a naked man in Mom's bedroom. "I mean, wait downstairs. With your clothes on, I mean."

"Right."

"No, I didn't mean it that way." I ducked my head into my T-shirt and pulled on my jeans. I could hear Simon moving around in the bedroom.

"You don't happen to see my suit anywhere, do you?" he called.

I looked down at the pile at my feet and picked out a man's dark blue jacket and pants. "Here it—" I began and then stopped.

A sheet of folded paper had fallen out of the inside pocket of the jacket. It fluttered open at my feet. I bent over and picked it up. It was some kind of document.

SUISSE UNION CREDITBANK OF ZUG
GENERAL CONDITIONS

The following conditions shall govern the relationship between the Bank and the customer.

1. **Due Care and Secrecy**
   a) The Bank undertakes to conduct all business transactions with due care and attention.
   b) In all matters between the Bank and the customer, bank officials and employees will observe strictest secrecy in accordance with Swiss banking law.
2. **Power of Disposition** The signatures of persons authorized to sign for the customer, which has been filed with the Bank, shall be binding until revoked by the customer.

3. **Communications of the Bank** Communications of the Bank shall be deemed to have been properly made if they have been dispatched to the last address given by the customer. . . .

"Elizabeth?" called Simon. "I can't seem to find my pants. Are you sure you haven't got them in there with you?"

4. **Incapacity to Act** The customer bears any damages caused by his/her own or third party's incapacity to act unless such incapacity has been published in a Swiss official gazette or communicated to the Bank in writing by an impartial third party.
5. **Verification of Signatures and Identity** The customer bears all damage resulting from the nondiscovery of forgeries or faulty identification unless the Bank is guilty of gross negligence.
6. **Amendments to General Conditions** The Bank reserves the right to amend the General Conditions at any time. Customer will be notified of amendments by circular letter. . . .

"Elizabeth? Are you all right in there?" He was knocking on the bathroom door.

7. **Applicable Law and Jurisdiction** All legal relations with the Bank are subject to Swiss law. Place of performance and of exclusive jurisdiction for all proceedings is Zug. All decisions are binding.
8. **Agreement** The undersigned agrees to all conditions and obligations represented herein. . . .

"Elizabeth! Can you hear me?" He was rattling the doorknob.

Signed on this, the 14th day of March, 1992 . . .

"If you don't open this door, I'll . . . "

Irving Meltzman.

"Here you go," I said smoothly, opening the bathroom door suddenly and handing Simon his jacket and pants.

He just stood there in the doorway in his shirt and socks and looked at me. "Are you all right?"

I looked right back at him. "Is there any reason I shouldn't be?" I answered.

"None that I can think of offhand."

"Well, there you go," I said.

"You mean there *you* go."

"Pardon?"

"To get Emily, of course," he said, shrugging into his jacket.

I am ashamed to admit that even this last flagrant example of Simon's duplicity—the deliberate withholding of the existence of Irving Meltzman's Swiss bank account—did not entirely extinguish the glow of previous events. As I drove pell-mell through town (I was only about three minutes late, but I hated the thought of all those other mothers running to their children while Emily waited, looking around expectantly), I found myself reliving, not the paper fluttering to the floor, but the kisses and caresses of the hour and a half before, with the result that I was actually saying things like "well, he probably hadn't had a chance to tell me," and "maybe he thought he was protecting me by keeping it from me," and other similar forms of dreck to myself.

But a Swiss bank account was what I finally came back to as I careened into the Hawthorne School driveway. So Irving Meltzman had had a Swiss bank account. Probably one of those numbered jobs, the kind of account where nobody looks twice at large, unexplained transactions. The kind of account favored by deposed heads of totalitarian countries and nuclear arms traders. The kind of account somebody like Irving Meltzman, on the run from the law and his investors, would naturally have thought of. The kind of account where thirty million dollars could sit in complete safety until such time as Irving decided to spend it. In retrospect it was all so obvious that there was hardly any satisfaction in finding it out. I screeched to a halt and hurried out of the car.

Most of the mothers were still there, hoisting squirming children into car seats. Denise waved at me from the driver's seat of her Pathfinder as she was pulling out. I could see Penny Johnson frowning and nodding her head seriously as she spoke with one parent, while another stood by, holding a boy by the arm, obviously awaiting a turn with the teacher. I could see one little girl—was that Rebecca?—jumping up and down, while her mother—Anne? Sue? Pamela?—checked her lunch box. I could see another little boy rolling on the ground, while a grimy-faced little girl waved a paper bag puppet in her adoring mother's face. The only person I could not see, in fact, was Emily.

I slid through the chattering, noisy crowd and made my way to the circle around Penny Johnson. She was just finishing up speaking to the woman with the little boy. ". . . but you feel there's been improvement?" I heard the woman ask anxiously.

"Oh, yes. Children of this age are just learning about which behavior is socially acceptable and which isn't," Penny reassured her.

"He has only bitten twice this week," admitted the mother. "And one time he didn't even break the skin."

So that's David, I thought.

David and his mother left, and Penny turned to me. "Why, Elizabeth," she said, looking surprised. "I hope there hasn't been any misunderstanding."

Misunderstanding? "Is something wrong?" I asked.

"No, of course not, I just thought . . . I didn't get the date wrong, did I?" asked Penny. "It was today, wasn't it?"

"Was today what?" I asked.

"The day that Emily was supposed to be picked up by her aunt and uncle," said Penny.

I felt my mouth go dry. "Her . . . ?"

"Well, after you called this morning—"

"I *called* you—"

"Well, not me, specifically. Didn't you speak with Fawn's assistant?"

"Fawn's assistant? Who is Fawn's assistant? I never met Fawn's assis—"

"All I know is that I got a message from the office that Emily was to go home today with her aunt and uncle and then, when they showed up, they had a note from you—"

"From me?" my voice squeaked.

"Yes, here it is." Penny unearthed a scrap of paper from her clipboard and handed it to me. "I hope there hasn't been a mistake," she repeated.

I stared down at the paper without seeing it. It took me a few minutes to focus. The writing did look similar to mine, although now that I was faced with it I realized that my writing wasn't all that distinctive.

To whom it may concern. This is to inform the Hawthorne School Beginning Threes program that Emily Halperin will be going home today with her aunt and uncle, Mr. and Mrs. Tumenas. If there are any problems, please do not hesitate to call to confirm.
Sincerely,
Elizabeth Halperin

I grabbed Penny's arm. "Did they say where they were going?"

"I—"

"Think! It's important!"

"You mean she hasn't come home yet?"

"Did they leave a message for me? Did they say anything? Which direction did they go?"

"I—well, I—oh yes, come to think of it, they said to tell you that they'd meet you at the ice-cream store. They—Mrs. Halperin? Elizabeth? Is there something wrong?"

But I was already in my car and flying out of the parking lot.

It was the longest four and one-half minutes I have ever spent. I couldn't breathe. I couldn't speak. I couldn't cry. All I could think was: Let her be there. Let her be all right. I drove up Route 183 and took a left at the monument. The ice-cream store was on Housatonic Street. There wasn't a space in front, so I just double-parked in front of the plate glass window and leaped out of the car. I'm not even sure I turned it off.

Let her be there. Let her be all right.

"Elizabeth! There you are!"

It was Alejandro. He was sitting at a table near the center of the store, a large hot-fudge sundae in front of him. To his right was Kristina with a banana split. To his left—

Was Emily.

She was sitting with her feet dangling, a dish of vanilla ice cream half eaten in front of her. She was animated and enthusiastic, and pink sprinkles dripped from her chin. She was obviously having a wonderful time.

Kristina pointed at me. "Look, Emily," she said. "There's your mommy."

Emily looked up. Her face broke into a huge grin. "Mommy!" she cried, waving her spoon in my direction.

I was across the room in three paces. "Emily!" I scooped her into my arms. "Emily!"

Emily squirmed in my embrace and tried to get back at her

ice cream. I held her firmly and stood up. "Emily, we have to go now," I said.

"But, Mommy, I'm not done yet," she protested.

Alejandro was on his feet. "Please, Elizabeth, do sit down," he said.

"I will not. How dare you—"

"You are understandably upset. Please, sit down. *Ira furor brevis*—"

"Don't you dare quote Goethe to me!"

"It's Horace. It means—"

"I don't care what it means! We're going straight to the police!"

Kristina made a quieting motion with her hands. "Please, please," she said. "The child. You will only frighten her."

"*Me?*" I was so angry I could barely spit out the word.

"Now, in the end, what is there to be so upset about?" urged Alejandro. "You see the child is all right. She is just having a treat."

"You object to the ice cream?" Kristina cut in solicitously. "I made sure she finished her lunch first."

"Oh, yes," agreed Alejandro. "And she did a marvelous watercolor for you at her little school. Let's see, we have it here somewhere—"

"I think it's in her backpack," Kristina supplied helpfully.

"Leave us alone," I told them, putting Emily down and taking her by the hand.

"Ah, but that's the one thing we cannot do," said Alejandro. "We regret frightening you, but circumstances forced us to consider this alternative."

"We needed to get your attention," Kristina murmured.

"Oh, right," I said. "What's the matter, ransacking my house wasn't enough?"

"We did not ransack your house," said Alejandro firmly.

"You just took my child."

"For an ice cream."

"To scare me."

"You are in bad company," warned Alejandro.

"You bet I am."

"You are trusting the wrong person," Kristina seconded.

"I—"

"He is not who he says he is."

"He is taking advantage of you."

"Look who's talking," I retorted. "Listen. In this country we have such a thing as kidnapping. You go to jail for it. For twenty years," I made up a number.

Alejandro shrugged. "She wants to go to the police," he said to Kristina.

"If she wants to go, I don't know that we can stop her," Kristina answered.

"You're damn right you can't stop me." I turned to go.

"We'll have to tell what we know, of course," Alejandro continued, shaking his head sorrowfully.

"You mean, that Elizabeth was at the construction site at the time of Meltzman's death?" asked Kristina.

I stopped. "I was *not* there at the time of his death," I said.

"And that afterwards she stopped outside of that little store—you know, the one where they made the excellent dough-nuts—to make a phone call," said Alejandro, ignoring me.

"Yes, that was the phone call to the police, was it not?" said Kristina. "The anonymous one." She paused. "They can trace the call."

"In this country you call an emergency number," Alejandro informed her. "But it makes no difference. They will have a record." Then he paused. "Afterwards she met a certain party at a restaurant nearby."

"The one where the hostess can identify her."

"She made an impression, I believe. She was disheveled." Alejandro paused. "And she was wearing high-heeled shoes," he continued thoughtfully. "I wonder what happened to those high-heeled shoes?"

"I can't say for the shoes, but her torn stockings were found in the ladies' room," Kristina supplied demurely. "I think I have them here somewhere," she threw in as an afterthought, pulling a cavernous pocketbook up onto her lap and beginning to search through it.

I squared my shoulders and turned back to them. "What do you want?" I asked through clenched teeth.

"You know what we want."

"I tell you, I don't have the money."

"But you know where it is," said Alejandro softly.

I stared at him. "No I don't."

"Why don't I believe you, Elizabeth?"

"Because you're not listening."

They paused and exchanged a glance.

"You have to excuse a certain desperation on our part, Elizabeth," said Alejandro finally, with a little droop to his shoulders, "but we are under an enormous strain."

"There are so many counting on us," murmured Kristina. "I don't know what will happen to them if we don't—"

"It is a terrible responsibility," Alejandro cut in. "I cannot let those who trusted us suffer more than they already have."

"Sadly, it is a case where the ends must justify the means," said Kristina.

"Justify them to someone else then," I told them, "and leave Emily and me alone."

"Elizabeth," said Alejandro sternly. "You must listen to us. We are your only hope." He stopped. "If you know something you must tell us."

Fat chance, I thought. "I know nothing."

"You are under the sway of a man who will betray you," said Alejandro.

That thought slowed me down.

"Think, Elizabeth," Alejandro commanded. "Before you just dismiss us. Who knew you would be out of the house this morning?"

"I—"

"How could your house be ransacked unless someone knew you would be otherwise occupied for some period of time?"

"I—"

Kristina leaned forward. "How do you suppose we knew you'd be late getting to the school today to pick up Emily?" she whispered.

I stared at her, horrified.

"*Le dernier acte est sanglant, quelque belle que soit la comédie en tout le reste,*" said Alejandro. "Pascal: 1623 to 1662. From *Pensées*. 'The last act is bloody, however charming the rest of the play may be.'"

Chapter

10

I got Emily out of there then. I grabbed her and her stuff and we went out the door to the car. I threw her backpack and lunch box into the back, helped her into her car seat in the front, hurried around to the driver's side, and started the car while I still had a foot out the door. I don't mind admitting that I was shaken by that encounter. In fact, my one thought was to get away from Alejandro and Kristina as quickly as possible.

But once inside the car I discovered I had another problem. Where to go? Home? No way was I taking Emily home until I was sure Simon had left. The police? For all my threats, I didn't trust them to protect us, not from this crowd anyway. I started driving around the block while I considered my various options.

Emily shifted in her seat. "Where are we going, Mommy?" she asked.

"I don't know exactly, sweetheart. I have to think for a moment."

Emily was quiet for a few minutes while we meandered slowly around town. She shifted again and then spoke.

"Mommy?"

"Yes?"

"I need to go to the bathroom."

Great, I thought. "Do you have to go badly? Can you hold it a few minutes?"

"I can't hold it."

Great.

I looked down the block. We were on Walker Street. Town hall was half a block away, right next to the police station. They have a public bathroom at town hall and you couldn't get much safer than that.

"Okay," I said, zipping into a parking spot. "Let's go."

Town hall is another historic Lenox landmark, although this one is kept in much better condition than the library. You go up the stone steps, and the first thing you see after going through the doors is a big marble entranceway with a high ceiling and a speckled floor. In front of you are two sweeping staircases, one on either side of some white columns, leading in a heart-shaped fashion to the second floor. To your immediate right is the administrative office where you pay your taxes or apply for a permit if you want to burn leaves in the spring. To the left are the offices of the selectmen. Straight ahead is a large auditorium where everyone votes in November and watches the local ballet school perform *The Nutcracker* around Christmas. The bathrooms are also straight ahead, right before the auditorium.

I locked the car (something I never do) and grasped Emily firmly by the hand. We ran across the street, up the steps, across the foyer, and over to the bathroom. I opened the door, turned on the light, and got us both inside.

Emily started tugging at her tights.

"Hurry up, sweetheart." The last time it took her so long to get out of her clothes that she peed all over her shoes. "Here, let me help you."

She regarded me with blue eyes. "I want to do it myself."

I watched and hoped as she tugged and pulled. Finally she got them down and hopped up on the seat. She looked at me again.

"Yes?" I said.

"I want pwivacy," she said with great dignity.

Six months of training and begging and it all has to coalesce now, I thought. "All right," I sighed, and went to stand outside the door.

It was still the lunch hour, so there weren't too many people around. I sort of sidled over to the entranceway, keeping one eye on the rest room door, to see what was going on. There was only one woman in the administrative office and she was sitting at a desk in the back eating a sandwich. There was no receptionist in the selectmen's waiting room. The door to the inner offices was ajar, however, and I could just hear voices coming from within. Good, I thought, we're not alone. I started to move back toward the bathroom when I heard Cubby's voice.

"You're telling us he never intended to put up a mall at all? That it was one big fake from the beginning?"

As quietly as I could, I crept over to the door. I could just see through the crack on the side.

It was the room where the selectmen held their official board meetings. It had a huge American flag on an eight-foot flagpole with a little golden eagle on the top, a fireplace trimmed in colonial red, a blackboard upon which were thumbtacked various maps of Lenox, a long, chocolate brown oak conference table with a glass top to protect the surface from scratching and a little bowl of white and gold mums in the center and four glum faces grouped around one side in black swivel office chairs. These were Joe Cobb, Forrest

McNulty, Paul Mahoney, and Marion Hollister Thornewood.

But there was a fifth person in the room. It was Chief Rudge. Chief Rudge was not sitting. He was standing in front of the conference table rocking uneasily back and forth and staring down glumly at the glum faces who in turn were staring back up at him.

"It would be premature to draw conclusions at this point," he began. "The investigation is far from—"

"Well, let's put it this way," said Cubby, crossing his Nikes under the table. "Has your investigation turned up any documentation dealing with contractors?"

"That would be a negative," admitted the chief.

"What about materials? Any contracts for materials?"

"Negative."

"And he never paid Timmy Culpo for the land?"

"That would be a positive," said the chief.

"You mean he did pay him?" said Cubby, sitting up a little.

"Negative," said the chief. "You said, 'and he never paid Timmy Culpo for the land,' and I said, 'that's a positive,' meaning yes, he did not pay—"

"Oh, never mind," said Cubby, sliding back down in his chair.

Forrest McNulty frowned and scratched his jaw. "Maybe we can attach his assets. Did he leave any assets, Chief?"

"That's a negative."

"What do you mean, it's a negative? He had a house, didn't he? He had furniture, didn't he?"

The chief's lips barely moved. "Mortgaged. Bank gets it all."

Everybody around the table got a little glummer.

Paul Mahoney removed his unlit cigar from his lips. "Let's face it, folks," he said. "We got taken." He paused. "I knew I never liked that guy," he said.

Marion Thornewood sucked on her glasses reflectively. In contrast to the others, who wore Eddie Bauer sweaters on top of jeans or Dockers, Marion was wearing a beige suit, stockings, and low-heeled pumps. Her jacket was clasped at the neck primly by a pin of dried roses that goes for forty-five dollars at Eviva, the fancy dress shop in town. Her hair, which was shoulder length, had been rolled in hot curlers for the occasion.

"Maybe we can get the state to pick up some of this," she said.

"Some of what?" demanded Forrest McNulty. "There's nothing to pick up. It's Timmy Culpo's problem. I feel sorry for Timmy, but the town's got no stake in this. If anything, we're ahead with that hundred thousand—"

The chief coughed.

"You have something you want to say, Chief?" Marion leaned forward encouragingly.

When the chief spoke, he directed his remarks to the head of the selectmen. "We've got a situation about that hundred thousand," he said.

"What situation is that, Chief?" asked Cubby.

"Victim didn't put up the money."

"He didn't? Then who did?"

"Certain investors," said the chief, looking down at the linoleum.

"Private investors?" asked Cubby.

"That's affirmative."

"From out of town?"

There was a long pause.

"That's a negative," said the chief.

Paul Mahoney played with his cigar on the desk. "Fact is, Cubby, a number of respectable local people put money into that mall."

"I can't tell you how much I'd like to see the state participate in this," murmured Marion.

Cubby passed a hand over his brow. "You got a complete list of investors, Chief?"

The chief removed a paper from his shirt pocket and handed it to Cubby.

Cubby looked at the sheet and whistled. Then he squinted at it. "These figures here on the side correct, Chief?"

"That's affirmative."

"They add up to substantially more than one hundred thousand. Where's the rest of the money?"

"The investigation is proceeding along official lines."

"In other words, you can't find it."

There was another long pause.

"That's an affirmative," said the chief.

Cubby laid the paper down on the table. "Well, this is an interesting turn of events. We've got a piece of land off Route Seven with an earth mover on it and precious little else that hasn't been paid for. We've got approximately two dozen influential citizens who are out-of-pocket anywhere from five thousand to twenty-five thousand dollars apiece and who are expecting to recoup their investment by virtue of a mall which Jonathon Nichols never had any intention of putting up."

The chief coughed again. "There is some indication that the victim used an alias."

"An alias? You mean, he wasn't who he said he was?"

"That's affirm—"

"Would you stop saying that, please? Just use yes or no."

"Yes," said the chief.

"Yes what?"

"Yes he wasn't who he said he was."

"Who was he, then?"

"A fugitive," said the chief.

"A—"

"Wanted by the FBI," the chief explained.

There was a shocked silence.

"Wanted? What was he wanted for?" Cubby asked finally.

The chief sighed. "Embezzlement."

They all looked positively miserable.

"Oh, that's great. That's just great," said Forrest McNulty, throwing his pen down on the table.

Everybody was silent. The chief shifted.

"How much land are we actually talking about?" Cubby asked finally.

"It's twenty acres, isn't it?" said Marion. "I thought it was twenty acres."

"That sounds about right," said Paul.

"Maybe we can get somebody else interested in it," said Cubby. "It's already zoned commercial. That's a plus."

"Hey, what about Andrew and Linda Gordon?" suggested Forrest. "They've got some money. Remember they sold the Primrose Inn to that New York woman last year? I've known the Gordons since—well, since they started that inn. A class act all the way. Maybe they'd like to start a mall," he said.

"What do they know about a mall?" demanded Paul Mahoney. "A mall is not an inn."

"I'm not saying they'll want to. I'm just saying maybe—"

"What's that land worth, anyway?" interrupted Cubby.

Paul shrugged. "Twenty acres on Route Seven? Maybe three quarters of a million. Not more than that."

"Maybe we should appoint a committee to look into it," said Marion. "See if we can't come up with some alternative uses—"

"I wouldn't," grunted Paul.

"I agree with Paul," said Cubby. "I think that, for the time being, we should keep this between us. No sense getting everybody agitated."

"Timmy's going to be a problem," warned Forrest.

"I'll take care of Timmy," Paul volunteered. "I've known the family for a long time."

"We'll proceed along those lines, then, unless someone's got something else to say." Cubby waited but nobody said anything. "I'm not telling anybody what to do, you understand, it's a matter for each individual's conscience, but if anybody asks *me* what's going on with the Nichols project, I'm going to tell them we've got a number of parties interested in the property, and we are in the process of evaluating their offers according to the best interests of the community. When we've considered all the factors, we'll come forward with the details. In the meantime, nobody should worry because their investment is safe with us."

There was a general nodding of heads around the table.

"Good. We're all agreed, then. About time to get back to work, then. Thank you all for your time." Cubby paused. "I'm beginning to think that it was lucky this guy was knocked off when he was. A couple of more months of Jonathon Nichols and the whole town might have had to declare bankruptcy."

There was a general scuffling of chairs then, so I scampered back to the bathroom. It suddenly occurred to me that I had been gone a long time. Of course, that wasn't unusual. I had once cleaned the entire kitchen in the time it took Emily to wash her hands. "Em?" I whispered, knocking tentatively on the door. "Are you all right?"

"I'm wiping," came back clearly through the door.

"Why don't I just come in and help?"

"I can do it myself."

"I know you can. I'll just come in and stand—"

"Elizabeth. I'm glad I ran into you," said a voice behind me. I turned quickly. There stood Detective Fineburg.

"I wasn't listening," I said quickly. "I was just waiting for Emily to come out of the bathroom. It takes her a long time. EMILY! HOW ARE YOU DOING IN THERE?"

"Listening to what?" asked Detective Fineburg.

"Nothing."

"Oh. You weren't listening to nothing," he said. He paused. "I guess that makes sense."

"I don't care what they said, I didn't do anything," I continued recklessly.

"What who said?"

"Uh—nobody."

"So you don't care what nobody said," said Detective Fineburg, nodding his head. "You know, Elizabeth, my conversations with you aren't like my conversations with anyone else."

"Right. EMILY! ARE YOU STILL THERE?" I called, a little desperately.

The sound of running water came clearly through the door.

"I flushed," Emily reported through the door.

I turned back to Detective Fineburg. He was eyeing me strangely. He's going to arrest me, I thought suddenly, and then Emily will never get out of the bathroom. Well, I'm not going to help him with it. "Do you have a warrant?" I demanded.

"A warrant?" he repeated. "For dinner?"

"Dinner? What dinner?"

"Oh. Umm, uh—would you like to have dinner?" he asked.

"Would I like to—you mean with you?" I asked, taken aback.

"Uhh, yeah."

"You mean you want to interrogate me over dinner? Is this some kind of new police training thing?"

"What are you talking about? I'm asking you out on a date."

My mouth dropped open. "A date? But I thought . . . I thought you thought I killed Jonathon Nichols."

"I never thought you killed Jonathon Nichols."

"Oh."

"The chief thinks you killed Jonathon Nichols," Detective Fineburg explained.

"Oh."

"I thought you killed your husband."

"You did? Then why—"

"I like to think of myself as an open-minded sort of person," he said.

"I see."

The door to the bathroom opened and Emily emerged. She had a big triumphant smile on her face. "I'm all done," she said.

"Congratulations," said Detective Fineburg gravely. He turned back to me. "So what do you think? Think you want to have dinner with me tonight?"

"Tonight? I'm sorry," I said. "I'm not leaving Emily tonight." I held her close to me.

"So bring her," said Detective Fineburg.

I think I can safely say that the restaurant Detective Fineburg took us to, Elizabeth's (named for the owner's wife, not me), is something of a phenomenon for the Berkshires. It certainly breaks all the rules. In an area that prides itself on white clapboard, green-shuttered country charm, the exterior of Elizabeth's two-story frame building has been painted a shade of hot pink most commonly associated with Pepto-Bismol or the fingernails of recent beauty-school graduates. In a place where people are so concerned about the quality of their environment that they don't allow fluoridation of the water, Elizabeth's continues to thrive despite the fact that it is located across the street from an abandoned General Electric industrial park that—and I swear to God this is the truth—has a sign on it that reads: "Warning: Hazardous Waste." It all goes to show, I guess, that here in the Berkshires there is no natural delicacy of feeling or aethestic scruple that cannot be overcome by a funky interior design, a Harry Connick Jr. tape crooning in the background, and a knockout Bolognese sauce.

It was the middle of the week after season, so it wasn't too crowded. Tom, the proprietor, looked up from his station behind the salad counter. Elizabeth's has an exposed kitchen. "Hey, Matt," he called.

"Hey, Tom," said Detective Fineburg. "You got room for us?"

"Don't I always have room for you?" asked Tom, bustling over. He was a short, thick man who in another life had certainly been either a marine drill sergeant or a professional wrestler. "You're three tonight? How about right in front here?" He led us to a corner table. "Hey, sweetheart," he said to Emily.

"Hi," said Emily shyly.

"You want to see how we make the pizza?" he asked.

"Uh, sure," said Emily.

"C'mon, then," said Tom.

We watched as Tom brought Emily to the kitchen area, where she was immediately surrounded by his wife and three of the four waitresses, the fourth waitress having just arrived at our table with two glasses of wine. "Is that your daughter?" she asked, setting a glass in front of me. "She's so cute."

"Thanks," I said.

"Want to hear the specials or will you just be having the usual?" she asked Detective Fineburg.

He looked at me. "What do you feel like?"

"Oh, let's have the usual, by all means," I said.

"Right," said the waitress. "A Mista salad for two and a half and a pizza Rustica coming right up."

"And some plain buttered spaghetti for Emily, please," I added.

"Sure." The waitress turned away and went to join the group around Emily.

"You eat here often?" I asked Detective Fineburg.

"Pretty often," he admitted.

"Do you like to be called Matt?" I continued.

"It's all right. Matthew would be okay also, though." He smiled. "Anything's better than Detective Fineburg."

"Okay, Matthew," I said, looking at him hard, "what are we doing here?"

I didn't mean to be so abrupt, but it had been a long, hard day and I was worried about a lot of things, so I didn't have much patience left. Although I'd successfully outwaited Simon earlier in the afternoon—he wasn't there by the time Emily and I finally made it back home and I'd cautiously opened the door—that didn't mean he wasn't coming back. And, as a result of my conversation with the Tumenases, I felt completely adrift. Was Simon a good guy or a bad guy? *Had* he arranged to keep me out of my house so that it could be searched and I'd be late for my child so she could be abducted? And there were other considerations. I'd locked my doors that evening, but that didn't mean I wasn't going to come home to another surprise. And now here was Detective Fineburg taking me out to dinner for God knows what purpose. I just didn't have it to play coy.

"What are we doing here?" I repeated.

Matthew took a sip of wine and wound his tie around his finger. There were pictures of Bugs Bunny all over it. The tie, not the finger. "Well, it's like this," he said. "When I first came to your house two years ago after your husband was shot, the minute I saw you I wanted to ask you out. Things weren't going too well between Maria and me at that point—we were already separated—so I figured we'd find out who killed Hack, close the case, and then I'd ask you out. But then we found out you inherited all the money, which gave you motive. Suddenly, you're the prime suspect, so I couldn't ask you out. Even after you were cleared—officially, anyway—the case was still open. I was sure that you didn't tell us everything you knew, so I still couldn't ask you out. And then Maria and I decided to give it another try, but it didn't work out, so after a year or so I thought of you again. And then, over the summer, I saw you at Tanglewood and I was going to come over when I saw you sit down on a blanket with that developer guy, so I didn't. And then I was going to call you, when the developer guy turns up dead and you're a suspect again, although personally I think it's unlikely you killed him, since in this case there's no motive, and besides, he wasn't killed by a Jeep. So I thought, if I have to wait to catch her until she's between murders again, I'll be waiting until I'm on Social Security, so I started following you around looking for the right moment but you're always with people so I had to wait until today when you'd finished eavesdropping on the selectmen meeting." He paused. "And that's what we're doing here."

"Oh," I said.

There was silence.

It's odd how you can think you know a person when you're used to seeing them in one capacity, and then when you see them in a different setting you suddenly realize you don't know them at all. That's what happened to me with Detective Fineburg. I'd already made up my mind about Detective Fineburg long ago, but that's when he *was* Detective Fineburg. Now he was someone named Matthew who was sitting across from me and looking at me funny. . . . The salad arrived.

"I'll get Emily," Matthew volunteered. He paused. "It will be nice eating with a family again," he said.

Actually, we did have a pretty good time. "How's your salad, Em?" I asked.

"It has apples in it," she said. "I like apples in my salad. Can I have apples in my salad at home?"

"*May* I have apples in my salad at home."

"May I have apples in my salad at home," Emily repeated.

"Yes, you *may* have apples in your salad at home."

Matthew laughed. "You're tough," he said to me.

Emily looked at him. "Who's that?" she asked me.

"That's Detective Fineburg, remember?" I told her.

"Matthew," said Matthew.

"What's a detective?" asked Emily.

"He's a policeman, honey."

"What's a policeman?"

"Good question," said Matthew. "I like to think of a policeman as a person who catches bad guys," he told her.

"Are there any bad guys here?" Emily persisted. She looked around.

"No," said Matthew. "There are no bad guys here."

"Where are they, then?"

"I don't know. Before you can catch a bad guy you have to have a clue," Matthew told her.

"What's a clue?"

"Well, I found one today, as a matter of fact."

"Weally?" said Emily, working another piece of apple onto her fork. "What was it?"

"It was a truck," said Matthew.

So they'd found Irving Meltzman's truck! I took a bite of salad to show I didn't care.

But Matthew was still talking. "A big shiny black truck with a little red racing stripe—"

"Like Mr. Nichols's truck?" asked Emily, crunching.

Matthew stopped. "Do you know Mr. Nichols's truck, Emily?" he asked, reaching for his wine.

"He used to let me drive it. I drove to New York," said Emily.

"Long trip," acknowledged Matthew.

"Where was it?" asked Emily.

"Where was what?" asked Matthew.

"Mr. Nichols's truck."

"It was . . . somewhere where it shouldn't have been," Matthew answered after a moment. "That's how I knew it was a clue," he added.

"Oh," said Emily. "Why—"

"Pizza, anyone?" said the waitress, clearing a space in the center of the table. She set the pizza down and then handed Emily her bowl of spaghetti.

"Great," said Matthew. "No matter how many times I eat this, I always—"

Beep. Beep. Beep.

Matthew sighed. "Excuse me," he said, and got up from the table. "Can I use your phone, Tom?" I heard him ask.

"What's going on?" Emily wanted to know.

"Nothing," I said, craning my head to try to catch the expression on Matthew's face as he spoke into the phone. "Eat your spaghetti." I caught a glimpse. "Eat fast," I added.

Matthew returned to the table. "I hate to—"

"I know," I said. "You have to go. C'mon, Em." I stood up. "We're leaving."

On the way home, Emily fell asleep in the car. When we got to my house, Matthew lifted her out of her car seat and carried her to bed. He looked at her as I took off her shoes and slipped her under the covers. "She's a sweet kid," he said.

"Thanks." I turned out the light and we tiptoed down the stairs. Matthew stood awkwardly by the front door.

"Thanks for the dinner," I said. "It was fun."

"Yeah. I had a good time, too," he said. "Uh, the pizza. I left it in the car." He started to turn. "I'll get it for you."

"Oh, no," I said. "You take it."

"You're sure? It's really good cold."

"That's okay."

"Well, thanks," he said.

There was silence.

"I suppose I had better be going," he said.

"Yes."

"Well, good night," he said.

"Good night. And thanks again."

He opened the door and started to leave. Then abruptly he turned back. "I have to ask you something before I go," he said. "Are you seeing someone?" he asked. "Someone else, I mean?"

"What?"

"I mean, I'm probably way out of line here," he said. "I know it's none of my business."

"No, I—"

"Just forget I said anything," Matthew said, and started to leave again.

I waited. He got halfway down the front steps and then turned back.

"Can I see you again?"

"*May* you see me again?" I said with a smile. "I'd like that," I said, and realized I meant it. I had had a good time with him.

He broke into a big grin. "Great! I'll call you." He started down the steps again.

"Uh, Matthew," I called.

He stopped. "Yes?"

"Where *did* you find Jonathon Nichols's truck?" I asked.

"Now, Elizabeth, you know I can't tell you that," he said.

"I know," I said. "I'm sorry. I just couldn't—"

"It's official police business."

"I know. It's my own fault for being so nosy. Please forget I said anything," I said.

"Just so you understand," he said.

"I do."

"Good. We found it abandoned in the woods just off Bean Hill Road," he said, and left.

Chapter

11

"I can't understand how it happened," said Fawn Woode-house. "Thank you for bringing this to our attention."

It was the next morning. Emily and I were in Fawn's office. "We have such tight controls about this sort of thing," she continued.

"Yes. I can see that. Would you call in your assistant, please," I said.

"Lucy? Of course." Fawn rose from behind a cluttered desk and walked to the door of her office. "Lucy? Would you come in here, please?" she called.

Lucy appeared. She was in her mid-forties, with long brown hair that fell straight down to her shoulders. "Yes?" said Lucy.

I stood up. "Lucy," I said, "I am Elizabeth Halperin."

"Oh, yes, I spoke to you on the phone yester—"

"And this is my daughter, Emily. Emily is in the Preschool Threes program with Penny Johnson," I continued.

"Oh, yes, that's such a wonderful program, don't you—"

"Emily is not to go home with anyone unless I come up here specifically and tell you so," I said firmly.

Lucy looked surprised. "Why—"

"No notes."

"Why—"

"No phone messages."

"I—"

"I don't care if the president of the United States himself asks to pick her up."

There was a pause.

"I see," said Lucy.

"Thank you, Lucy," said Fawn. "I think I hear the phone ringing."

Lucy left. I stood up with Emily and turned to go as well. Fawn came out from behind her desk, arm extended. "I can't tell you how sorry I am for this misunderstanding," she said. She seemed genuinely sorry. "The Early Childhood Division is indeed a special world. I so enjoy working with you and Emily. May I just say that I hope that you will not let a small mix-up like this one prejudice your feelings against the entire school."

Fawn smiled. "Along those lines, may I ask a favor? The annual student auxiliary fund needs a parent coordinator, and frankly I think you'd be perfect for it. There isn't much to it. You simply write a letter to each parent in Emily's class, asking for a tax-free donation. The amount of the donation is entirely up to the parent, although we do suggest a target figure for each family of—"

"Sorry," I interrupted, "but I'm already doing gift wrap," and hurried Emily out the door.

I took Emily inside the Preschool Threes' classroom and repeated to Penny the admonition about pick-up. When I came out, Denise was in the parking lot, getting into her Range Rover. When she saw me, she got back out again.

"Oh, hi, Elizabeth," she said in that breathy way she had, as soon as I was close enough to the car to hear her. She was dressed in a monogrammed tennis outfit. Around her neck was a gold necklace from which hung a charm of crossed tennis racquets. The handles of the tennis racquets had tiny little diamonds on them. "I was just on my way to the club for my lesson. Do you play tennis? I love it. I have such a good teacher. Do you know Ilya Sieradzki at Berkshire West? He does this kind of yoga tennis. I've been going to him now for almost a month. . . . It's great, I really feel like I'm getting somewhere. Of course, he's seventy-five dollars each time, but William said, if you're going to do something you might as well do it right, so I'm up to about five lessons a week now. If you want, I can see if he'll take on someone new—"

"Uh, no thanks."

"Actually, I'm thinking of starting Amber. Do you think three is too young to play tennis? William wants her to start as soon as possible. But he's so competitive. Is Emily taking tennis lessons?"

"Uh, no, not—"

"Well, maybe you should think about it. William says it's never too early to—"

"Listen, Denise—" I cut in.

"You know, Elizabeth," said Denise, "I always enjoy these little talks. . . . I just wish we could have them more often. Would you like to have coffee?"

"Coffee? Well, sure, sometime—"

"I mean right now. At that cute little coffee shop in Lenox."

"But what about your tennis lesson?" I asked.

"I'll move it back. After all, what's more important," said Denise, "a little tennis or a real talk between friends?"

"So I told William, 'William, we simply have to do something special this year for Amber's birthday.' She's getting to the age where her friends are important to her."

We were at the cute little coffee shop in Lenox. I had a café latte in front of me. Denise had a cappuccino, but she'd been so busy talking she hadn't had a chance to taste it yet.

"Oh, that reminds me!" said Denise suddenly. "I was supposed to call William." She looked around. "I wonder if they'll let me use the phone here," she said. "It won't take a minute. I think I'll just ask. . . . Will you excuse me for a moment?"

She got up and I saw her approach the man behind the counter. She spoke a few words and the man nodded and smiled and lifted a phone onto the counter. She picked up the receiver and began to dial.

Boy, will he be sorry, I thought, and looked around for something to do while I waited.

Luckily, there is always a ready supply of newspapers at the coffee store—even some of the out-of-town ones like the *Boston Globe* and the *New York Times* are left in a rack on the wall. But today I wasn't interested in the national news. Today I just wanted to see the *Berkshire Eagle*. Perhaps Matthew's beeper going off last night had meant there was a break in the case. He'd already broken police confidentiality, or whatever it's called, by telling me about finding the truck.

Whatever small lingering misgiving I might have had over taking advantage of my relationship with Matthew to elicit information was immediately dispelled when I looked at the Berkshires section of the paper.

"MURDER VICTIM'S TRUCK FOUND," read the headline.

Humph, I thought. So much for my influence with Detective Fineburg.

A key piece of evidence in the suspected murder case of Jonathon Nichols, the Berkshires developer found dead late last Saturday evening, was found in the woods off Bean Hill Road in Lenox yesterday. Working together, state and local investigators, in cooperation with the FBI, which has been brought in to help with the case, found Mr. Nichols's truck, which had apparently been missing since the night of the accident, some distance off the road. Mr. Nichols's body had been found earlier at the site of his proposed mall at the corner of Route 7 and Housatonic Street in Lenox.

Police investigators found the vehicle, which was a late model black four-by-four Ford pickup, after receiving a tip earlier in the week that a truck matching the description of the victim's was sitting abandoned under a maple tree some twenty-five yards into the woods off Bean Hill Road. According to Lenox Chief of Police Ned Rudge, although otherwise in perfect working condition, the vehicle was found to contain scratches and hair and blood samples on the left front fender consistent with the type of hit-and-run injuries sustained by Mr. Nichols. Asked by *Eagle* reporters if he believed that the Ford pickup was, in fact, the murder weapon by which the Lenox developer met his untimely demise, Chief Rudge expressed optimism while urging caution. "We are not ruling out that possibility at this stage in the investigation," he noted, adding that the vehicle would be impounded so that further forensics tests could be conducted, including a thorough examination for fingerprints.

The presence of the abandoned truck over two miles away from the site of the suspected murder, together with an earlier discovery of tracks of high-heeled shoes at the scene, brings up the question of whether the crime was committed by multiple suspects. "Either that," agreed Chief Rudge, "or the actual perpetrator had one or more accomplices." Pressed further, he added that "it was now the prevailing theory that at least two people were involved in the murder, one to drive the truck to its place of concealment, the other to follow in an as-yet-unidentified vehicle."

Chief Rudge dismissed questions about the presence of FBI agents in what began as a local investigation as "routine."

In a related issue, Marion Hollister Thornewood, Lenox town selectwoman, announced yesterday that several individuals were interested in the property left by Mr. Nichols, and that the Board of Selectmen was currently reviewing proposals. "It is only a matter of time before the project is taken over by the appropriate developer," she said. "The contracts and plans left by the late Jonathon Nichols, which were required by the Board in case of just such an emergency, are sufficiently detailed to allow for a smooth transition to a new owner."

Anyone with any information relevant to the murder investigation should contact . . .

I put the paper down and glanced over at Denise. She was still on the phone. I sighed, took a sip of my café latte, and ran my eye down the rest of the first page of the Berkshires section. I was about to turn to the comics when an article in the lower left-hand corner stopped me.

"FOREIGN TOURISTS KILLED IN FREAK ACCIDENT," it said.

Naaawww, I thought. Couldn't be . . .

A husband and wife touring the Berkshires from Europe were killed instantly yesterday when they apparently leaned too far over the edge of the rocks at the top of Monument Mountain and fell into the gorge below. The two, who have been identified as Alejandro Tumenas and his wife, Kristina,

[oh my God]

had climbed the mountain at what police estimate to be approximately the hour of sunset, and then lost their footing near the top.

Although Monument Mountain, located in Great Barrington, is a popular spot for hikers and tourists, there were no eyewitnesses to the accident owing to the lateness of the hour. The bodies were discovered only after a party of hikers from

Canyon Ranch, armed with flashlights, noticed the couple lying inert on the rocks below.

While it is unusual for two people to fall, police theorize that one of the two was trying to save the other, resulting in both going over together. Although autopsies will be performed, as is the routine in cases of accidental death, the police said that, at this time, there is no indication of foul play. Most likely the two were simply inexperienced hikers. Police point to the footwear of the woman, particularly, as being inappropriate for the degree of difficulty of the terrain.

In the light of the accident, the Great Barrington Chamber of Commerce hastened to reassure other visitors to the area. "Monument Mountain has historically been a safe and healthy addition to the landscape," said Max Dolan, president of the chamber. "Thousands of tourists climb it every year. I can't remember something like this happening in my lifetime before."

Police and park district officials are using the occasion to remind hikers of basic safety rules. Always wear appropriate hiking shoes. Sneakers or rubber-soled shoes may not provide the necessary support or traction. Always keep to the path. Don't lean out too far over the rocks. . . .

"Interesting article, don't you think?"

I jerked my head up with a start. There stood Ed.

"Well written," noted a second voice.

And Frank. Both in full tennis regalia.

"Chock-full of useful information," added Ed. "May we join you, my dear?" he asked, sitting down next to me. "Terrible thing," he said, taking the newspaper out of my hand. "What was that couple's name? Tumenas? What could have possessed them to go hiking at such an hour?"

"And such a difficult climb, too," said Frank, sitting on my other side.

"And from what I understand, they were not a young man

and woman. And not at all in the condition of serious hikers," Ed continued.

"Like us," said Frank.

"Elizabeth," said Ed, drawing a little nearer, "why do *you* think they might have elected to take such an arduous undertaking at such an unusual hour?"

"Yes," Frank agreed, "if they got into trouble on the trail, they would have been quite alone." He had moved perceptibly closer as well.

"I have no idea," I said, suddenly glad Denise was in the room, even if she was still on the phone.

"Neither did we," said Ed. "But then we talked it over and came up with a theory. Would you like to hear our theory, my dear?"

"Not particularly," I said.

"Well, here it is anyway. We thought, perhaps, they were going to meet someone," said Ed.

"Someone who had promised them something," said Frank.

"Like information," said Ed.

"About some money, perhaps."

"Quite a lot of money," said Ed. "The same money that we are interested in, even. But you know what happened instead?"

"I have an idea," I replied.

"Poof!" said Ed, flicking his fingers outward.

"They were pushed," Frank translated earnestly.

"And that leads to the next question," said Ed. "Why would anyone have done such a thing?"

"And *who* would have done such a thing?" asked Frank.

"Not yet," said Ed, frowning.

"Sorry," said Frank.

"Where was I? Oh, yes, why would anyone have done such a thing? Perhaps someone had a grievance against them. Did you know anyone who had a grievance against them, Elizabeth?"

I was silent.

"But maybe it wasn't a grievance at all," Ed continued.

"Maybe it was just the all-American spirit of competition."

Frank looked at Ed. "Did they play tennis?" he asked interestedly.

Ed ignored him. "If this theory is correct, it seems that there are only three possibilities to answer the question of who did it." He looked at me. "You might have done it," he said. "Did you do it, Elizabeth?"

"No," I said.

"We didn't think so," said Frank.

"Secondly," said Ed. "*We* might have done it. Frank, did we do it?"

"That was so long ago," said Frank, "I don't seem to remember."

"That does happen," said Ed.

"Although not that often," Frank added quickly.

Ed moved in closer. I could feel his elbow in my side. "And then, of course, your friend Simon might have done it. Too bad he's not here so we can ask him and he can say *he* doesn't remember. But, really, Elizabeth, it doesn't matter much to you. If Frank and I did it, it means we are starting to get desperate, and that, in turn, means you are in serious danger. In that case, your only alternative would be to tell us what you know. If your friend Simon did it, it would mean that *he* is getting desperate, which means, in turn, that you are in serious danger. In that case, your only alternative is to tell us what you know so that we can protect you."

"Why wouldn't I tell Simon all I know and have him protect me from you?" I asked.

"Because Simon is not to be trusted." Ed peered at my face. "But I think you already know that, don't you, my dear?"

"No, I don't know that at all. What makes you think I know that?"

"Elizabeth, you *are* hiding something," said Ed.

"No, I'm not. And what makes you more trustworthy than Simon?"

"Why do you trust Simon so much? Just because he's young and good-looking?" sneered Ed.

"We may be slower," said Frank, "but we're very thorough."

"Or did he give you that line about working for the British royal family?" said Ed.

I flushed. "I'm not going to talk about Simon," I said firmly.

"Oh, I don't mind your talking about me," said a voice overhead. "But I think it would be only polite to ask me to sit in on the conversation."

We all looked up at once. There stood Simon.

He was so tall and strong and smooth and powerful and well-dressed that I didn't know whether to throw my arms around him as my savior or make a run for the door. So I just sat there as we all watched him come around the table and draw up a chair on the other side.

"We were just discussing the unfortunate incident on Monument Mountain," said Frank.

"Ah, yes. Professor and Mrs. Tumenas. Very unfortunate indeed. A terrible waste of a good education," noted Simon. He turned to me. "How are you, Elizabeth?"

"Feeling a little crowded at the moment," I said.

Frank and Ed immediately pushed their chairs back away from me.

"I wouldn't worry about that, Elizabeth," said Simon. "These two were just leaving."

"What if nobody leaves?" said Frank.

"What did you have in mind?" asked Simon.

"Well," said Frank, "thirty million dollars *is* a lot of money. Maybe we could come to an arrangement."

"You mean where everybody gets a share of the money and we all ride off happily into the sunset?" asked Simon.

"Something like that," said Ed. "After all, *we* didn't push those people off the cliff."

"Neither did I," replied Simon. He turned to me. "Elizabeth, did you push those people off the cliff?"

"No," I repeated.

"Undoubtedly a strong gust of wind, then," said Simon.

"I suppose we could settle for that," said Ed.

"Yes, let us not allow a technicality to interfere with an otherwise amicable situation," commented Simon. He paused. "So, what do you know?" he asked.

Frank and Ed exchanged an uneasy glance. "You go first," said Frank.

"Right. The money is in a Swiss bank account," said Simon.

I stared at him. He crinkled his forehead ever so slightly in my direction.

"Oh, you already knew," said Frank, with some relief.

"Well, now that you mention it, yes," said Ed. "It's not that we were holding anything back. . . ."

"Suisse Union Creditbank of Zug, in fact," continued Simon.

"That was our understanding as well," admitted Frank.

Simon looked across the table. "Well?" he said, and waited.

"It can be done," said Ed, finally. "They don't know yet."

"You've confirmed that?" asked Simon.

"We had somebody check it out," Frank admitted.

I couldn't help myself. "*Who* doesn't know yet?" I asked. "And what don't they know?"

"Suisse Union Creditbank of Zug doesn't know yet that Irving Meltzman is dead," said Simon, not taking his eyes off Ed.

"That's because the name that was released to the papers was not Irving Meltzman, but Jonathon Nichols," supplied Ed.

"And, anyway, news doesn't travel that fast from the Berkshires to Switzerland," explained Frank. "The Swiss papers are unlikely to pick up a story from America unless it is on the front page of the *New York Times* or the *Washington Post*."

I stared at Simon. "So, if they don't know that he's dead,

they won't know to release the money to the next of kin, or the government, or . . . "

". . . and therefore there is a very slight possibility—" began Simon.

"—that we can still get the money," finished Ed and Frank in chorus.

Get the money! That was kind. Steal the money was more like it. And Simon working with these two! But then sanity kicked in.

"Get the money?" I repeated. "Why, don't be ridiculous. You'd have to get someone to impersonate Irving Meltzman and his signature, fly that person to Zug, hope the bank manager doesn't recognize him as an imposter—"

"Irving Meltzman was only in Zug for one day three years ago," said Ed calmly, looking down at his fingers.

"Just to make the deposit," confirmed Frank.

"That meant the bank manager only saw him once," said Simon.

"How do you know?" I demanded.

"Because they found his passport," said Simon calmly. "Didn't you?" he asked Ed and Frank.

"Well, if you're going to be careless enough to leave an important document like that lying around . . ." said Ed.

"In your safe," noted Simon.

"Wherever." Frank waved an arm airily.

"Still," I persisted, "the imposter . . . "

"Makeup," suggested Ed.

"Plastic surgery," put in Frank.

"An actor." Simon shrugged. "Hired for the part."

"But you'd still need the account number," I said. "Without the account number . . ." I became aware that they were all looking at me.

"Yes, the account number," said Ed.

"The account number *is* absolutely necessary to the success of the operation," agreed Frank.

"Funny you should mention that, Elizabeth," said Simon.

"Wait a minute. You think that I—"

"Elizabeth! Are these some of your friends?" asked Denise.

I'd forgotten all about her. But there she stood, beaming down at everyone.

"I'm sorry I took so long," she continued, "but you know William. You just can't get him off the telephone. William is my husband," she explained to Frank, Ed, and Simon. Her gaze lingered on Simon just a second longer than on the other two. "He's a personal injury attorney. . . . Am I interrupting anything?"

"Uh, no, not at all, Denise," I said. "Please, sit down."

Denise sat down. The whole table was quiet.

"I am interrupting something," said Denise. "I'll just be going—"

"No, no, Denise," I interrupted. "I want you to meet my friends. This is Ed Pasquini and Frank Plishtin. And I believe you've met Simon before."

"Pleasure to meet you, my dear," said Ed.

"Always happy to meet a friend of Elizabeth's," said Frank.

"You're looking even more charming than at the fair," said Simon.

"Thank you." Denise blushed. She turned to Frank and Ed. "Oh, do you play tennis?" she asked, noting their outfits. Then, without waiting for a response, "Have you ever tried Ilya Sieradzki at Berkshire West? He does this kind of yoga tennis. If you want, I can see if he'll take on someone new, or" —she brightened—"perhaps you'd like to join me. We could play doubles with Ilya. I've got time reserved in fifteen minutes—"

"Oh, no, we couldn't," said Frank.

"Much as we'd like to, my dear," said Ed, who had been critically admiring Denise's figure.

"Of course you could," Simon said firmly.

"Would you and Elizabeth like to come as well?" asked Denise. "We could take turns—"

"Oh, no, thank you, but I'm afraid I'm not dressed for tennis," said Simon. "You three run along, though," he said. "Elizabeth and I have some catching up to do."

"Oh, I see," said Denise, smiling at me.

"Some other time," I murmured.

"It seems we are going to play yoga tennis," said Ed to Frank. He turned to Simon. "About that other matter . . ." he began.

"Don't worry," said Simon lightly. "I'll take care of it."

"Where can we get hold of you?" asked Frank.

"I'll be in touch."

Denise, Frank, and Ed made a move toward the door. On their way out I saw Frank turn to Ed.

"Does yoga tennis involve new positions?" he asked.

"We can only hope," Ed replied. "Denise, my dear," he said, holding the door for her. And then they were gone.

I was left alone with Simon.

Chapter

12

We just stared at each other across the table for a moment. It was very quiet.

What to do, what to do?

Then Simon grinned at me, a long, slow, melting grin.

The grin infuriated me. How dare he, after everything that had happened, just take it for granted that I would fall in line because he has a great smile? I will not speak to this man again as long as I live, I vowed to myself suddenly. Instead, I will glower at him until he goes away. Accordingly, I arranged my features into what I was sure was the appropriate mixture of anger and scorn. Take that, I thought.

But Simon seemed unaffected. He just took a sip of coffee and munched on his scone.

I glowered some more.

Finally he spoke. "I thought that went rather well, don't you?" he asked.

I am not speaking to you, I thought.

"Until I came in and saw them with you, I was afraid that

they had somehow gotten the account number on their own."

Go away, I thought.

He took another leisurely sip.

"Perhaps while they were ransacking your house."

"They were the ones who ransacked my house? How do you know that?" I demanded.

"Well, it wasn't the Tumenases. They didn't have the time. And it wasn't me," he added, looking directly into my eyes. "I was with you." He paused. "But perhaps you don't remember," he said.

"I'll tell you what I remember," I burst out suddenly. "I remember that you kept me occupied so that my house could be broken into and my child taken. I remember that you asked me to come and help search Irving Meltzman's house with you but didn't bother to share what you'd found. I remember that once you found what you thought you were looking for, you disappeared, and have only come back because you need something else." I took a quick breath and continued hotly. "And now I discover that you are perfectly willing to share information with a pair of disreputable old lechers who may or may not be FBI agents, but who are most certainly thieves, information that, incidentally, you saw fit to withhold from *me*, so that you are now in cahoots"—yes, I actually used that word— "with those two and you've had the nerve to drag me into it and not only that, ask if it went well. Well, I've only got one thing to say to you—" I was so angry I couldn't think of what the one thing was, so I just shut my mouth. *Now* I will never speak to this man again, I thought.

But Simon was speaking. "What is it that you want, Elizabeth?" he asked.

"I'll tell you what I want. I want the *truth*."

"Right," said Simon genially. "I'll tell you everything I know."

I stared at him.

"Right," he said again. "Do you want to ask questions, or

shall I just begin? I'll tell you what," when I still hadn't replied, "I'll just meander about, and you can interrupt where you—"

"Did you kill the Tumenases?" I interrupted him.

"I did not."

"Who did? Ed and Frank?" No way, I thought. Those two?

"They must have."

"Why?"

Simon shrugged. "They might have been getting too close, Ed and Frank didn't want to split, or worse, get cut out altogether."

"Does that mean they killed Irving Meltzman as well?"

"I'm not sure, although it's beginning to look that way," Simon admitted.

I stood up. "Denise," I said.

"She's all right. They know she's not involved."

I stared at him. "But they're killers."

"Not like that. She's perfectly safe, unless you count their torturous senses of humor," Simon remarked. "They'd consider her an innocent bystander. The FBI takes great pains never to jeopardize the lives of innocent bystanders."

I felt my mouth form a perfect O. "You mean to tell me that those two are really—"

"FBI? Well, not anymore. But they were," said Simon. "Up until last year, that is. Then they were stuck with mandatory retirement."

"But if they're retired—"

"They weren't happy about it. They'd been assigned the Irving Meltzman case and they wanted to finish it. They argued for an extension, they argued to be taken on as consultants, they pointed to their many years of experience, but it was no use. The federal government is apparently quite firm on this point. Everyone who gets to a certain age retires, in order to save money. It has something to do with the Republican freshmen, I believe," he concluded vaguely.

"But I don't understand," I said. "If they're off the force—"

Simon shrugged. "I think they refer to it as the Bureau. In any event, they turned turncoat, for lack of a better word. Started tracking Meltzman on their own. Somewhere along the line it occurred to them that thirty million dollars was quite a bit of money." He paused. "Apparently they were not particularly impressed with the size of their pension, either."

"How do you know all this?" I asked.

"I know people they know. A number of people in the Bureau are sympathetic to them. They get help. That's how they found out about Suisse Union Creditbank of Zug. They called their people in Switzerland. Also how they got the passport out of the safe."

"But if you know all this, why don't you stop them?" I asked.

Simon looked surprised. "They're doing pretty well. Why should I stop them?" he asked.

"But the Tumenases . . . "

"The Tumenases were professionals. They knew the risks," said Simon firmly.

"Professional whats?" I asked.

"Professional thieves, of course. They've pulled off quite a number of robberies in Europe, mostly having to do with art and insurance fraud. The Oxford-don routine is apparently especially effective in art circles. This was rather out of their depth, but I suppose the amounts involved lured them. They must have heard about it in England. Irving Meltzman had a number of English investors," said Simon. "Word gets around. Also, I'm sure it was getting a bit hot for them on the Continent. The American venture probably looked both safe and lucrative to them."

"But the book," I insisted.

"What book?"

"The book on ancient Greece that Alejandro wrote."

"Anybody can write a book, Elizabeth," said Simon. "In fact, in my opinion, they usually do."

"Were they . . . dangerous?" I ventured, thinking of Emily.

"Oh, yes. Extremely. Especially Kristina. Until yesterday I had them pegged as Meltzman's killers. Kristina can be so volatile." He peered at me. "Are you all right?"

"Yes, I—" I swallowed, thinking of Emily eating ice cream with Kristina. "How do you know about them, Simon?"

"Oh, everybody knows about them," he said carelessly. "They've even made the papers in Italy and France. You can look them up yourself if you'd like."

"If everybody knows about them, why didn't anybody arrest them?" I asked.

"They were very good. Always a step or two ahead of the police. It isn't unusual," Simon told me. "Change countries, change aliases, have friends. . . . Think of the Israelis. They usually know who they're after. Sometimes it just takes them awhile to catch up."

"Kristina said you were working with them," I said flatly.

"She was lying."

"She said she and Alejandro knew that I'd be late getting to the school yesterday to pick up Emily. She meant that you were supposed to keep me busy at home while they went to get her. How would she know that, Simon?" I asked.

"I don't know. Probably she and Alejandro drove by your house and saw my car in your driveway. It's a pretty distinctive car," said Simon. "And, anyway, you weren't more than a few minutes late getting to the school that day. I'll bet if you checked, you'd find that the Tumenases picked Emily up fifteen minutes or so before the regular dismissal time. She was bluffing you, Elizabeth."

I was silent.

"Anything else?" asked Simon. "Or will that be satisfactory? It seems to me that we have covered a fair amount of territory—"

"What about you?" I said.

"What about me?"

"Who are you, Simon?" Looking right at him.

"Right," he said. He paused. "Are you sure you want to know?"

"Just tell me," I said, mentally preparing myself for the worst. Professional thief like the Tumenases, I thought. That would explain the safe at Meltzman's house. No, wait. The coolness under pressure. The negotiation with Ed and Frank. A mercenary, perhaps.

"Very well. I'm—"

The clothes. Dear god, a hired assassin. An English hit-man. A—

"—a chartered accountant," said Simon.

I blinked at him. "A what?" I asked.

"An accountant." He had removed his wallet from the inside pocket of his sport coat. He opened it, removed a little white business card, and presented it to me.

Simon Montgomery Smith, read the card. Chartered Public Accountant.

"It's in Japanese on the back, if that's any help," he pointed out.

I turned the card over. It certainly looked like Japanese.

"I don't believe it," I said. "An accountant!"

"Perhaps this will help," he suggested. He opened his sport coat again. This time he removed a pair of reading glasses. He put them on.

"You've got to be kidding. An accountant?" I said. Then I stopped and thought. "Wait a minute," I said. "What about getting the safe open when the police couldn't? And how come you know so much about the FBI? And what about making a deal with Ed and Frank? An accountant! You don't dress like any accountant *I* know," I continued. "And what's an accountant got to do with Irving Meltzman's thirty million, anyway?"

Simon looked distinctly uncomfortable. "As it turned out, one of my clients invested quite a large sum of money with Irving Meltzman and his hotel scheme on my recommendation, and is now threatening to sue me, and I thought, if I recovered the money—"

"Oh, really, Simon, this is absolutely the most idiotic thing I've ever heard. You must think I'm—"

"I'm sorry I didn't tell you right off," said Simon, "but I'm sure you appreciate my predicament. I don't generally go around telling people my profession. I've noticed that it tends to result in a glazed look and a certain predilection towards boredom." He shook his head. "I especially did not want that to happen with you," he added after a moment.

"Oh, come on."

"Seriously now, Elizabeth. If you had known I was just a chartered accountant trying to save my own skin, would you have found my story credible?"

That gave me pause.

"But the safe," I persisted.

"Already open when I got there. We might easily have surprised Ed and Frank just as the police surprised us. I think they left in a hurry."

"Your knowledge of the Tumenases."

"The *Financial Times*."

"Ed and Frank."

"Scotland Yard came to interview us three years ago when the Meltzman case first broke. I got friendly with some of the chaps. We used to go out to the pub after work. They told me about Ed and Frank."

"Your negotiating skills."

"Acquired with some difficulty at university."

"Your clothes."

"Acquired with much less difficulty from Harrods." He paused. "Believe me, Elizabeth, I wish it were different. Nothing would please me more than to be able to impress you by boasting of something romantic, like Interpol or even British Intelligence. But the plain truth is that all this is simply business."

"But you're negotiating with murderers!" Was I starting to believe this?

"I believe that here in the States that is called 'swimming with the sharks.' Sometimes you have to get a little dirty in order to get a deal done. Surely you remember that from your own Wall Street days, Elizabeth. Actually, as these things go, I've found negotiations with Ed and Frank to be refreshingly straightforward. Try having a go with some of our competitors sometime. Now that's—"

"And the money?"

"Belongs to my client," said Simon firmly.

I was silent.

"I'm sorry I told you," said Simon. "It's happening already."

"What is?" I asked.

"The inevitable letdown that occurs whenever I disclose my profession," he said, his gray eyes locked on mine.

"Oh, no," I said, blushing. "It's just that—"

"You're disappointed."

"Oh, no, really, I—" When had he moved his chair so close to mine?

"You were hoping for something a little more . . . exciting." His fingers played with my wrist.

"On the contrary. I mean, I swear it doesn't—"

"Shall we say dinner tonight, then?"

"Dinner?"

"Something intimate. Unless you're otherwise occupied."

"Oh, no, I—I mean—"

"Shall we say nine? There's something I have to do first," he said. I could feel his breath on my neck.

"Nine? Oh, no, I couldn't—"

"You feel differently."

"No, really, I—"

That's when he kissed me. Right there in the cute little cof-fee shop in front of the waiter behind the counter and the sour-faced woman who runs the health food store sitting at the next table. And it was a great kiss. All right, I admit it. I kissed him back.

He let me up for air. "Nine o'clock," he said.

"Nine o'clock."

"I'll pick you up."

"You'll pick me up."

"We'll talk more then."

"We'll talk more then," I echoed.

He left.

I watched him go.

So Simon is an accountant, I thought, as I saw him climb into the Jag and ease his way out of the parking lot.

Right.

You might very well wonder how I could even consider seeing Simon again. After all, the Tumenases had just been killed, and despite appearances, I had a hard time believing that Ed and Frank had done it. And yet . . . and yet . . . I felt safe with Simon. I did. Whatever he was, he wasn't a hardened criminal and he wasn't a killer. Sometimes you've just got to go with your gut instincts, I decided, as I left the coffee shop.

I stepped outside. It was a beautiful morning. Town looked cheerful and inviting, not too crowded. Ed and Frank were with Denise and I'd seen Simon leave myself. Perhaps a walk would help me think. Besides, there was something I'd been intending to do this morning in town, although for the life of me, with everything that had already happened, I couldn't think of what it was. Oh, well, it would come to me. . . . I set off down Main Street.

I took the same walk I always do. Down Main Street, past the library to the monument. Take a right at town hall, swing over by Yokun Avenue, and up again to Main Street. It's nice, quiet, and sunny at this hour of the day. A good route for thinking. And this is what I thought:

Break into somebody else's numbered Swiss account. What nonsense! Impossible—well, actually, upon reflection, if the bank manager *had* only met Meltzman once, and *if* the bank remained ignorant of the murder, and *if* the account number could be found . . . they were right, it might just be possible. Swiss banks, for all their reputation for secrecy, aren't very different from other commercial banks, I realized. And Swiss bank employees were very likely the same as other commercial bankers I'd known. Diligent enough but certainly not infallible. I could think of half a dozen bank vice presidents I'd known from my days on Wall Street who would have fallen for such a scheme. Why not a Swiss banker?

But the account number. Where would Irving Meltzman have hidden it? Did he write it down at all? Perhaps he just memorized it. But no, he'd have been afraid of forgetting it. He seemed to have kept scrupulous records of everything. But why hadn't it been in the safe like all the other documents? That was the most likely place to have kept it. Well, it wasn't there, I thought, because if it were, neither Ed, Frank, nor Simon would still be hanging around town.

Maybe he kept it on him. That way it would always be with him. But no, it would be too easy for somebody else to get. Perhaps he buried it in his garden. Kind of hard to refer to it, then, if he'd had to flee town suddenly. Where, where, where . . .

"Ms. Halperin? Elizabeth? Excuse me," called a voice several paces behind me.

I turned to the sound of running feet. There was Paige the librarian hurrying after me.

"I hope I'm not bothering you," she blurted when she got close enough to slow down. "I saw you walk by the library and I was afraid you hadn't gotten my messages."

Of course. That was the errand I'd forgotten. Paige had been leaving messages on my answering machine, asking me to drop by the library. "I'm sorry, Paige," I said. "I should have phoned.

I've been meaning to stop by, but things have been so hectic."

"Oh, it's no problem." She waved a manila envelope triumphantly in my direction. "I've got it!" she said, beaming.

"Got what?" I asked.

"That article you wanted that wasn't on our computer," said Paige, her face falling a little.

Article? What article? Oh, she must mean the early piece on Meltzman. "Really? Why, that's terrific, Paige," I said.

"You're sure? I thought you said you wanted it. . . ."

"Oh, I do." I remembered more clearly now. "But I thought it was going to take several weeks?"

Paige looked a little embarrassed. "Well, actually, when I found out they had it in Albany I just took a quick drive over there on my day off," she said.

"You didn't." Albany is an hour's drive from Lenox.

"Oh, it was no trouble at all. I knew you wanted it, and I thought, well, since I didn't have that much to do yesterday anyway I'd just go see if I couldn't intercept it before it went through channels . . . "

I took the manila envelope. It wasn't going to tell me anything I didn't already know, of course, but I couldn't very well tell her to send it back. It would be like kicking a puppy. "Thank you, Paige," I said warmly. "You are really very helpful. In fact, you're wasted in your present position."

Her face brightened. "You think so?" she said.

"Oh, yes, I—" I stopped. A group of cyclists wearing expensive fitness equipment had just pedaled past us.

"Ms. Halperin? Elizabeth? Are you all right?"

"Hmm? What? Oh, it's nothing. For a moment I thought I . . ." I was still watching the cyclists. Now, who was that in front on the right? That cyclist wearing the black spandex with the hot pink stripe down the side? I knew that person from somewhere. But where?

"I have to be getting back to work now," said Paige. "If you're sure you're all right," she added worriedly.

The cyclists had turned the corner at Main and Walker Streets. "I'm perfectly all right, thank you," I said, "but I have to go now," and on an impulse, I started to run.

I ran to the corner and stopped. The cyclists had already turned off Walker and onto Kemble Street. Even if I ran the block down to Kemble Street, I'd never catch up. They were moving too fast.

It's probably nothing, anyway, I thought as I turned away. Just my imagination. Someone-who-looks-like-someone-I-used-to-know kind of thing.

I sighed and turned around abruptly to go back to my car. As I did so, someone bumped into me. Someone large and solid and male, wearing a lumberjack shirt and work boots. It was Tim Culpo, the man who owned the property that Jonathon Nichols had pretended he was going to build a mall on.

"Oomph!" I said, almost falling over.

He must have been behind me the whole time. I don't think he was expecting me to turn around so quickly because for a moment he had a very unpleasant look on his face.

Tim Culpo, I thought. The man who sold the land to Jonathon. It suddenly occurred to me that he might know something. Maybe Jonathon told him something, something important, and he doesn't know it. Maybe . . .

"Excuse me," Tim muttered.

His eyes had narrowed as I stood watching him. Reflexively, I took a step backward. I hadn't realized how strong he must be until he'd bumped into me. And the hard expression in his eyes . . . it was almost scary. . . . I decided against interrogating him and instead hurried along.

When I looked back, he was still watching me. He had a very strange look on his face.

It was time to get Emily. I didn't want to be late, so I ran back to the car, tossed Paige's offering in the backseat, and took off.

Emily was there this time, and I gave her a big hug. Denise was there, too. Despite Simon's assurances, I was so relieved to see her that I almost gave her a big hug, too.

"How was the tennis match?" I asked.

"Oh, you mean Ed and Frank. We didn't get to play," she confided. "Almost as soon as we got there, one of their beepers went off—I think it was Ed's—and they had to go. It was such a shame, too, because they were really very sweet and I think Ilya might have done something with their backhands."

"Too bad," I murmured. "They didn't mention where they were going, did they?"

"They said something about meeting someone about the Josh," said Denise.

The Great Josh Billings Runaground was an annual competition that, over the years, had become every bit as important an event in the Berkshires as the Boston Pops concert. Thousands of people came every year from all over the country to compete. The Josh, as it was called, consisted of a twenty-six-mile bicycle race followed by twice around Stockbridge Bowl in a canoe and ending with a 10K run. Most people competed in teams of four—a cyclist, two canoers, and a runner—although it was possible to compete as an iron man or iron woman and do the whole thing yourself. Afterward, the town of Lenox throws a big party on the grounds of Tanglewood, complete with live bands and barbecue. It must be this Sunday, I realized. That's why there were so many cyclists in town. They were in training.

"Are you competing in the Josh?" asked Denise.

"No. Are you?"

"No, but William is." Denise hesitated a moment. "Some of us are planning to get together afterward, so that the children can play and listen to the music. . . . Maybe you and Emily would like to come."

I smiled at her. "Thank you. We'd love to," I said.

*   *   *

After that I resolutely put the whole Irving Meltzman affair out of my head and concentrated on playing with Emily. We went to the playground and rode the merry-go-round, swang on the swings, and climbed the monkey bars. Afterward I gave her dinner and a bath, read her a book, and tucked her into bed. Then I got ready for Simon.

I'd decided to surprise him and have dinner waiting for him when he arrived, rather than going out. Emily and I had shopped and I had a nice little supper ready on the stove, a bottle of wine cooling in the fridge, and an apple-and-cranberry pie from Suchele's bakery for dessert. I changed my clothes, brushed my hair, and put on some makeup. I turned on some soft music, lit the candles, and sat down to wait.

I waited and waited and waited. At nine forty-five I poured myself a glass of wine. At ten o'clock I turned off the oven. At ten-fifteen I had another glass of wine. At ten-thirty I threw out the nice little supper. At ten forty-five I attacked the pie, blew out the candles, and went to bed.

He never came, he never called.

Someone else did, though. At seven-thirty the next morning, the phone rang. It was Matthew Fineburg. He said: "Good morning, Elizabeth. I really shouldn't be telling you this, but I thought you should know that the bodies of Ed Pasquini and Frank Plishtin were just found floating in Stockbridge Bowl."

Chapter

13

"*What?*" I had been standing in the kitchen shaking Cheerios into a bowl for Emily, and I nearly dropped the receiver into the box.

"I'm sorry to have to be the bearer of sad tidings," said Matthew.

"I—I—how did they . . . how did it happen?" I asked.

"I'd rather not discuss it on the phone," said Matthew.

"Of course not," I murmured automatically, shoving the Cheerios in front of Emily.

Matthew cleared his voice. "I don't suppose you could come down and talk about it this morning?"

"Come down where?"

"To the station."

"The Lenox Police Station?" I repeated. "Why?"

"Umm, well, the chief and I would like to have a word with you," said Matthew. "It's nothing serious," he assured me, "it's just—"

"It's just what?" I asked.

"Well, your phone number was found in the pocket of one of the victims, and since it was the only phone number on either of them, naturally we'd like to talk to you about it."

I was quiet.

"Elizabeth? Are you there?"

"When do you want me?"

"Well, we've got a few people here we're talking to already . . . How about around nine o'clock?"

"All right."

"And, Elizabeth?"

"Yes?"

"Please try and make sure no one else you know dies in Lenox before you come and see us," said Matthew.

"Would you please describe the relationship you had with the deceased, ma'am?" asked Chief Rudge.

We were sitting in the interrogation room at the Lenox Police Station. It was a small rectangular room with cinder block walls and one of those cheap metal conference tables. The chairs were of the high-school folding variety. Chief Rudge sat at the head, a pad and tape recorder in front of him. Matth—Detective Fineburg sat to his right and I sat across from Detective Fineburg.

It had been something of a struggle just to get here. Town had been filled with reporters and television news vans. Five corpses in Lenox in the space of one week (counting the Tumenases') was big news in the neighboring cities of Albany and Springfield, and I'd even seen a Boston logo on one of the vans as I'd wriggled through the crowd in front of the police station in order to get inside for this interview. But it wasn't just the press—it was the police. Between the murders and the Great Josh Billings Runaground set for Sunday, the cops obviously weren't taking any chances. There were enough blue uniforms on Main Street to compose a parade. And there had been a number of plainclothes guys in bad suits hanging around the reception area of the Lenox station, drinking coffee and making notes on clipboards. One of them had even tried to get into the interrogation room with us, but the chief had locked him out by tilting a folding chair against the door handle.

"I didn't have any relationship to the deceased," I said, a little too sharply. I was a bit put out. I'd come promptly at nine, after dropping Emily off at the Hawthorne School, and they'd made me wait. But also, I felt sure that the chief was putting the worst possible connotation on the word, and I wanted to nip that one in the bud. It was bad enough having been connected to Jonathon Nichols. I don't think I could have taken people thinking I went around with Ed and Frank.

"But you knew them," Detective Fineburg pointed out.

"I've spoken with them," I acknowledged.

"What did you talk about, ma'am?" asked the chief.

I opened my mouth to speak. I knew I had to say something, I'd known I'd have to say something for over an hour now, since I'd received Matthew's phone call alerting me to the situation. And I'd also known from that moment that, whatever I elected to tell them, the one thing it could not be was the truth. I knew what would happen to me if I told them I knew that Jonathon Nichols was not Jonathon Nichols at all, but Irving Meltzman; if I told them that Ed and Frank had been intending to steal Irving Meltzman's millions; or that there was a Swiss bank account only Simon and I knew about because we had broken into Irving Meltzman's safe before they had.

"Oh ... tennis. Mexican restaurants. Touristy sorts of things," I answered vaguely. Did I imagine it or did Detective Fineburg look relieved?

But the chief plugged on. "When was the last time you saw them?" he asked.

"Yesterday morning."

The chief duly noted this.

"Where did you see them?" asked Detective Fineburg.

"At the coffee place in town—"

"Berkshire Coffee Roasting?" suggested the detective.

"Yes."

"About what time was this?" interrupted the chief.

"Oh, in the morning," I said. "About this time of the morning, I guess."

"And you discussed"—the chief turned back a page on his notepad—"'tennis and Mexican restaurants'?"

"I don't remember, exactly."

"You don't remember something that happened yesterday morning?" Detective Fineburg asked softly.

"Well, it wasn't like it was a long conversation," I hedged. "We just sort of . . . ran into each other." I waved my arm in the air to indicate total coincidence.

"You don't happen to remember if they said something about going canoeing, do you, Elizabeth?" asked Detective Fineburg.

"No, I don't believe they mentioned it."

"You wouldn't happen to know what they were doing in town in the first place?"

"No."

"Just visiting, perhaps?"

"Perhaps," I agreed.

"Where were you last night, ma'am?" the chief broke in.

Not this again. "I was at home."

"Can anyone vouch for you, ma'am?"

"Well, Emily was with me."

"How old is Emily again, ma'am?"

"Three. Actually, three and three-quarters," I corrected myself.

"No one else knew you were home?" asked the chief.

"That's a negative," I said before I could stop myself.

The chief threw me a dirty look.

"Elizabeth, can you think of any reason why Frank Plishtin would be carrying your phone number around in his pocket?" asked Detective Fineburg quickly.

"No."

"Did he call you often?"

"He never called me."

"Had you told him to call you?"

"No."

"But he must have been intending to call you," Detective Fineburg persisted.

"I have no idea what he was intending to do," I said.

"Do you swim, ma'am?" asked the chief suddenly.

"Swim? Of course I swim," I said. "Why?"

"Police business," grunted the chief. "Would you categorize yourself as a below-average swimmer, an average swimmer, or an above-average swimmer?"

"What?"

"Just answer the question, ma'am."

"Well, I—I guess I'm a pretty good swimmer," I acknowledged.

The chief nodded as if to say "I thought as much," and made a note in his pad.

I turned to Detective Fineburg. "What's all this about swimming?" I asked.

Detective Fineburg looked down at *his* pad. "The victims' canoe was overturned and they were found drowned," he said. "We are hypothesizing that their boat was deliberately capsized and that there was something of a struggle in the water."

I stared at him, then turned to Chief Rudge. "You're saying you think I—"

"I'm not saying anything, ma'am."

"You think *I* swam out into the middle of Stockbridge Bowl and overturned their canoe at night and then held them underwater until they drowned?" I continued, incredulous. "Both of them? Of all the ridiculous accusations—" I stopped suddenly.

"No one is accusing you of anything," Detective Fineburg hurried to reassure me.

But I wasn't listening to him. Having been confronted with the facts of the crime, I couldn't very well ignore the implications. Someone had either boated or swum out to the middle of Stockbridge Bowl, a lake several miles long and at least two miles wide, overturned a boat containing two older but well-trained FBI agents, and drowned them. Who could have done such a thing?

Only someone young and strong could have done a thing like that.

Chief Rudge said something. I forced myself to pay attention.

"What? I'm sorry, I didn't hear what you—"

"I asked how you knew it was the middle of Stockbridge Bowl, ma'am?" asked the chief impassively.

I looked at Matthew. He was looking down at his pen. I suddenly realized that I wasn't supposed to say anything about his call to me. He'd been watching out for me, trying to warn me. I'd get Matthew in trouble if I said he'd told me.

"I said—" I began, confused.

"You said 'the middle of Stockbridge Bowl.' How did you know that that's where they were found?" repeated the chief.

Only someone who knew Ed and Frank were looking for the account number. "Uh—I don't know that."

"But you just said the middle. Why not 'the edge of Stockbridge Bowl' or 'the north end of Stockbridge Bowl' or—"

"The middle of—it's just an expression," I replied.

The chief nodded again and wrote. "And what time of night would that have been?" he asked after his pencil stopped moving.

Only someone whom Ed and Frank would have been willing to meet at night out in a canoe in the middle of a lake. "What?"

"You said their canoe was overturned in the night. How did you know that?" asked the chief.

"I don't know it."

"Well, then why did you say it?" asked the chief, pencil poised.

"I don't know, I guess I just assumed it was at night." *Only someone who had been free last night.*

"Is it your habit, ma'am, to make assumptions about criminal investigations?"

"Of course not, I was just—" *Only someone who had killed before.*

"I think that will be all," Detective Fineburg broke in, hastily. "You're free to go now, Elizabeth."

Only Simon.

The realization that Simon was, after all, the killer, left me sort of rooted to my seat. I just stared dully at the chief and Detective Fineburg as they pushed back their chairs and stood up.

"Elizabeth?" asked the detective. "Is everything all right?"

No, everything most certainly was not all right. Once I walked out of there it was open season on Elizabeth Halperin. I was the only one left.

"Elizabeth?"

I eyed Detective Fineburg as he said this. As badly as I'd wanted to be out of here only five minutes ago, that's how badly I now wanted to stay. But the only way to stay would be to tell them the truth, and how could I do that with the chief standing right there looking at me like that?

"You have something else you'd like to say, ma'am?" the chief prompted, as though he'd read my mind.

Mechanically I rose from my chair. "I'll just—" Maybe I could get Detective Fineburg alone.

"Here," said the detective obligingly. "I'll walk you to the door."

We walked out of the interrogation room toward the main doorway. Out of the corner of my eye I saw the chief following us.

We were almost to the door. "You're sure you're okay?" asked Matthew.

"I—" I threw a backward glance at the chief and then looked up at Matthew beseechingly.

He seemed to understand. "Uh, Chief?" said Matthew. "Could you bring the next one in without me? I'll be there in a minute."

The chief frowned but turned into an anteroom. "Who's next?" I heard him ask. "Oh, yeah. Would you come this way, please, sir?"

Matthew turned back to me. "What is it, Elizabeth? Do you know something?"

"Yes," I said, grabbing his arm. "Yes, Matthew. You've got to help me. I know—I know who—" The words were almost out when I felt a strong hand on my elbow and a familiar presence loomed over me.

"Good morning, Elizabeth. I hope you slept well?" said Simon.

Simon! But how could it be? Where had he . . . ? But of course. There was the chief with him. It was he who was next for questioning and had come out of the anteroom.

"I'm sorry about last night," Simon continued smoothly. "I have an excellent explanation, I assure you."

I just continued to stare frozenly at him. For once he didn't look like he'd stepped out of the pages of *Gentleman's Quarterly*. His suit was wrinkled. His tie was askew. His cuffs had mud clinging to them. In fact, he looked like he'd spent the night in a field.

"Last night?" Matthew repeated. He sounded like Detective Fineburg again.

Simon ignored him. "Might I have a word with you, Elizabeth?"

"I was just leaving," I said quickly.

If Simon were here, it must be because they thought he knew something . . . they were having him in for questioning.

Maybe they already suspected him. Maybe they didn't need my evidence at all. Maybe I could still get out of this alive *and* jail free. After all, I didn't really know anything, not as much as Simon, anyway.

"Right. It won't take a moment." Simon squeezed my arm a little.

I looked up at Matthew again.

Matthew turned to Simon. "I'm afraid we're on a tight schedule this morning," he said in his best detective's voice. "If you'll just follow Chief Rudge, we'll be right with you," and he motioned Simon down the hallway.

"I quite understand. However, this is singularly important," said Simon, trying to catch my eye.

"I'm sure it is. Chief?"

Chief Rudge stepped foward. "Mr. . . ."—he eyed a clipboard—"Smith. This way, please," he enunciated distinctly, crossing his arms in front of him.

Simon released his hold on my elbow. "I stand defeated," he acknowledged with an amused glance at Matthew, who had assumed a protective stance in front of me. "Another time perhaps, then, Elizabeth."

I didn't say anything.

Matthew followed after Simon and the chief until they were both safely inside the interrogation room. "Now. What's all this about, Elizabeth?" he asked, turning back.

But I was already out the door.

I have no idea why I did that. Turned and fled, I mean. All I had to do was to tell Matthew that Simon was the murderer—that he had murdered five times, to be precise—and give the explanation. But instead, I panicked.

I literally ran through the crowd waiting outside the police station. Some of the reporters tried to stop me, but I flung myself into the Jeep and backed out quickly. If I was going to tell the police, I wanted five minutes' time to plan out what I was going to say. I wanted to sit down and literally sketch out what had happened and see how it looked on paper. I wanted, in other words, to *think*.

Where to go? Somewhere close. Not home, though. Somewhere public. And quiet. But where, in this crowd of people, could I find someplace quiet, someplace that wouldn't be surrounded by reporters or cops? I drove around the block. And there it was, looming up in front of me.

The library.

The proof against Simon Montgomery Smith, I wrote. Testimony of Elizabeth Halperin.

I had found a deserted corner in the magazine room and had settled into one of those big leather chairs that I'd always found so comforting and that seem to be endemic to country libraries. I was balancing a manila envelope I'd found in the back of the Jeep on top of a stack of *Popular Mechanics* magazines in order to take notes.

It hadn't taken five minutes to see that I had no choice now but to go to the police. Simon was the killer; Simon had killed five times in pursuit of the Suisse Union Creditbank of Zug bank account number; and even if I had the number (which I didn't) or was close to getting the number (which I wasn't), and gave it to him, there was no saying he'd just go away and leave me in peace. Face it, Elizabeth, I thought glumly as I stared down at the back of the manila envelope, you know too much.

Hence the testimonial. Write it all down, I told myself. Start at the beginning. Then go and hand it in to the police. It will probably mean getting into some trouble, but at least you'll still be here. And don't hold anything back, I warned myself. You are the only one who can send Simon away long enough so that he is no longer a threat. Nothing halfhearted or he'll only get seven years or something like that and you can be sure the first thing he'll do when he's out is to come after you.

That was enough to get my pen working.

(1) On the night Irving Meltzman died, Simon Montgomery Smith confessed to me that he had been at the site where Irving Meltzman a.k.a. Jonathon Nichols was killed earlier that evening.

(2) On the same night, Simon Montgomery Smith revealed a knowledge of Irving Meltzman's activities that indicated that he had been pursuing him for some time.

(3) Simon Montgomery Smith was extremely interested in the thirty million dol—

"Elizabeth?"

I looked up from my writing. There stood Paige. She was smiling at me in her most friendly and helpful fashion.

Uh-oh, I thought.

"Hello, Paige," I said, as coldly as I could, trying to cover my writing with my arm. Go away, Paige, I thought.

But Paige didn't go away. "Was it helpful?" she asked.

"Was what helpful?" I returned, frowning. Go away, Paige, I thought.

"The article on Irving Meltzman. I see you have it with you. Are you taking notes on it or something?"

The article . . . ? Oh. That's what was in the manila envelope. "Uhh," I began.

"May I see it? I didn't really get a chance to look at it when I picked it up," said Paige, bending down to give it a closer look.

"Why don't we look at it together?" I said graciously, sliding the article out with one hand and turning the envelope over on my lap with the other.

"Great!" said Paige, squatting down next me. "Is that him?" she asked, pointing at the picture that appeared at the top of the first page.

But I didn't answer.

"What does it say about him?"

I still didn't answer. I was staring at the picture.

"Elizabeth?"

I dropped the article on my lap and, to her great surprise, threw my arms around Paige.

"Elizabeth? Ms. Halperin? What's going on?" she asked, rocking back on her heels.

"I love you, Paige," I said solemnly.

For there, staring up at me from the front page of the article, was the answer to the mystery.

Chapter

14

"GOOD MORNING, RANCHERS!"

This greeting was issued by a young woman, short, attractive, and apparently possessed of a natural effervescence that would give Perrier a run for its money. She had tousled blond hair and thickly muscled legs and was wearing a pair of navy blue shorts and a white T-shirt with the Canyon Ranch emblem plainly visible across her right shoulder. Around her neck was a whistle.

It was the start of the early morning walks at Canyon Ranch. Every morning at precisely seven o'clock, it appeared, the spa offered a two-, three-, or four-mile guided walk as a service to those guests who weren't already in the gym or the indoor pool or (sacrilege) still lying in bed, worn out from the previous day's activities. Those guests who wished to take advantage of the Berkshires' brisk morning air, the program coordinator assigned to me had advised, assemble in the driveway in front of the main spa building for prewalk stretching.

So here I was in the Canyon Ranch driveway touching my

toes and swinging my hips in preparation for the morning walk, doing my best to blend in, all the while surveying the crowd on the driveway, looking for a murderer.

I was at the ranch on a one-day pass known as a Spa Day, which included lunch and two services (facial, haircut, manicure, pedicure, or massage) and ended promptly at five o'clock in the afternoon. It usually didn't start until eight o'clock in the morning, but I had specifically asked if I could start with the walk. All classes, such as aerobics, weight lifting, and step, were free with a Spa Day, my program coordinator, an earnest young man in his twenties also wearing shorts and a T-shirt, had explained. Well, in a manner of speaking, I thought. The Spa Day cost $280.

"Good morning," the thirty or so of us stretched along the driveway echoed back politely if self-consciously at the instructor. It was Saturday morning and the ranch was booked solid with weekenders. I had been a little late getting to the stretching, having first had to drop Emily off at Soji's house at six-thirty.

"I CAN'T HEAR YOU!" bellowed the instructor.

"GOOD MORNING," we hollered back, like lemmings.

"I *STILL* CAN'T HEAR YOU!"

"GOOD MORNING!" we shouted.

I pulled my visor down glumly over my sunglasses and reflected that, on a prorated basis, I was paying somewhere between $25 and $30 for this.

Not only that, but I had had to endure Soji's scorn before breakfast. She'd come out of her house while I was pulling Emily, still half asleep, from the car. Soji was wearing an oversized tie-dyed T-shirt, a beaded Indian necklace, and earrings. Her hair was falling in her face. She had sleep in her eyes. She looked young and fresh and unbelievably sexy.

"So what is this big emergency, anyway?" she yawned at me, taking in my gym shorts and sneakers.

That was how I'd gotten her to baby-sit at such an early

hour. I'd figured it was safest for Emily to come to her. "I can't tell you," I said, reaching into the backseat and emerging with a bag. "Here's Emily's stuff," I said. "Keep her here. Don't take her back to the house until I come for her."

Soji nodded. "Sounds cool." She squinted. "You want to leave a number or anything?"

I hesitated. "If you need me, call . . . Canyon Ranch," I said, "and have me paged."

A pained expression crossed Soji's face, but she didn't say anything.

I knelt down beside Emily.

"Good-bye, Em," I said, giving her a big hug. I squeezed her extra tightly.

"Good-bye, Mommy."

"Wish me luck," I whispered in her ear, reluctant to let her go.

I felt her soft lips tickle my earlobe. "Why?" she breathed.

"It's a secret."

"Oh." She leaned into my ear again. "Good luck," she whispered loudly.

"Thanks," I whispered back, and relinquished her.

Soji reached out for Emily, who snuggled into her arms. "You want some pancakes?" she asked.

"Uh, sure," said Emily, and I watched as the two strolled into the house.

This had better work, I thought grimly as I got back into the car.

"SWING YOUR HIPS TO THE RIGHT!"

I swung and forced my attention off the instructor and onto my fellow guests. It was difficult to see, there were so many of them. That woman standing next to the man in front of me wearing the matching leopard-skin running tights and black windbreaker, was that . . . ? No. What about the one to the right in the hot-pink-and-neon-green print jogging suit? Too tall. The one in the corner in the walking shorts? Too old.

"WE ARE OFFERING THREE WALKS THIS MORN-ING: BEGINNING, INTERMEDIATE, AND ADVANCED. THE ADVANCED WALK GOES AT APPROXIMATELY A TWELVE- TO THIRTEEN-MINUTE-MILE PACE, COVERS FOUR MILES, AND RUNS ABOUT ONE HOUR. PLEASE DO NOT ATTEMPT THIS WALK UNLESS YOU HAVE KEPT UP WITH THE LEAD OF THE INTERMEDIATE WALK. ALL THOSE WISHING TO TAKE THE ADVANCED WALK, LEAVE NOW WITH RICK AND KATHY. THE REST OF YOU, SWING TO THE LEFT!"

The vast majority swung to the left. Four people broke off from the main group and started walking purposefully with two guides. I squinted after them. Three men and a woman with long frizzy hair. I let them go.

"THE INTERMEDIATE WALK GOES AT APPROXI-MATELY A FIFTEEN-MINUTE-MILE PACE, COVERS THREE MILES, AND RUNS ABOUT FORTY-FIVE MINUTES. ALL THOSE WISHING TO TAKE THE INTERMEDIATE WALK, PLEASE LEAVE NOW WITH ANNA AND STEVE."

A much larger group broke off this time, at least twenty people. I scanned them closely as they marched by. No, no, no . . . was that? No.

"I'M DARLENE AND I'LL BE LEADING TODAY'S BEGINNER WALK, WHICH GOES AT APPROXI-MATELY AN EIGHTEEN- TO TWENTY-MINUTE-MILE PACE, COVERS TWO MILES, AND RUNS ABOUT HALF AN HOUR. WE WILL STAY ON PROP-ERTY TODAY. LET'S GO!"

The eight people left started filing out one by one behind Darlene. They were mostly women in their sixties and seventies. I was out of luck. Oh, well, I still had the rest of the day. With a sigh, I turned to go.

"WHERE ARE YOU GOING?"

Startled, I turned around. Darlene was walking backward and shouting at me.

"I, uh, I was just—"

"PLEASE STAY IN LINE!"

"But I don't want—"

"PEOPLE DON'T LEAVE ON MY SHIFT. EVERY-ONE WHO COMES OUT COMPLETES THE WALK. NOW, PLEASE FALL IN. YOU'RE HOLDING EVERY-ONE UP!"

Half an hour later, after solemnly marching around the grounds alongside a seventy-two-year-old woman from New Jersey who had recently had her gallbladder removed, I finally managed to escape Darlene and get back inside the main spa building.

Canyon Ranch is divided into three buildings, rather like the three sides of a big Y. All three are linked by corridors, so that nobody has to go outside if they don't want to. One building houses the main reception desk and the guest rooms. The second contains the dining room and the health and healing center. The last, which constitutes the stem of the Y, is the main spa building. This is where you find the gyms and the indoor tennis courts, the weight room and the pool, skin care, the beauty salon, and the men's and women's locker rooms. It was also, I reasoned, the most likely place to find someone, since one way or another, it looked as if some time during the day, everyone, staff and guests alike, would find their way to the main spa building.

I stopped in front of a large bulletin board across from the main spa desk. It listed the time and place of the activities offered that day.

I looked at the clock. It was seven forty-five. The first class didn't start until eight-thirty. That gave me a chance to look around. But where to look first?

Grrrr, said my stomach.

Of course. Most people were probably eating breakfast. I walked briskly in the direction of the dining room, keeping the brim of my visor pulled down.

There was quite a line in front of the dining room. I tried to angle my way to the front so I could see in to where people were sitting.

"Excuse me," I said politely to the woman in front of me. "I just want to—"

"Wait your turn," she snapped. She was short and round and was wearing a white bathrobe. I had heard that the guests at Canyon Ranch went everywhere, even to meals, in their bathrobes, but up to this minute I hadn't believed it. "Can't you see there's a line?"

"But I'd just like to—"

"I paid my money. I was here first," she announced to the woman standing next to her.

"I heard that some of the people who come here *are* pushy," the other woman agreed.

So I waited. When I got to the front of the line, a young, attractive woman smiled warmly at me from behind a desk. "Table for one?" she asked.

"Umm, well—" I hedged, trying to see around her into the dining room. I didn't want to sit down and be recognized. I felt strongly that the element of surprise was vital to my plan. Actually, to tell the truth, I didn't exactly have a plan yet, just the element of surprise, so naturally I was reluctant to give it up.

The hostess saved me, however. "Room number?" she asked smoothly, pencil poised above a seating chart.

"Uh, I don't have a room number. I'm here on a Spa Day," I told her.

"Oh," said the hostess. "Oh, I'm afraid that only lunch is included in the Spa Day. . . ."

I began to be aware that the guests lined up behind me were getting restless. Canyon Ranch was obviously a place where meals mattered. Get this over with, Elizabeth, I told myself. You're drawing attention to yourself.

"Can't I just . . ." I spied a huge bowl of fruit in the center of the dining room. I could walk to it, scan the room, and get out with something to eat without attracting undue notice, I felt. "Can't I just take a piece of fruit?"

"I'm afraid not," said the hostess.

Two hundred and eighty dollars and I couldn't get a banana? I was irked. "What do you mean?" I demanded.

"I'm sorry, we have very strict rules here at the ranch. We can't make an exception. If we did it for you, we'd have to do it for everyone, you see," said the hostess. She was still smiling warmly.

"All right." I sighed, starting to turn away. "I'm sure the doctor was being overly cautious anyway. . . . The medication will probably work just as well on an empty stomach. . . . He didn't seriously mean I'd drop dead." I affected a little laugh.

The hostess stopped smiling warmly. People dropping dead at the Ranch was obviously something else that mattered.

"Very well," she said finally, lifting the velvet cord to the dining room. "But just this once."

"Oh, I wouldn't dream of trying this again," I told her sincerely, and slipped into the dining room.

I kept my head down and my sunglasses on. There must have been fifty people in there eating apple-and-currant pancakes (no butter, no syrup) and egg white omelets with dry whole wheat toast. I got to the bowl in the center of the room. No, she wasn't in the corner. No, not in the back. I scooped up a banana *and* an apple—take that, I thought—turned back to leave, and caught just a glimpse of long red hair leaving . . .

She was here. I knew it.

As quietly and inconspicuously as possible, I followed the

woman I'd seen on the bicycle the other day, the red-haired woman from the Hawthorne School fair, out the door and down the long corridor back to the main spa building.

She went right to the women's locker room and disappeared inside. I stood outside behind a large cactus, counted very slowly to twenty, and then poked my head in the door. She wasn't in sight, so I slowly and quietly slid in and looked around.

"Can I help you?" It was the attendant behind the desk.

"I—uh—" There she was, halfway down the room, tying her sneakers! Her head was down, I don't think she saw me, still—I whirled around so my back was to her and I faced the attendant. "I—" There was an open closet filled with white bathrobes behind the desk. "I—I'd like a bathrobe, please," I said, as quietly as I could.

"Certainly. Could I have your robe tag, please?" asked the attendant, who was dark and thin and wore what I now knew to be the regulation Canyon Ranch T-shirt and shorts. Her name tag read "Cathy."

"My what?"

"Your robe tag. You should have received it when you checked in and were assigned a locker."

"I'm here on a Spa Day." I was all but whispering.

"Oh. In that case, your program coordinator should have included it with your folder," said Cathy.

Folder? I did dimly remember a folder, but it was in my gym bag, which was in the car, which was parked in the guest parking lot, which was at least a fifteen-minute walk away. "That's all right," I hissed. "I don't really need a robe."

"But you can't get a locker without it, either."

". . . or a locker." I was desperate to end this conversation. With my back to her, I couldn't tell where the red-haired woman was or if she had noticed me. "I'll just . . . "

But Cathy was ringing a little bell on the side of the desk and calling down the length of the locker room. "SHARON! CAN YOU TAKE OVER AT THE FRONT, PLEASE? I HAVE TO TAKE THIS GUEST OUTSIDE AND SEE ABOUT HER LOCKER ASSIGNMENT!"

Everyone within fifty feet looked over at me.

Sharon came bounding over.

"Come on," said Cathy. "I'll take you out to the front spa desk."

I mutely followed her out.

It took awhile to get my locker assignment and robe tag because without my folder they had to call my name up on the computer to verify that I had, in fact, paid for my Spa Day. But the computer lines were down, so I had had to run to my car and retrieve my gym bag with the folder inside. Then, after they gave me a locker assignment, Cathy had heaped a bathrobe and several towels into my arms and then insisted upon taking me on an extended tour of the locker room.

"It's really not necessary," I tried, shouldering my gym bag and lifting my chin to see over all the terry cloth.

But Cathy was not to be denied. "Even lockers on top, odd lockers down below," she said, walking briskly down one aisle and up another. "In the center here are the showers. Farther down is the sauna and the whirlpool. We also have an inhalation room, which is a small steam room with eucalyptus spray. Here is your locker. If there's something you want and don't find, just ask. Have a nice day," and she left me.

I dumped the towels and bathrobe and the gym bag on a bench in front of my locker and then sank down on top of them. This was not going well. I had lost the element of surprise. I had lost the woman with the red hair. I had lost my sunglasses. What next? I thought glumly.

At the next locker a woman in her fifties with sausage curls and green spandex observed me sympathetically, then leaned over.

"I saw Julia Roberts naked," she confided, and left.

I had a busy morning. At nine o'clock I weight-lifted. No red-head. At ten o'clock I stretched. No redhead. At eleven o'clock a young male fitness instructor in gym 4, sporting an Arnold Schwarzenegger body and a T-shirt several sizes too small, demonstrated a particularly demonic-looking machine that was supposed to do something wonderful for your thighs. I was just edging my way out of the room when I saw her.

She was at the back of the room where they kept the free weights, wearing black. Black halter stretch top. Black spandex shorts. Evil-looking black leather gloves with the fingers cut out, and a black leather weight belt, wider in the back and studded with silver. Her long red hair was tied back with a black bow. Her nails were the same color as her hair.

I quickly ducked behind the partition where they keep the StairMasters. Gym 4 had two whole walls devoted to mirrors and two walls devoted to plate-glass windows. If I got up on one of the StairMasters, I could keep an eye on her activities through the reflection in the opposite wall mirror. There would be the added benefit that, if I was already working out, none of the staff would feel compelled to ask me if I wanted help with one of the machines and blow what little cover I had left. I got up on one of the StairMasters and started climbing, keeping my head down and watching covertly through the glass.

She had a personal trainer, I soon realized. Another young guy with big muscles. I was beginning to understand the attraction of the place. He was helping her with the weights.

"More," I heard her sort of snarl, lying on her back with a bar across her chest.

"You sure?" the personal trainer asked.

"Just put it on."

Silently he added weights to the bar, then crouched over her, ready to catch the bar if it fell. I held my breath. She was so thin . . . Could she really lift all that?

She lifted. "One," counted the trainer.

"Two."

"Three."

"Four . . . "

My jaw dropped. She lifted fifteen times. He helped catch the bar on the final lift. She laid back on the hard little bench. Then she looked up at him.

"Again," she said.

I had to wait forty-five minutes before he left her. I was on the StairMaster the whole time. My legs were killing me. I made a vow: If I do get through this I will never, ever go near a Stair-Master again.

Finally, it was eleven forty-five. Time to get ready for lunch. The gym cleared out as if somebody had screamed "Fire!" But not the red-haired woman. There was a line of at least fifteen treadmills in front of the mirrored wall. She started running on the one at the far end.

I got off the StairMaster, reached into my gym bag, and removed my Walkman. I fastened it around my waist with an athletic belt. I hit a button.

Now, I thought, and started walking in the direction of the treadmills.

I lied a little when I said I didn't really have a plan. I did have a plan. A trifle sketchy, perhaps, but sound nonetheless.

All I had to do was to get her to confess. I was a mystery writer, it's true, but, more important in this case, I was a mystery *reader*. I knew that there had yet to be a mystery invented where the guilty party didn't break down and confess to every detail of the crime under questioning by the protagonist. It had worked with Sherlock Holmes, it had worked with Agatha Christie; my goodness, it had worked with Batman.

Now, like Agatha Christie herself, I would get my confession. There was a tape in my Walkman, but it wasn't set to play, it was set to record. Lots of people exercise wearing Walkmans and mine was right out there, ready to catch her entire confession.

It was just a question of the correct approach to the interrogation. I eyed her as I sauntered over to the treadmills; she looked like the antagonistic type. I could be antagonistic.

She was running smoothly and easily, but I could see she was watching my approach in the mirror. I took the treadmill next to hers and started it on slow. We were the only two people in the room.

I scowled at her.

She ignored me.

Okay, so I won't *start* with antagonistic, I thought. I'll start with friendly. I'll get her talking. I smiled warmly.

"Hi," I said, still smiling. "Do I know you?"

She didn't acknowledge the salutation but kept her eyes fixed straight ahead. Her face was set with determination.

"This is my first day," I announced brightly.

She still didn't answer.

"Have you been at the Ranch long?" I asked.

This time she spoke. "About two weeks," she rasped. She reached over and increased the speed at which she was running.

"Oh," I said. "Maybe you can help me then. You wouldn't happen to know if the ranch offers a canoe trip, would you? I'm not a very good swimmer but I thought I'd like to try—"

"I wouldn't know," she interrupted.

"Well, what about—"

"Do you mind?" she demanded. "I'm trying to concentrate."

"Oh," I said.

We treadmilled for a while.

"I'm *sure* I know you," I persisted, after a few minutes. "Aren't you from New Jersey?" I asked.

She rolled her eyes and kept running.

I snapped my fingers. "I know!" I exclaimed heartily, as though I'd just this second thought of it. "Weren't you—"

The red-haired woman hit the red Stop button on her machine abruptly. She waited until the treadmill had come to a full stop and then turned to me.

"I couldn't possibly know anyone as rude as you are," she said, and changed to a treadmill farther down the row.

Hmm, I thought. I think I'm breaking her down. I followed her. This time I didn't bother to get on the equipment.

"I do know who you are," I said abruptly (and as loudly as I could). "You're Tasha Meltzman, Irving Meltzman's wife. Yes, you are," I hurried along, not waiting for her to respond. "You're Tasha Meltzman and you killed your husband in a fit of rage by running him over with his own truck last Saturday night."

I had her attention now. She was watching me through the mirror.

"You didn't kill him for the money, like everyone thought," I continued recklessly. "You killed him because you were angry with him. Angry that he'd taken your money to get started and then left you. Angry that he'd gotten thinner and tanner and better dressed after he left you. Angry that he'd started dating other women. You were jealous," I told her. "It was a jealous rage.

"You'd been trailing him all this time. You never gave up. Then you saw his picture that day in the *Times*. You came right up to Lenox. Naturally you stayed here, at the Ranch. You're a spa person. You just registered under your maiden name, Tasha Itzkovitz.

"It didn't take you long to realize that you weren't the only person looking for him. You knew he'd taken the money, you guessed they hadn't given up either, but you had an edge on the others: you knew his habits, where he'd be likely to mess up. It didn't surprise you that he'd allowed himself to be photographed for the newspapers. That's just the way he was. He couldn't help himself.

"So you hung around town and waited. Tried to flush him out. Watched the others watching for him. Checked out the site. You knew he'd eventually go back there. And you suspected he'd gotten involved with another woman. It wouldn't take any trouble at all to find out that he'd been seen with someone called Elizabeth Halperin. But you were so busy tailing him you didn't have time to figure out who I was. That's why you didn't know me at the Hawthorne School fair," I told her. "You thought you'd ask around, but you asked the wrong person."

I glanced up at her. Her eyes were narrowed. It's working! I thought.

"So you went after him. Sent him a note or a fax or something under a different name that got him to the site that night. Told him something that scared him. That's why he phoned me right before he went. But you were there at the site first, hiding in the dark. You didn't take a car. You didn't need one. You just ran there from Canyon Ranch. It's not very far. Three miles, max.

"You waited until he drove up. Of course, he used his truck. Maybe you weren't even expecting to kill him. Maybe you just wanted to confront him. To say your piece, whatever. But then he got out of the truck and left the keys inside, and you went on gut instinct. You slipped into the driver's seat, caught him in those big headlights, and mowed him down. He never had a chance, he was that close. He didn't even know who you were until you were right on top of him. With everyone after him, he wasn't expecting you. That's why he looked so surprised at the end."

I took a breath. Tasha had slowed the machine. She was no longer running. She was winding down.

"After you killed him, you just kept driving. You must have gotten out of there right away because others came almost immediately after you, and they didn't see anything. Perhaps you drove around for a while, just cooling off. But eventually you ditched the truck on Bean Hill Road. Bean Hill Road's only about half a mile from the ranch. It wasn't a particularly smart move but it ended up working in your favor. Nobody thought about Canyon Ranch. Nobody thought that the person who did all this might be a fitness enthusiast. Instead, the police think it was at least a two-person job. That somebody tailed the truck."

She wiped her face with her towel.

"I'll bet you sweated it out that night, back in your room," I said. "You probably had to stop yourself from checking out first thing in the morning. It would have been a tip-off. It would have made you look guilty. So instead you took your aerobics classes. Maybe had your hair done, went for the sunset hike. Tried to look normal and not-guilty.

"And you know what? It worked. After about two days you realized that no one suspected you. And why should they? you thought. There wasn't any way the police could have known that Irving Meltzman's ditched wife Tasha Itzkovitz had turned up here in Lenox to murder him. And even if they found out about you, it's not like anyone had seen you leave or reenter the spa that night. It's nothing to sneak out of Canyon Ranch through the employee parking lot in the back. There's no guard, no fence. After dinner on a pleasant evening there's no reason why a guest should walk inside, through those long corridors. Many people just go outside and cut across the circular driveway to their rooms. That's what you did that night. Only you didn't go to your room. You just kept going, through the employee parking lot—out the back way onto the street. So as far as anyone here at the ranch knew, you had dinner and spent the rest of the night in your room watching complimentary videos on the VCR.

"But that wasn't all," I went on. "Once you started to get comfortable with the idea of not getting caught, you started to focus in on the money. Why should one of these other creeps get it? you must have thought. What had Irving Meltzman meant to them? You were the rightful heir. But if you went about it legally—waiting for the authorities to discover the alias, the uncovering of the will and the inevitable hunt for the missing funds—you wouldn't end up with squat. Once the U.S. government got involved, you could be pretty sure that the money wasn't going to go to Irving's grieving widow. So now you began to shadow the people who were hunting for that thirty million. The Tumenases. Ed and Frank. Simon. When someone got too close, you got rid of them.

"You started with the Tumenases. They must have been easy. Another note. Let's make a deal. Meet me on Monument Mountain. You were familiar with Monument Mountain, of course. That's where Canyon Ranch goes for its sunset hikes. They probably don't keep lists here of who signed up for what hike, but you're pretty distinctive. I'll bet if the police interviewed the guides here, several of them would be able to remember that you took that hike quite often in the two weeks you've been here. Sure you did. You were scoping it out.

"And the Tumenases would have been caught unawares. Not that they weren't looking for someone; they weren't looking for *you*. The Tumenases were focused on Ed and Frank and Simon. They didn't know there was anyone else in the game. You could have gotten very close to them that way. Chatted them up. Put them at their ease. Talked about food, or something. They wouldn't know you from Adam. They'd be busy watching for someone else. You could have inched them slowly over to the side and then—the old one-two push and over they go. They must have been so tired from the climb that you could have blown them over. Once again, the police would never think of you. They don't know you. You're too thin. They haven't seen you work out. You weren't even there when the bodies were discovered. You waited for the sunset hike to come back down the mountain and discover the bodies. In all the excitement, you just slipped into the Canyon Ranch van and drove home with the other hikers like you were with them all along."

I was pretty fired up now. I'd been waiting for this for some time.

"Ed and Frank were a little more difficult, but nothing you couldn't handle. Once again, you caught them by surprise. They thought that Simon had killed the Tumenases. They would have been looking for Simon. Not a woman.

"How did you do it?" I asked. "Did you take them out in the canoe yourself? No, of course not. They didn't think they were meeting you. They would have been out on the lake already in their rented canoe, maybe with a couple of flashlights, squinting into the distance, watching for Simon to come paddling up for the meet. That would have made it easy for someone swimming quietly to get in very close and tip the canoe. There would have been a short struggle in the water, but you had surprise on your side. Their eyes wouldn't have been acclimated to the dark. You might even have hit them over the head with one of the paddles. Or just dived down and held their feet underwater. For all their talk, Ed and Frank weren't immune to the effects of age. They had weak hearts. That wouldn't have helped them. I'll bet," I said, eyeing her closely (she had stepped off the machine and was just standing there, listening to me), "that you're a pretty good swimmer. I'm sure there's someone here who has seen you practicing laps in the pool . . . "

She opened her mouth, but I hurried on. I wanted to get it all in.

"That left Simon and me. I'll bet you were pretty confident that the police would try to pin all this on Simon. Especially when you bumped me off. How were you going to do it?" I demanded. (Push her over the edge, I thought.) "Throw a pair of dumbbells at me? Mow me down with your bicycle? Well, it's all over now, Tasha," I declared. "The police already know. They . . . they . . ." I had a sudden rush of inspiration. "They found your fingerprints on the steering wheel of the truck," I proclaimed triumphantly. "They've tracked your movements. They know you were on Monument Mountain on the same day as the Tumenases. They found your footprints near the spot where they fell. They . . . they . . . they'll be here any minute. The absolute best thing that you could do is to give yourself up. Cooperate and hope for leniency. Make a clean breast of it. Just say, yes, I did it," I urged, moving in for the kill. "You know you want to get it off your chest. All you have to do is admit it. Just say, yes, Elizabeth, you're right. It all happened just the way you said it did. I did it. I did it all."

I finished all in a rush and stood there, breathing heavily. Tasha Meltzman considered me for a moment and then opened her mouth.

"That is the most ridiculous story I've ever heard," she said. "I don't know who you are but you are badly in need of psychiatric treatment. If you speak to me again, I'll call the program coordinator."

And she turned on her heel and left.

Chapter

15

I just stood there, openmouthed, and watched her go. I had been so sure—I clutched.

Had I been wrong? What if that woman *wasn't* Irving Meltzman's neglected wife, Tasha? What if I had so much wanted it *not* to be Simon that I had leaped at straws? Had accused a total stranger of . . . I felt my face blush hotly. I had just made a complete and utter fool of myself. And spent two hundred and eighty dollars to do it.

I dragged myself out of the gym, up the stairs, and into the women's locker room. I looked at the clock. Twelve-fifteen. My whole diatribe had taken less than half an hour.

I sighed and stood in front of my locker. The place was empty. Everyone was at lunch. Even Cathy was missing from her accustomed place behind the desk in the front. I sort of slumped down on the bench. I was embarrassed and confused and exhausted. Every muscle I had hurt.

Well, I'm here, I thought suddenly. I already paid my money. I might as well get something out of it. What had

Cathy said? There's a Jacuzzi all the way in the back? Fine. I'll just lie there and bubble my troubles away. Or maybe I'll just drown myself.

I changed out of my clothes and into my robe. I stored my gym bag in the locker and padded down the long aisle, through some glass doors and into a warm, steamy room, also deserted, filled with lounge chairs and magazines. There were *two* Jacuzzis, one warmer than the other. I slipped out of my robe, hung it up on one of the little hooks they had placed conveniently on the side of the wall, and eased my way into the hot Jacuzzi on the right. Aaahhh. The first nice thing to happen all day. I settled back in the water and closed my eyes. Maybe I'll stay and have my hair done or something after all, I thought.

The next thing I knew, my head was being pushed underwater. What . . . I struggled, came up for air, and was forced back down again. Someone had an iron grip around my neck. I could just barely make out a white robe, red nails, red hair . . .

"*You!*" I heard her spit out the word. "You've got some nerve coming around here. Well, you saved me the trouble of going after you tonight. I'd been saving you for last."

I made a huge effort and got my head above water for an instant. I coughed and choked. She forced my head back down again.

"You thought you could get away with it, didn't you?" she hissed. "Stealing another woman's husband. You went after him, didn't you? You probably hounded him, never let him alone. My poor Irving! I'll kill you!"

She held me under, I struggled. The water was terribly hot and overchlorinated. Suddenly, she seemed to reconsider. She brought my head up high enough so I could hear her.

"But it wouldn't be smart to just finish you off after all this without getting the money," I heard her say. "So here is what you are going to do. You are going to tell me that account number. I am going to let you up for one second and you are going to give it to me." She brought my head up a little further but maintained her grip.

I coughed and choked some more. "I don't have the account number," I managed, right before she held me under again.

I tried holding my breath as long as I could but I was starting to lose it. Little dots were clouding my vision. I could feel my body relax. Another second and all my air would be gone. . . .

Suddenly, I felt her release me. I came up, gasping and choking. Arms on either side of me lifted me out. "Elizabeth! Are you all right?"

Cough, cough, choke.

"Elizabeth? Can you speak?"

"Yes," I gasped, "yes, I'm . . ." My vision cleared. I looked up. "Simon," I said, looking to my right. "Simon, how did you . . ." I looked to my left. "Matthew?"

There they were, both of them. They were both bending over me.

"Elizabeth?" said Simon. "Are you hurt?"

"Do you think we could lift you up?" asked Matthew.

"I . . . I . . ." Between the heat and the water I was so confused. How had they gotten there? Where was—"Tasha!" I exclaimed suddenly. "Tasha Meltzman! She's getting away!" I tried to sit up.

"Don't strain yourself, Elizabeth," said Matthew quickly.

"Lie quietly," said Simon.

"NO, no, you don't understand." I gripped Simon's arm. "It's Irving Meltzman's wife." I turned to Matthew. "She did it all. She's getting away. You're letting her get away."

Suddenly, we all heard screams coming from inside the women's locker room. "Aahhh!!" "Eeehhh!!" Some of the guests must have come back from lunch. "What's going on here?" "Watch it! She's got a razor!"

Matthew stood up. "What the . . . "

"Hurry, hurry," I told him. "You don't know her. She'll get away!"

And then, suddenly, I heard *him*.

"POLICE DEPARTMENT."

More screams. Lots of screams. "AAhhh!" "EEhhh!" "What's *he* doing here?"

The glass doors were flung open and Tasha Meltzman backed into the Jacuzzi room. She was wild-eyed and holding something in her hand. Matthew and Simon made a move toward her, but before they got very far, the sturdy figure of the chief appeared.

"STOP WHERE YOU ARE, MA'AM," intoned the chief.

Tasha Meltzman glanced furiously from the chief to Matthew to Simon and, finally, to me. She hesitated.

"DROP THE WEAPON, MA'AM."

There was silence. Then Tasha smiled sweetly. "Is there some sort of problem, Officer?" she asked.

"LAY THE WEAPON ON THE FLOOR."

"There must be some mistake," I heard Tasha say. She tried to laugh. "This is just a safety razor. I was about to shave my legs." She laid the razor on the floor.

"PLEASE PUT YOUR HANDS UP."

Tasha flushed. "I'm going to report you," she warned.

I couldn't take it any longer. I stood up, dripping, and broke away from Matthew and Simon. "Chief! Chief!" I cried, as I ran over toward him. "*She* did it! She did it all! *She* killed Jonathon Nichols. *And* the Tumenases. *And* Ed and Frank! And she tried to kill *me!*"

The chief didn't respond. He had a very strange look on his face.

I looked at Matthew. He also had a strange look on his face.

I looked at Simon. He also had . . . "What's the matter with everyone?" I demanded.

Then I remembered and looked down at myself.

I was naked.

*   *   *

The chief handcuffed Tasha and took her away. Matthew and Simon fell all over themselves handing me a robe, which I accepted with quiet dignity. Simon, of course, had already seen me naked, and Matthew, well, I guess that wasn't so bad . . . but the chief . . . the chief . . .

"Ohhh," I groaned, knotting the belt and sinking down on one of the lounge chairs.

Simon sat down next to me and patted my hand. Matthew had gone off to disperse the crowd. There were quite a few faces peering interestedly at me through the glass doors.

"Better now?" Simon asked. "That was pretty close."

"What are you doing here?" I asked. "How did you know?"

"The wonder is that I didn't know sooner," he said. "It wasn't until I saw Ed and Frank's canoe turn over—"

"You saw their canoe? Where were you?"

"I was on the shore, trying to see in the dark. I'd been shadowing them all day. When they rented a canoe, I knew something was up. That's why I never made it to your house that evening." He paused. "I wasn't particularly sanguine about their commitment to our deal. It had occurred to me that once they had the number there was very little chance of their sharing it with us unless forcefully reminded of their obligation. I figured I'd let them make whatever aquatic connection they'd arranged and then nab them as they came ashore." He shook his head. "Problem was, they never came ashore," he said.

"But you said you saw the canoe tip—"

"In a manner of speaking. They had flashlights and were shining them all around the lake. They were clearly looking for something. I, on the other hand, was without benefit of light. To shine a light would have been to give myself away. So I contented myself with watching their lights. Then, all of a sudden: no more flashlights."

"Did you see another boat?"

"No, and that was what stumped me for a bit, I must say. At

first I thought perhaps they'd found what they were looking for and I'd lost them. But I realized that they still would have needed light to get back to shore. It was cloudy, as you might remember. It was only then that I suspected an accident, or foul play. But how could it be deliberate? There wasn't anyone there."

"What time was all this?" I asked.

"About ten-thirty, maybe eleven. Well, I sat there and waited, then spent the rest of the night hunting about. At about five, some amateur boaters came by and explained that they were in training for some terribly important event—"

"The Josh," I put in.

"—and I was just about to shove off when who should come floating by, facedown, but our former partners."

"Ed and Frank," I said.

"Right," Simon agreed. "A rum deal, as they say at the pub. Anyway, after that it was difficult to leave. Someone had called the authorities, and naturally, after they found out I'd been there all night, they wanted to have a bit of a chat. That's how I came to be at the police station that morning," he said. "I must say, you weren't particularly friendly," he continued, looking at me.

I blushed. "I thought you did it," I said simply.

"Right. Detective Fineburg relayed that sentiment. In fact, he kept me there all day and most of the evening. He was most reluctant to let me go," said Simon.

"That still doesn't explain how you came to be here," I said. "And in the company of Mat—Detective Fineburg." I coughed.

Simon leveled a frank gray gaze at me. "He's not a bad sort of chap," he said. "He was simply concerned for your welfare. Once the real villain surfaced, he had no problem—"

"But how *did* the real villain surface?" I interrupted. "How did you know about Tasha? And how—"

"You're not the only one around here who knows some-thing about detecting, Elizabeth," said Matthew, who had come up behind us. "Of course," he continued, "I had access to FBI reports. I suppose you'd consider that cheating."

"Search the room?" asked Simon.

"Uh-huh," said Matthew.

"Find anything?" asked Simon.

"Oh, not too much," said Matthew. "Some weights. Dark clothes. An underwater flashlight. Scuba equipment . . . "

"Scuba equipment!" I exclaimed. "So that's how she did it!"

"Yes," Matthew agreed. "That's how she did it. But that's not what interests me. What interests me is how *you* did it, Elizabeth."

I got up, walked over to my locker, and came back with my gym bag. I unzipped it and came up with a piece of paper. I handed it to him.

"An old *Barron's* article?" said Matthew. "From 1987? You've got to be kidding."

"Look at the picture above the title," I said. "That's her, standing next to him. Tasha. It tells all about their life together. She's the one who gave him his first stake."

"But how did you know she was here at Canyon Ranch?" asked Matthew.

"I met her at the Hawthorne School fair," I said. "She was wearing a sweat suit that said La Costa. That meant she was a spa person. Spa people stay at Canyon Ranch. Also, once I hypothesized it was her, a lot of little details fell into place. The position of the truck, for example, and the way the Tumenases were killed. . . . It just all seemed to make sense."

"I'm beginning to have a new respect for the printed word," said Matthew, handing the paper back to me. He paused and looked me over. "You feel well enough to come down to the station and make a statement?"

I nodded.

"Okay, get dressed and I'll meet you there," said Matthew. He got up to go.

Simon rose slowly to his feet. "You didn't, by chance, find anything else in her room?"

"That all depends," said Matthew. "What were you looking for?"

For a long moment the two men stared at each other in silence. Then Simon spoke.

"Oh, nothing," he said. "Nothing at all."

"Mommy!"

"Emily!" I bent down and hugged her. "Emily!"

We were outside of the Lenox Police Station. I'd already given my statement and had arranged for Soji to bring Emily to me. I was outside standing with Matthew when they drove up.

Soji handed me Emily's bag. "Here's her gear," she reported. "She was great."

"Did you have fun?" I asked Emily, still holding on to her.

"Uh-huh," said Emily. "We read stories and painted pictures and guess what, Mommy!"

"What sweetheart?"

"We even went to a pond and saw a *frog*," said Emily.

"No," I said.

"Yes. Can you even *believe* it?"

I laughed and stood up. "Thank you, Soji," I said. "I don't know what I would have done without you."

"No sweat," said Soji. She crouched down. "Bye, peanut," she said to Emily. "See you next time."

We watched her drive off. "So what now?" I asked Matthew.

"Now? Now she gets charged. We do more investigation. We look for forensics, see if she'll—"

Emily pulled on my shorts. "Look, Mommy," she said.

"Just a second, sweetheart. Mommy's talking," I said.

"But, Mommy. Look. It's Mr. Nichols's truck," she said.

I looked. Sure enough, there in the station parking lot was the truck.

Matthew addressed Emily. "You're right," he said. "That is Mr. Nichols's truck. We're keeping it here so we can run tests on it."

Emily ran over to the truck and we followed.

"Mommy, I'm going to drive to New York!" she announced.

"No, honey, you can't drive today," I said. "You can't touch the truck."

"Why not?"

"No one can touch it," said Matthew. "We need it just the way it is."

"Oh," said Emily. She stared at the truck.

"So that's it?" I continued with Matthew. "You don't need me anymore?"

"Well, I wouldn't say that," he said, giving me a look.

I remembered the Jacuzzi and blushed.

There was an awkward silence.

"There is one small matter, though," Matthew continued thoughtfully. "The high-heeled slippers."

I stared at him.

"I'm sure you read that tracks of high-heeled shoes were found around the body."

I nodded.

"Obviously, Tasha Meltzman didn't run to the site in high heels," said Matthew. "There must be some other explanation."

I nodded.

"I suspect that Irving Meltzman met someone else earlier at the site," Matthew continued. "Someone unrelated to the actual crime. The meeting might even have occurred a day or two before. There's no way of telling."

"That sounds good," I sort of croaked.

"It would be a shame to drag that person into this," said Matthew, looking deeply into my eyes. "If I could just be sure those shoes would never show up . . . "

"I'm sure," I answered instantly, "that whoever wore those shoes has gotten rid of them by now."

"You know, that's just what I thought." He paused. "I'd better be getting back inside," he said, making no move to go. "The chief'll be needing me."

I nodded. "Thank you, Matthew," I said softly.

"Can I—uh, may I call you?" he asked.

"Yes, you may," I said.

Matthew laughed. "I'll call you," he said, and went back inside.

I watched him go. So that's it, I thought. It's over. No more killings. No more worry. I wondered, though. If Matthew knew about my high heels, did he also know about the money? I couldn't tell. It didn't really matter, anyway. The secret of the bank account number would die with Irving Meltzman. I wonder what will happen to all that money, I thought. I suppose the Swiss authorities will eventually be told and there will be a search and the whole thing will disappear in legal fees. . . . I sighed.

I turned my attention to Emily. She was staring at the truck, counting. "Six—four—eight—" she was saying. "Nine—one—four—" She stopped. "Is that right, Mommy?"

"Is what right, honey?"

"The numbers. Six—four—eight—nine—"

"Where are you looking, sweetheart?" I interrupted, puzzled.

"There." She pointed at the truck. "One—four—"

"Where?" I knelt down until I was just her height. Oh, of course, the license plate. Eye level for a three-year-old. "Do it again, puddin'," I said.

"Six—four—eight—nine—one—four," she read again.

"Yes," I said. "Yes, that's just—" I stopped.

Something about the license plate on the truck was strange. It wasn't a regulation plate. Regulation plates on new trucks like this one in Lenox have three numbers followed by three letters. This one just had numbers. A vanity plate.

Pleased with herself, Emily began again. "Six—four—eight—"

Naaawww, I thought. Couldn't be.

"Nine—one—four—"

Wait a minute. What was that he'd said? "Most valuable truck in the county"?

"Six—four—eight—"

Put a number on a piece of paper and it's obvious. Put the paper in a safe or lock it in a drawer and it's noticeable. But a number on a license plate? It's unobtrusive. And it's always there if you need it.

"Nine—one—four—"

It was like him. He would have considered it a big joke. Like he was putting something over on everyone. Here they were falling all over themselves for the number and it was right out in the open where everyone could see it. It was the sort of risk he loved to take.

Very slowly and calmly I put my hand over Emily's mouth. She looked over at me, surprised.

"Thank you, Emily," I said gravely. "Thank you very much." I paused. "And now, how about a cookie?"

Chapter

It was the next morning, Sunday, the day of the Josh. They'd gotten a perfectly beautiful day for it. Clear autumn blue sky, no wind, cool in the morning but warming fast now. Much better than last year when it was so stormy that the canoes tipped over.

The finish line was at Tanglewood. It was such a big race and there was such a diversity of ability among the participants that the last racer wouldn't cross the finish line until early afternoon. Emily and I stood with the crowd that lined the driveway and cheered the winner and the first few runners-up as they ran the last few yards. Then we ambled over to where a band was playing to meet Denise and Amber and their friends.

"Hi, Emily," said Amber, running up.

"Hi," said Emily.

"You want to dance to the music?" asked Amber.

"Okay," said Emily, and they joined a group of children who were twirling on the grass in front of the band.

Denise pulled on my arm. "Do you know everyone?" she

asked. "This is Sue and Harold, Rebecca's parents, and this is Mary, Dean's mother, and this is . . . "

Everyone was friendly. We watched the children, listened to the music, sniffed the aroma of barbecued hot dogs wafting from the various outdoor vendor stands. I chatted. I relaxed. I drifted.

There was a very large turnout. I recognized just about everyone I knew from town. Roberta was there, from the dentist's office, and the woman who ran the ice-cream store and the man who ran Wholesome Harold's and baked those delicious cheesecakes. I saw Judge Clarkson standing with the Hunklers and some other members of the Lenox Club. In spite of myself, I couldn't help surveying the crowd. Maybe Si—I heard the screech of a microphone and turned my head.

The sound came from a podium that had been set up just to the left of the finish line. Assembled on the podium was an impressive array of local politicians. All of the select people were there, of course, smiling and waving and wearing little green baseball hats that said "The Great Josh Billings Runaground" in white letters on the crown. Our Republican state senator and our Democratic state representative, both of whom were up for reelection, were there, on opposite sides of the podium, smiling, shaking hands, calling into the crowd, and doing their best to ignore each other. There were appointed officials from the Parks and Recreation Commission, the Planning Board, the Finance Committee, and the Conservation Commission. About the only person up there who didn't have anything to do with the running of the town was Tim Culpo. He was almost unrecognizable. Not only was he wearing what were obviously the only sport jacket and tie he owned, but he was . . . *smiling*.

The microphone stopped screeching, and the head of the selectmen stepped forward to address the crowd. "It is my distinct honor to welcome all of you to the Great Josh Billings Runaground," Joe Cobb said. "I know that you're all just as proud of the contestants as I am, so the first order of business is to give all of them a big hand."

Everybody clapped and cheered.

"You're probably wondering what all of us are doing up here. Well, since this is one of our most notable outdoor events, we all thought that it would be just the right place to make an announcement."

He turned to Tim Culpo. "Timmy, step up here."

Timmy shuffled over. Joe Cobb put his arm around him. He turned back to address the crowd. "I would like to announce the creation of the Timothy Culpo State Park, at the corner of Route Seven and Housatonic Street," he said. "Culpo Park will be one hundred and fifty acres of preserved woods with three miles of groomed nature trails. I would like to thank our state representative and our state senator, without whose help this would not have been possible, as well as my fellow selectmen—and women—and the various members of the Planning Board, the Parks and Recreation District, and the Conservation Commission for their tireless efforts in making this possible."

He turned to acknowledge the others on the podium. There was a sprinkling of applause. The photographer from the *Berkshire Eagle* snapped a picture.

"But most of all," Cubby continued, "we have to thank Timmy Culpo here for making available to the town such an important parcel of land which we all know he could have just as easily sold to a developer. I want to thank him for this donation to our town."

Timmy's smile vanished. "Donation?" he said in a voice that would have been audible to the crowd even without the benefit of the microphone. "I thought you said the state's paying me my million-two."

"Well, of course, Timmy, you'll be reimbursed by the state," Joe Cobb said quickly as Paul Mahoney came up with a smile and led Timmy to the back of the podium. "That's what the Commonwealth of Massachusetts Open Space Bond Bill is all about. . . ."

* * *

So they did it after all, I thought as I drifted away from the podium and the rest of the speeches. Got the state to pick up the tab for the Irving Meltzman fiasco. Now they could return the one hundred thousand in permit money to the local investors (you don't need permit money for a state park) and probably even find a little extra in interest to make up for the additional sums Meltzman had taken, and everybody would be happy. It all goes to show, I concluded, still unconsciously surveying the crowd, what can be accomplished if you put your mind to it, particularly in an election year. . . . I saw him.

He was leaning against the Vietnamese shrimp-roll stand. It was a wonder I hadn't seen him before. Except for Timothy Culpo, he was the only one in the entire crowd wearing a sport jacket.

I pulled on Denise's sleeve. "Could you do me a favor?" I asked. "I have to go talk to someone. Could you watch Emily for a moment?"

Denise looked where I was looking. "Oh! Of course," she said. She smiled. "Take your time," she added.

I started over toward him, but he had already spotted me and met me halfway. "You look beautiful, Elizabeth. No one would believe you had a harrowing experience just yesterday morning," he said, taking my hand and leading me away from the crowd, toward the parking lot.

"Thank you," I said. "Canyon Ranch has promised to cut my hair whenever I want if I refrain from telling the newspapers that I was almost drowned in their Jacuzzi."

"Sounds like a worthwhile arrangement," said Simon.

We walked for a moment in silence.

"So what happens now?" I said.

"Now? I go back home."

"And where is that?"

"London. Care to join me?" he asked.

The question was tossed off so matter-of-factly that I wasn't sure I had heard him properly.

"You mean, go to London with you? When are you going?"

"This afternoon."

"For how long?"

He looked at me. "For as long as you like. I have rather a nice flat in St. John's Wood. There's plenty of room for you . . . and Emily, of course. I'm right next to Regent's Park."

Emily and I in London? The idea had possibilities.

"It's three stories," Simon continued, "with a garden. Library, front parlor, dining room, kitchen on the main floor. Upstairs, master bedroom and bath, two bedrooms with adjoining baths, a smaller parlor which could be converted into a boudoir for you or perhaps a playroom for Emily. Third floor, more guest bedrooms . . . "

"Really. It sounds very impressive. I guess chartered accountants are paid pretty well in London," I said. "I can see why you would want to keep your position."

He stopped, then grinned.

"But, then, you're not an accountant, are you, Simon?"

"I'm afraid not," he conceded. "Are you disappointed?"

"Horribly. What are you, then, Simon?"

"Is it really important that you know precisely, Elizabeth? Isn't it enough that you know me as a person?"

"I'm afraid it is important," I said.

"Right," he said. "Well, I work for the royal family."

"Look, Simon," I said, "it doesn't matter anymore. You don't have to try to impress me. I don't care. I don't care if you're a thief. I don't care if you're a garbage collector. I just want to know the truth."

"But that is the truth, Elizabeth. One of the princesses invested a portion of her divorce settlement with Meltzman. She hasn't much head for business, but, unfortunately, she's got an unerring sense of scandal. The queen asked if I could retrieve her investment for her. That's all."

"Oh, right, I'm supposed to believe that the queen just rang you up, invited you to tea, and then asked if you could do her this one small favor?"

"Something like that," he said.

"Well, that shouldn't be too difficult to verify," I said. "I'll just call the British ambassador to the United States and ask if he knows a Simon Montgomery Smith and could he vouch for him. Do you want to wait here while I make the call? It might take me a little while to get through."

"I'm afraid calling Hubby won't do much good," said Simon.

"Hubby? Who's Hubby?"

"The British ambassador. He'll be forced to deny that he knows me. Obviously, this is being carried out unofficially."

"Obviously," I agreed, and laughed. "Serves me right for asking," I said. "Here." I handed him a slip of folded paper.

He opened it, scanned the numbers quickly, and the expression on his face changed.

"You found it?"

"I didn't find anything."

"Where was it?"

"Just take it," I said, "It's only eleven o'clock in the morning. If you leave right now, you may still be able to catch a flight out of Kennedy and make it to Switzerland in time for the opening of business Monday morning."

"Elizabeth," he said, and kissed me.

I kissed him back. Then I watched as he got into his car.

"You're sure you won't change your mind?" he asked.

I shook my head.

He started the car. As he was driving away he stuck his head out the window. "Don't you even want to know what happens?" he called.

"Sure." I waved. "Drop me a postcard or something."

And that was that.

Epilogue

Of course I gave Simon the account number. What else was I going to do with it? I certainly wasn't going to Switzerland. It wasn't my money. And giving it to the police . . . that was just a big waste of time. They'd just give it to the FBI, who would give it to the Treasury Department, who would officially petition Suisse Union Creditbank of Zug for the funds. Suisse Union Creditbank of Zug would bring the matter to the attention of the Swiss authorities, who would intercede in defense of that country's privacy restrictions. The international legal community would become involved. The result would be years and years of wrangling, lawyers' fees, bankers' fees, court fees, arbitration, taxes, damages, penalties. By the time the original investors were identified and located, there wouldn't be more than two cents left to redistribute. That just did not seem a fitting way to end the adventure. And Simon, I knew, would get it done if anyone could. He might be a congenital liar, but he was extremely competent.

I thought I would feel badly when Simon left, and I did. Let's face it, it's not often that a genuine handsome prince waltzes into your life, asks for your hand (sort of), and then waltzes out again. Maybe I shouldn't have been so picky about his not ever telling me the truth. After all, nobody's perfect. But, strange to say, I didn't feel *that* bad. This probably had something to do with my starting to write again. I may not have much of an imagination, but I am able to recognize a perfectly serviceable plot, particularly when it just drops into my lap that way. And then Matthew started calling almost immediately, and took Emily and me out to dinner at Elizabeth's, and this time I actually got to eat the pizza.

One thing did bother me, though. Did Simon get the money or not? For a week or so after he left, I half expected a letter, a postcard, a fax, some sign that he'd succeeded. But nothing came. And, after a while, I stopped watching for it.

Until the morning of October tenth.

On the morning of October tenth, I dropped Emily off at school, kissed her good-bye, chatted with Penny Johnson and Denise and some of the other mothers hanging around the cubby room, and was just about to go back to the parking lot for my car when I heard:

"*Elizabeth*."

I turned. It was Fawn Woodehouse. She was just sort of standing in the cubby room looking at me. She had a very strange expression on her face. For a moment I had to look down and check to see if I was wearing clothes.

"Yes?" I said. I was.

"*Elizabeth*." She was having trouble speaking. She had her arms raised in front of her. For a moment, I was afraid she was going to try and hug me, but she restrained herself at the last second and contented herself with just repeating my name. "*Elizabeth*," she said.

"What?"

"How ever can we thank you?" she asked.

"What are you talking about?" I demanded.

She'd been twisting a piece of paper in her hands; now she handed it to me.

I looked down at it. It was an order form, with an attached

check. It was difficult to make out the signature, but apparently someone from Great Britain—from Windsor Castle, actually—had ordered two thousand rolls of gift wrap from the Hawthorne Day School and credited me with the sale.

Naaawww, I thought. Couldn't be. . . .